He had died in terror.

The hands flung out as he'd fallen, perhaps running too hard, running like hell from the wreck of the freighter, running in terror. His face showed that much. He had died screaming.

Not far away there was something black showing in the sand. It was plumage and as I pulled it upwards the wing rose, scattering sand, and then the gross black body with its bald head dangling, the hooked beak agape. The bird, like the man, had died screaming . . .

ADAM HALL

The Tango Briefing

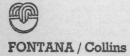

FONTANA / Collins

First published by Wm Collins 1973
First issued in Fontana Books 1975

© Elleston Trevor 1973

Made and printed in Great Britain by
William Collins Sons & Co Ltd Glasgow

To
Bernard and Jane Horsfall

CONDITIONS OF SALE
This book is sold subject to the condition that
it shall not, by way of trade or otherwise, be lent,
re-sold, hired out or otherwise circulated without
the publisher's prior consent in any form of
binding or cover other than that in which it is
published and without a similar condition
including this condition being imposed on the
subsequent purchaser

CONTENTS

Chapter One

BIRDSEYE

I came in over the Pole and we were stacked up for nearly twenty minutes in a holding circuit round London before they could find us a runway and then we had to wait for a bottle-neck on the ground to get itself sorted out and all we could do was stare through the windows at the downpour and that didn't help.

Sayōnara, yes, very comfortable thank you.

There was a long queue in No. 3 Passenger Building and I was starting to sweat because the wire had said *fully urgent* and London never uses that phrase just for a laugh; then a quietly high-powered type in sharp blue civvies came up and asked who I was and I told him and he whipped me straight past Immigration and Customs without touching the sides and told me there was a police car waiting and was it nice weather in Tokyo.

'Better than here.'

'Where do we send the luggage?'

'This is all I've got.'

He took me through a fire exit and there was the rain slamming down again and the porters were trudging about in oilskins.

The radio operator had the rear door open for me and I ducked in and the driver hooked his head round to see who I was, not that he'd know.

'You want us to go as fast as we can?'

'That's what it's all about.'

Sometimes along the open stretches where the deluge was flooding the hollows we worked up quite a bow-wave and I could see the flash of our emergency light reflected on it.

'Bit of a summer storm.'

'You can keep it.'

They were using their sirens before we'd got halfway along Waterloo Road and after that they just kept their thumb on it because the restaurants and cinemas were turning out and every taxi was rolling.

Big Ben was sounding eleven when we did a nicely controlled slide into Whitehall across the front of a bus and he put the two nearside wheels up on the pavement so that I could get out without blocking the traffic.

'Best I could do.'

'You did all right.'

Most of the lights were on in the building but the place sounded dead as if they'd made up their minds at last that the only thing to do was run. I used the stairs and went straight into Walford's room but he wasn't there and I had to barge into Field Briefing before I could find anyone.

'Where's Walford?'

'Sprained a ball.'

'Oh for Christ's sake.' I pulled off my trenchcoat and shook the rain off the collar, throwing it on a chair. They've never done anything about the environment at the Bureau: it's a fridge or an oven according to the season and this was August. 'Walford told me to get here, fully urgent.'

'That's right.'

Tilson was always like this: try blasting his eyes and he'd ask if you'd care for some tea.

'You mean he's not in the building?'

'All that matters to me, old horse, is that you are.' He picked up a phone, not hurrying. 'Quiller's come in. Cancel those last two cables, revamp the board and warn Clearance for tomorrow morning.'

He put the thing down and eyed me amiably.

'How were the geishas?'

'Listen, if Walford's not here, who do I see? Who's my director?'

'Director?'

'It *is* a job, isn't it?'

'As far as I know, old horse.'

'Then I want some orders.'

'What's the rush?'

I turned away so I wouldn't have to look at his pink amiable face. He wasn't doing it deliberately; this was just his character and maybe they'd put him in charge of Field Briefing because that's when your nerves tighten up a whole octave higher, right on the brink of a mission. Maybe they thought his sleepy-eyed approach to the thing would calm us down. It was driving me up the wall.

'Look, they whipped me over the North Pole and spat me

ut of the airport and we screamed the place down getting
ere in a squad car and now you ask me what's the rush, so
or God's sake get on the blower and find out.'

He rocked gently on his swivel chair.

'Care for a spot of tea?'

'Is Carslake in the building?'

'He's running the Irish thing.'

'Well, get me some orders.'

It's the routine reaction: most of the shadow executives
et it the minute they know there's a mission lined up with
heir name on it. We call it the shakes, the blues, the doom-
angers, but it's the same thing, a kind of sudden love-hate
elationship with the job that's been giving you the kicks you
sked for all along the line, the same job that's going to kill
ou off one day when your guard's down or your luck's out
r you've finally lost that fine degree of judgment that has
far kept you alive.

So when you know there's a mission you get an urge to run
he other way and you can't do that because you're com-
itted, so you run to meet it instead, head down and blood
p but with that little cold knot in the stomach.

'The only orders I know, old horse, is that you're to piddle
f home.'

'What did they get me here for, then, so bloody fast?'

'We just wanted to know you were physically available for
is one, and we couldn't be sure of that if you were mooning
ound Tokyo.'

It made sense and the speed went out of me and I crossed
the open window and stood with my back to the rain,
atching his face now because I wanted all the info I could
t without asking too much.

'What were the signals you just cancelled?'

'We were going to warn Smythe and Bickersteth to stand
. One's in Bucharest and the other's hanging around in
serve on the Pakistan show.'

'You were going to pull them out for this job?'

'If you couldn't make it.' He flattened his pink hand and
ted it, watching the light flash across his nails. 'And now
u have. Or have you?'

'What the hell does that mean?'

'Well, you might not like this one.' He gave a shy smile.

The knot in my stomach got colder.

9

'Why? Is it a bastard?'

'Oh I don't mean that, old horse. Anyway, the thing
you're here physically and all you have to do now is go hom
and get a good night's zizz.' He leaned forward to look at
pad on his desk. 'Tomorrow they're running a film show f
you at –'

'It would've been quicker to pull out Smythe and Bicke
steth, wouldn't it?'

'Much.'

'Someone wants me particularly for this one.'

He smiled boyishly.

'That's right.'

'Who?'

'Not absolutely sure. Tell you in the morning.'

'Is there a director lined up?'

'Sort of.'

'Who?'

'They haven't told me. Honestly. Or I'd tell you, wouldn
I?'

'If it suited you.'

'That's the way we do things, isn't it? We don't like y
people to have too much on your mind. Gives you indigestio
Now why don't you just buzz off and –'

'Where's this film show?'

'Air Ministry. Nine ack-emma mañana – will you be there

'All right.'

'Room 43, Squadron-leader Eastlake. Code-intro's "Bir
eye", okay? Then you can tootle back here and I'll give y
the rest and you can get cleared.'

I stood watching his smooth cherub's face for a bit a
thought again about what he'd said – *you might not like t*
one – and then got it out of my mind and picked up t
trenchcoat and slung it round my shoulders because it w
too stinking hot to put it on.

'What's the area?'

'I think you'll need tropical kit.'

'Oh my God.'

'It's a shame,' he smiled amiably, 'in winter they send y
to Warsaw, don't they?'

'Why did they want me for this one, specially?'

'It's a solo mission, apart from the director in the field. Y
like working alone, don't you? So it ought to suit you do

the ground.'

Suddenly it struck me that they'd deliberately got Walford ut of the way so that this bland little angel-face could andle me softly, softly, till they'd caught their monkey. This b was a bastard and they'd picked the only one who'd take on out of sheer bloody-mindedness because he knew that nyone with a bit of sense would refuse. It had happened efore and now it looked like happening again. If I let it.

'Get you a taxi?'

'I'll walk.'

'In this rain?'

'It'll cool me off.'

'We could put it down,' he said comfortably, 'on the ex- nses. Let's say the operation's running, as of now.'

'From what I can smell about this one you can stuff it, ong with the taxi-fare.'

er breasts were marbled in the greenish light and her face oked cold and blind. The shadow of the window cut half ross her body, leaving her long legs in darkness, silvered th moisture.

The rain had stopped a long time ago but now and then a amond drop flashed down from the guttering. Taxis were ll about, their tyres hissing along the roadway; in here the was stifling, even with the window open.

She moved and I looked down at her, she'd opened her es and they were brilliant in the half-dark.

'Okay?' she asked.

'Okay.'

She smiled and uncurled herself, getting off the bed and aking her hair out, moving lazily in the glow from the eet lamps, her hands idly smoothing her body as she etched a little, her eyes closing again as she took pleasure ply in being alive, turning slowly in a kind of dance and getting I was here.

I hadn't meant to be.

But Tilson had seemed so certain they'd got me, and he uldn't be stupid enough to think I'd take on *any* kind of . He knew enough about the background to know that finally fall for this one after I'd put up a preliminary eal to show I had a choice.

So I'd gone dripping wet into a phone-box and tried four

11

numbers before I could find anyone with enough time c
their hands to take in a nerve-case who wanted a woman an
wanted her badly because he knew that once the mission w
running he wouldn't get another chance and that if som
where along the line a wheel came off she'd be the last on
he'd ever have.

'You're quiet.'

'I was watching you,' I said.

She smiled again, just a lazy movement along her mout
'You weren't.'

Her name was Corinne. I'd only seen her twice before b
we liked things the same way, it was a kind of natural.

'There's another job,' I said, and found my clothes.

'How long for?'

'You can't ever tell.'

She got her cigarettes and held one out and I shook n
head and she lit up. 'Where is it this time?'

'Italy. Whole coach-load, want to see the Tower of Pi
before the bloody thing falls down.'

I dropped my keys and she picked them up, stooping nak
in the light, giving them to me, smiling with her brilliant eye
'I just can't see you doing it.'

'Why not?'

'I just can't see you standing up with a microphone an
saying on the left there's the statue of Marco Polo and c
the right there's the Co-operative Spaghetti Works.'

'Well, I've got to do something for a living.'

The smoke curled across the slanting light, quickening to
air current from the window.

'I wish I was going with you.'

'On a coach-trip in a heatwave?'

'It'd be a different kind of grind, and there'd be you.' S
moved around the room, unconsciously making stylized tur
on her slim bare feet. 'You know something? It isn't the c
throat bitchiness of the competition that gets us down in t
end, it's the strain on the shoulders, lifting our arms to g
in and out of the dresses. You're right on the point
throwing it in, then you get a break and see your face
the front of *Go-Girl* so you think you've hit it big, and you
back in the grind again.'

I tied the second lace.

'You ought to get married.'

'Oh futz, spare me the suds and the sink.'

'Someone with a sack of loot.'

I got my coat and we kissed and I opened the door and
looked back and she was standing perfectly still in the small
airless room, the after-rain smell coming in and the light
striking obliquely across her, across a thin willowy girl with
blue-veined breasts and a slowly-dying smile as she watched
me go, a girl called Corinne whom I'd met only twice before
and wouldn't, maybe, ever see again.

Room 43 was on the fifth floor and I was standing by the
window when he came in.

'Sorry I kept you. You're Mr Gage?'

'Yes.'

'I'm Eastlake.'

'You've got quite a birdseye view from up here.'

'Appropriate word.' He was going to add something but
the phone buzzed and he picked it up. 'Squadron-leader
Eastlake. Yes, I told him to get three while he was at it.
Well, tell him to pull his finger out, and listen, I'm going
along to Projection and I don't want anyone to come barging
in, so put someone on the door.'

I came away from the window and he gave me a slow
probing look, wondering what a nondescript civilian was
doing in here with a code-introduction. I'd used the name
Gage because that had been stuck on for Tokyo and if they'd
changed it when they'd arranged this meeting Tilson would
have told me.

'Let's go along. Nobody with you?'

'No.'

In the small room smelling of acetate and overheated guide
mechanism he introduced me to a WRAF operator and three
flight lieutenants: 'Hinchley was piloting this sortie, Pierce
was navigating, and Johnson's the photographic interpretation
officer responsible for the analysis of the imagery material.
Can we have those curtains drawn, someone?'

There were three or four rows of tip-up seats and we sat
down and the WRAF hit the button and threw a desert on the
screen and I remembered Tilson saying, 'I think you'll need
tropical kit.'

Eastlake said: 'Ask what questions you like as we go
along, will you? We did this with a cluster of four 35mm

13

Nikons and a restricted field of 25 degrees. Filters we
yellow, green and two reds and the film's been cut and join
for continuity, all right?'

'What altitude?'

'Sixty-five thousand feet.' He'd hesitated a fraction becau
it was classified so I thought this must be the Mk II versi
of the Albatross and started looking for missile installatio
dolled up as mosques.

But so far there was only desert, a sugar-brown terra
filling the screen and looking like a sheet of corrugated car
board with a fold here and there.

'What are those rocks?'

'Shale upthrust, nothing very high, perhaps twenty or thir
feet.'

The pattern of dunes and rills spun slowly as we circl
clockwise so I focused my eyes on the centre but couldr
see anything.

'This isn't a dummy run?'

'No. These are the pix we went for.'

I still couldn't see anything interesting on the screen but
was beginning to see a lot more of the job that Tilson ar
those other bastards were trying to pitch me into: a stinki
Robinson Crusoe lark in an area defined on this frame-sc
three miles across with nothing in it but a bunch of roc
and something else so small that only people like these cou
see it.

The ground resolution looked close on ten-tenths, with
shade of grain on the light-exposed side of the shale upthr
but the rest very clear, and I began getting frustrated becau
they'd sat me down to show me something and they knew
couldn't see it and I felt a bit of a lemon.

'Have you got those rocks on a static 3-D viewer?'

'We have, but I wouldn't bother.'

Eastlake had obviously been briefed. Last night Tilson h
just told me to keep the rendezvous and that was all, so
hadn't reported at the Bureau this morning on my way he
but they'd briefed these chaps to run this film without telli
me what I had to look for and there must be a good reason

The desert spun and tilted, the group of rocks changi
shape as the angle of view turned through its conic vect
the light-and-shadow corrugations of the dunes shifting

14

finition like water flowing in slow motion. It was all I could
see.

'Can we have a few stops?'

The squadron-leader spoke to the girl and she began breaking it up into ten-second runs and I still couldn't get it. The
whole scene's slow revolutions were becoming mesmeric and
I shut my eyes to prevent strain, viewing for a few seconds
and trying to coincide with the rhythm of the stops, resting
at intervals and waiting till the after-image had faded under
my closed lids. I knew now why they'd been warned not to
tell me what I was expected to look for: the interreactive
process of eye and brain can play tricks and sometimes you
can see things only because you've been told they're there.

'Would you like some run-backs?'

'We can try.'

He told the girl and the scene began swinging anti-clockwise at precise intervals with five-second stops. It didn't make
any difference: I was looking at the same thing in a mirror.
There's no point in run-backs unless you think you've spotted
something and want to recap and I hadn't spotted a bloody
thing and I was getting fed-up. The heat of the projector
was adding to the heat of our bodies in here and there was
nothing much left to breathe and I thought it'd be nice if a
girl came round with a tray of Dairymaid.

The dunes flowed under my eyes.

Swing. Stop. Run-back.

The projector droned.

I kept wanting to look at the rocks but Eastlake had said it
wasn't worth bothering with. They weren't interested in the
rocks. And it was no good asking them for a clue because
the object of the exercise was that I should see the target for
myself, avoiding the risk of conditioned illusion.

Swing. Stop. Run-back.

The dunes were becoming a mirage. The dunes and the
rocks and the flow of light and shade across the scene were
beginning to swirl in a slow-moving vortex and I was losing
track of perspective.

'Would you like us to back-project against a –'

'What? No. Run it back. Run it back, will you?'

The scene swung to a stop.

'Tell me when –'

'Yes.'
Anti-clockwise. The shadows flowing and the angle –
'Stop.'
'This frame?'
'Back another fraction.'
The sprockets whirred again and stopped.
'Yes, that's the one. I've got it now.'

Chapter Two

OVERFLIGHT

'It didn't take you long.'
'You're joking.'
The WRAF shut down the projector and we all stretched
our legs.
'It took us a bit of time ourselves,' said Eastlake, 'even
though the navigator had seen it through direct binocular
vision.' He showed me a couple of dozen stills and blow-ups
and filter-screen montages on the static viewers but they
weren't any clearer, and even the still they'd taken from the
frame of the movie strip didn't have the same definition. I
asked Johnson about that. He was the interpretation officer.
'It doesn't seem possible,' he said, 'does it? When you look
at the still you're looking at exactly the same picture as the
one on the strip – but there's some data missing, all the same.
The eye hasn't got anything for immediate comparison. It's
the movement through the projector that leads the eye over
the changing pattern till it suddenly sees an inconsistency.
That's what happened with you.'
Eastlake cut the viewer lamp and someone pulled the
curtains and stopped sharp when I said: 'What sort of plane
is it?'
Someone gave a nervous cough.
Squadron-leader Eastlake said: 'Don't you know?'
'If I did, I wouldn't ask.'
It was perfectly all right if the Bureau had its reasons for
pitching me in here without any briefing, but if their idea
was to get me steamed-up about this thing then people would

have to answer the questions I wanted to ask them or it was no go.

'Thank you, Phyllis. That's all we needed to see.'

When the WRAF went out and shut the door the pilot and navigator and photo-interpretation bod stood looking at their shoes and Eastlake said:

'Mr Gage has been fully screened.'

They relaxed a bit and one of them offered a package of gum around and nobody wanted any and the pilot said:

'We were told to look for a medium freighter.'

'You think this is a medium freighter?'

We were grouped by the static viewer. On the blown-up still it didn't really look like an aeroplane at all but now that I'd seen it on the movie strip I could accept the smudgy configuration on the sand as an aircraft with one wing dislocated at the root end.

The interpretation officer didn't say anything. The navigator shrugged.

'All I'd say from the pix is that it could be. From what I saw through the binocs I'd say it's not military and not very big. If I had a bet on it I'd put it down as a light or medium twin-prop short-haul commercial transport.'

'Not just because that's what you were told to look for and expected to see.'

He smiled lopsidedly. 'What can we ever do about that? Once we're told what kind of target to look for, we're to an extent conditioned.'

I was feeling it difficult now to look away from the static viewer. In the illuminated central frame the picture wasn't very big: it had been blown up to the point where the grain would start blurring the definition. The ribbed background of dunes was perfectly clear but the grey ashy smudge could be anything – or nothing, just a fault in the processing – but even from sixty-five thousand feet they'd seen it was some kind of aircraft and now that they'd found it the Bureau had cabled Tokyo fully urgent and I was here looking at this vague configuration on the photographic plate that was the focal point of the mission they were trying to sell me.

'Where is it?'

Eastlake spoke before the others could start worrying. The people with No. 2 Fighter-Reconnaissance Squadron RAF spent most of their time taking the sort of pictures that

17

nobody really wanted to reprint as post-cards for the tourist trade. This was one of them.

'Longitude 8°3′ East by Latitude 30°4′ North.'

'Tunisia?'

'Algeria.'

'When did the plane come down?'

'We weren't informed. Our job was to look for it and take pictures if we found it.'

'From sixty-five thousand feet?'

'It's the highest we go.'

'You could've gone lower.'

Someone coughed again.

I thought I might as well push them right up against the wall so that they'd either have to answer my question or throw me out.

'Did you get official overflying permission?'

I counted up to seven.

'Did we what?'

Very slowly I said: 'Did you get official permission from the Algerian government to overfly their territory and take those pictures? Or did you go up to the maximum operational ceiling because the view was better?'

This time I was at nine before the pilot said:

'Actually, neither.'

It was just their natural disinclination as secret reconnaissance men to trust an unknown civilian with the whole score. Eastlake had told them I'd been screened and they'd obviously been briefed to give me all the info they could, but they still didn't like it.

I suppose the pilot thought that if things had gone this far it couldn't do any harm to go the whole way and the squadron-leader would slap him down in any case if he made a mistake.

'You see,' he said with a perfectly straight face, 'we were tooling around in Malta on a friendly visit and then we got these orders from on high. So we planned a suitable exercise and went in at our best altitude so we wouldn't annoy the scheduled airlines. Then we sort of lost our way a bit and after we'd got back on course for home we found Charlie here had made a silly mistake and left all the cameras running. I really don't know what things are coming to, in this mob.'

The squadron-leader was looking out of the window. He didn't say anything.

'You must have been tracked by radar.'

'Bound to have been.'

'How long were you overflying Algerian territory?'

'Not long enough to sort of cause too much comment.'

'Did they put up interceptors?'

'Don't actually know. You see, from that height we can go rather fast in quite a short time, by pointing things downwards.'

It was all I wanted to know and I left it at that.

When Eastlake took me down the corridor he said: 'Where exactly do you fit in with this little circus?'

'You can't see much from those photographs. I suppose they'll send me in to have a closer look at the bloody thing.'

There was nobody around in Field Briefing so Tilson sat me down and folded his chubby hands and said:

'Well, what shall we talk about?'

I said I wanted to know who my director would be if I took the job on.

'It depends who can get there first.'

'Where?'

'Tunis.'

'Who's been sent for?'

'I'm not really –'

'You're a liar –'

'Now why should I want to –'

'Oh for Christ's sake stop poncing me about, will you?'

He sighed gently. 'They asked for Loman.'

'As my director in the field?'

'That's right.'

He looked at his pink shiny nails.

I got up and walked about and thought of saying no, I'm not working with that bastard, but he was waiting for me to say that and I didn't want to give him the pleasure of being right.

'What's the mission, Tilson?'

'I'm not sure I –'

'Oh come on, don't waste my time.'

He looked up amiably and said: 'Are you in a hurry?'

I turned away and did some more walking and thought of saying no, I'm not in a hurry, but he'd got me and we both knew it and I was fed-up because they'd hijacked me into

19

a new mission the fastest way possible: by holding back and keeping off and letting me get interested without anyone coming to interfere.

Yes I was in a hurry.

We can refuse a mission. We can refuse to work at the kind of thing that's not our speciality or the kind of thing that we've proved in the past to be beyond our particular talents. We can say no, this one sounds too political or complex or dull or dirty or dangerous and we can say we don't like the director or we don't like Bangkok or Warsaw or Tunis. We can say we've got a cold or we can just tell them to go and find someone else without even giving a reason. It works all right because if a shadow executive lets himself be forced into an assignment he's a dead duck and they know that and it doesn't suit their book.

But if we refuse a mission it means we have to hang around and wait for another one to come up and it gets on the nerves the waiting. So in the end we'll take almost anything if it looks as though there's a break-even chance of getting out alive. Today I wasn't interested in that because the chances are always as good as you want to make them. They knew what I was interested in today.

The ash-grey smudge on the photograph.

It was just a medium twin-prop short-haul commercial transport and all it had done was to come down in the desert but the nearest anyone had got to it was sixty-five thousand feet and nobody else had dared to go any closer.

So I wanted to.

And they'd known I would.

'What's the timing on this?'

Tilson raked for a folder.

'Immediate.'

'You mean when I'm ready.'

'That's right.' He was opening the folder. 'So long as you're ready immediately.'

'Fill me in, will you?'

He looked up patiently. 'I'm afraid I can't, old horse. All I know is they want you to go and take a look at that thing you saw at the Air Ministry. Loman will spell it all out for you when you reach Tunis.'

'How long have I got for clearance?'

'There's a plane at 13.50 so you'll just have to do every

20

thing as quick as you can.'

On my way through the building to Credentials I passed Napier, one of our Admin. types.

'Hallo, Quiller, I thought you were in Tokyo.'

'So did I.'

'We're leaving your cover name as Charles Warnford Gage but there's a change in the cover itself. Excuse me.'

While she answered the phone I checked the papers.

C. W. Gage, geophysical consultant attached to Societé Petrocombine's South 4 drilling-camp in the Tunisian complex. Specific contract, exploration and preliminary assay, until October, optionally renewable, previous contracts with platinum-prospecting consortia, UK and Belgium. Returning from one month's routine leave.

When she'd got off the phone I asked who'd designed this one.

'Mr Egerton.'

'When?'

'It came through late last night.'

They'd been so bloody sure of me.

'It's a new camp, is it?'

'First assays, yes.'

Egerton had his faults but I'd take any cover he worked out for me. This one was very smooth because a geophysical consultant attached to a prospecting company hoping to strike oil was going to keep his mouth shut: it was the perfect excuse not to talk and that was fine because I didn't know anything about survey work.

In Firearms they wanted me to try out a new club-snout rapid loader they'd just had in from Italy and I told them where to put it.

'Take one of these compacts, then. Slung holster.'

'How long have you been here?'

'Me? Three weeks.'

'Look, there's my signature, so just put *Weapons drawn — none.*'

'Oh *you're* the one.'

Codes and Ciphers gave me a third-series seven-digit duplication set-up with normal contractions, transferred numerals and no blanks. The alert phrase was 'wherever possible.'

'Christ, don't they know that one by now?'

'It's never been blown.'

'There's a first time for everything.'

Accounts had passed their stuff on to Travel and I picked the Caledonian air ticket, two hundred dinars, travellers' cheques and an American Express card. The existing will and testament to stand as it was, no new codicil.

Then I went back to Field Briefing but Tilson said nothing fresh had come in.

'Has Loman arrived in Tunis yet?'

'There's been no signal.'

'Where's he coming from?'

'Nobody said.'

Tilson wouldn't necessarily tell me. He'd tell me precisely what Admin. wanted me to know and nothing more. Sometimes we bitch about this but it's based on logic because if an executive goes out on a mission with his head stuffed full of background info that doesn't directly concern him it'll take his mind off the job in hand and that can be dangerous. Last year Webster was found mixed up with the propellers of a Greek coaster in Trieste because he'd got himself involved in the political aspect of a perfectly straightforward penetration job and blew his cover by sending signals when he should have been concentrating on a fast in-and-out documentation snatch.

If you work for the Bureau you've got to work to the rules and they're strict. The Bureau doesn't officially exist. If it existed it couldn't do the things it's been designed to do: things that could never be countenanced even at Cabinet level. So if you get into a jam in the course of a mission you can count on London to help you but only up to a point: the point where they see there's a risk of exposing the Bureau, of letting it be seen to exist. Then they'll cut you off and you'll know it because the set's gone dead or the contact doesn't show up and then God help you because London never will.

Up to that point they'll look after you and one of the ways they do it is by keeping you short of information that you don't really need at the time.

'What made them pick Loman for this one?'

'No idea.'

Loman was a bastard but he was third in the ranks of the really high-echelon directors simply because he was brilliant at his job. The ash-grey smudge on that photograph must be hellishly important for them to send a man like Loman in.

'Did he ask for me?'

'Everything's been so quick,' Tilson said apologetically. 'No one's had time to tell me anything.'

So I asked the only kind of questions he'd be able to do anything with.

'What contacts in Tunis?'

'None. There'll be an Avis car waiting for you at the airport, dark blue Chrysler 180.'

'Rendezvous?'

'Hotel Africa, *Les Caravaniers* Bar on the 5th floor, 18.00 hours today. No code, just recognition.'

'What do I do if he's not there?'

'Rdv at hourly intervals till twenty-four hundred and then send us a signal. Code name for the mission is *Tango*.'

'Noted.' I belted my mack. 'Got any transport?'

'Car and driver standing by for you below.'

I turned away and an odd thing happened.

There is no ceremony at the Bureau. The only human contact in this ancient and featureless building is made when a shadow executive reports for briefing and clearance or when he comes in from a mission. Nobody exists here because the Bureau itself doesn't exist. We call each other by the names we're given: except to the top echelon people our own names have never been known.

Tilson had been here long enough to lose his soul to the sacred bull: the Bureau. He knew what we really were, the shadow executives: we were so many ferrets to be released down a hole and left there to hunt in the dark, to pursue the sinuous ways of the warren and to emerge blinded by the light, bloodied and embattled, triumphant or dismayed, or never, on occasions, to emerge at all.

Object achieved.

Executive withdrawn.

Mission failed.

Executive deceased.

Deceased or replaced or overdue or home and dry and drunk as a lord because this time we pulled it off and nothing worse to show than a flesh-wound from a glancing shot. Nobody cheers, nobody grieves. Only the results are important.

The J-class sub in the Black Sea has augmented missile potential and rejoins the Med. flotilla tonight on orders from Tikhomirov.

The Cuban national in Room 39 of the hotel opposite the dais where General Fernandez will speak tomorrow had a Marlin 336T .35 telescopic rifle with 4X scope among his possessions; appropriate action taken; his sister has identified him at the morgue.

The Temple of Heavenly Light near Kuchêng has a central minaret comprising concealed guidance ramp with 17-degree inclination towards the Russian border and accommodation for warhead armament in the Z-phase ICBM category. These are the photostats taken from the original designs.

We are nameless and speak in ciphers; we are homeless and work among strangers; and if we can claim identity then it lies in the sacrosanct and classified files somewhere in this building whose doors are as nameless as we.

So it was odd that Tilson should do so human a thing as to get up from his desk as I turned for the door, and stand there awkwardly with his plump arms folded and his round pink head on one side as he watched me go.

It told me that however much or little they'd briefed him about this mission, he knew that it was deadly.

'Take care,' he said, 'old horse.'

Chapter Three

SHOCK

We began sweating as soon as they opened the door and by the time we'd crossed the tarmac to the Tunis-Carthage No. 2 Airport building the soles of our shoes were hot and I thought oh you bastards, sending me to Africa in a heatwave

Vous n'avez rien à déclarer?

Rien.

A man in a fez waving a chalked board: PETROCOMBINE SOUTH 4. Half a dozen drillers were heading towards him bearded and sunbaked and one of them half-seas over. That was meant to be my mob but so far I didn't sense any kin

surveillance so I didn't join them just for the look of the
ing.

Avis? par là, m'sieur.

Merci.

Another chalked board: MR ROBINSON.

If anyone was here to meet Mr C. W. Gage they wouldn't
alk it up on a board and I took the long open passage to
e *Consigne* and back and then double-checked the main
ll before I tapped at the window and noted that in Tunis
ey not only try harder but they look prettier while they're
ing it.

'Yes, Mr Gage, we have a Chrysler waiting for you.'

'Any messages?'

London would contact me here if there was any change of
an and you never know your luck: Loman might have
ked a kidney on a camel and I could go home.

'There's no message.'

She led me outside with a light jigging high-heeled step and
studied the blue-black hair and the silky eyelashes and the
ite flashing smile as she showed me how to open the door
d where the steering-wheel was and everything, then I
pped the belt on and began butting a gangway through the
ck of clapped-out Minicabs towards the main gate.

There was a crosswind along the Khaireddine Pacha and
tall feathery eucalyptuses blew restlessly against the sky.
don't like wind: it disturbs me. I began checking the
rror because in this trade you can't always tell when a
her's been bust somewhere along the line and even in the
st few hours of a new mission you can sometimes pick up
ks.

This evening it looked all right and I started wondering
ere they'd pulled Loman in from: there was obviously a
p on because they'd bounced me Tokyo-London-Tunis with
y one night-stop and had to leave the final briefing for
cal Control. The last I'd heard of Loman he'd been setting
a classified document snatch at one of the ministries in
nn and he wasn't the kind of director who'd appreciate
ng turned round in the middle of an operation. This was
other reason why I knew this aeroplane thing must be
ictly urgent.

hadn't been briefed yet but there was one obvious aspect
this job: Control in London didn't only want me to go

25

and have a look at that wreck in the desert – they wanted r
to go and have a look at it before anyone else could.

So I kept a routine check on the mirror.

If anyone had ricked a kidney it was the poor bloody can
because Loman was there in the *Caravaniers* Bar at the Ho
Africa at precisely 18.00 hours and he got up right aw
without looking at me and signed his bill and went out.
waited thirty seconds and followed him.

I know people by their walk. The eyes are expressive b
if you're good at it they can be used for hiding things. E
there's nothing people can do about their walk becau
locomotion is a life-long habit and it expresses their attitu
towards the environment.

Loman walks like a bird, his hands behind him like ne
tucked wings, his head turning frequently from side to si
in case there's something to peck at: he never misses a
thing and if you get in his way he'll peck you to death.

The Arab room was at the end of a tiled passage and
was waiting for me there, his bland face half masked by
shadows of arabesque screens. There were no chairs he
just cushions massed along the stone plinth and on a d
where incense burned in a brass bowl. Light came from lam
high in the atrium outside where tropical plants grew, th
leaves like sword-blades and their shadows sharp.

'Where were you?'

'Tokyo.'

'You're still under flight-disorientation?'

'I'll settle down.'

He nodded and got a map out but didn't open it.

There was a flap on all right and it shook me. The pa
was too fast. The minute they'd slung this op at Loman
direct he must have said *I want Quiller for it* and he had
even asked them where I was, couldn't care less. The pa
ought not to be as fast as this right at the outset of a missio
people could make mistakes in the planning stages and th
could be dangerous, could be fatal.

Then I knew suddenly how much the flight had upset
personal clock because there was something sticking out
mile and I'd only just seen it. This wasn't a new mission
had been running for some time and it had seemed to
blowing up and they'd thrown it at Loman like an unexploc

mb because of all the high-echelon directors he was the
e who could stay cool enough not to drop it.

I could feel the whole network quivering.

Someone's mucked it, have they?'

He didn't answer.

It wasn't a good start because he knew I was bloody
noyed. I watched him while he moved around a bit, his
all feet nervous, the light glinting on his polished-looking
d and the neat polka-dot bow-tie and his brightly-polished
es: and I remembered what I thought about Loman the
t time we worked together – I could stand his massaged
e and manicured hands and immaculate tailoring and
brilliant reputation for efficiency if only he'd have the
ce to make a human gesture now and then, leave his fly
zipped or something.

He still wouldn't answer because he hadn't been given
ugh time to work out the initial phase of the operation,
that was his problem and I wanted to know the score so
aid:

How bad is it?'

He turned on me fussily.

There's no need to panic.'

Just let me in, Loman.'

knew I shouldn't rush the poor little bastard but it was
hangover from the Tokyo-London bounce and maybe the
d here, disturbing me. That was for Loman too: it's part
a director's job to kick out any kinks in his executive's
che and set him running straight when the whistle blows.

You've seen the reconnaissance photographs?'

Yes,' I said.

We want you to go and inspect that aircraft. You knew
, of course.' He began haltingly, but already I could see
decided to shoot me the whole thing before he'd got it
up in his own mind, because yes, I was panicking, and
had to do something about it. 'It's a medium cargo
chine and its call-sign in the phonetic alphabet code is
go Victor. After a routine take-off in the UK one of the
toms and Excise officials noticed what appeared to be a
e signature on the freight declaration form. An enquiry
made and subsequently the Special Branch was called in.
this time Tango Victor was reported missing.'

ind gusted across the atrium and the green sword-blades

27

quivered. I watched Loman thinking. He thought with h
feet, placing them neatly together, turning and taking sho
steps as he square-searched the data and decided how mu
to tell me, how much to leave out: because the executive
the field has to go in with his nerves tuned like a cat's a
his wits light and if he's been overloaded with too much in
on the brink of the mission he's going to sprain his bra
when he needs it most.

'The findings deriving from the Special Branch enqui
were significant enough to persuade the Minister that t'
RAF should attempt to locate the aeroplane, put a fix on
and take photographs. This, as you know, was accomplishe

He talked like a bloody schoolmistress.

'How did they know where to look?'

He spread out the map on the dais.

'Its course was known, and it was last heard of in an ar
where a violent sandstorm had been reported. The RAF ma
their initial reconnaissance sortie on the assumption th
Tango Victor had been forced down by it. This was prov
to be correct.'

Carte Internationale du Monde Sheet NH-32 – Ha
Messaoud Area – Scale 1/1.000.000 – Longitude 6-12, Latitu
28-32 – Elevations, dunes, rock outcrops, reefs, wells, oas
camel-tracks, so forth.

'Is this the sandstorm area?'

'Yes. The cross is the site of the wreck.'

South in the Great Eastern Erg. Nearest camel-track alm
thirty miles away, Tunisian frontier ninety miles, nothing e
but sand, not an oasis, not even a well, not even a palm-tree

'No wonder they didn't survive.'

'The conditions were unpropitious, highly.' His manicu
finger whispered across the map. 'This oasis, Sidi Ben Ali,
the nearest point of habitation in Algeria itself. Control s
O'Brien there to assess the local situation and report. He v
briefed to find out whether any other party knew wh
Tango Victor had come down, and if so, who that party v
and whether it had any intention of going out to exam
the wreck. Unfortunately London received no report.'

He turned away as he said that. Not that he had a
scruples: his tone was petulant. It had been remiss of O'Br
to fail in this most elementary of tasks and there was
excuse for clumsiness.

'Was he actually found?'

We always hope that when it comes it'll be short and sweet, bullet in the brain or something.

'His incinerated remains were found on a rubbish tip. Some Arab boys had heard a disturbance and told the police. Despite the condition of the body there was evidence that O'Brien had been subjected to interrogation –' he turned to me quickly – 'but the most exhaustive checks throughout the network have established that this was ineffective. All signal matrices are intact and codes, access facilities, safe-houses and personnel-monitoring units reveal no indication of surveillance, blowing or penetration. This aspect, at least, is satisfactory.'

I went on looking at the map.

There were six of us at the Bureau with the suffix 9 to our code name: *Reliable under Torture*. Now there were only five. That's not many. It's not many because there's only one way of earning a 9 and nobody ever sets out to get it, I mean it's not a basket of fruit or a marble clock, and they don't add it to your dossier posthumously because the whole record goes into the shredder once you've bought it. All the 9 means is that you've got yourself in a jam at some time and been pulled and got out again without blowing your cover or the mission or the whole network and with enough of you left in one piece to go on working. It also means that those bastards in London are going to pick you for the jobs where there's a high risk of the opposition treading all over your face when they want to know the time, and that sort of selection makes for a brisk mortality rate and that's why there aren't many of us. Five.

'Am I taking over from O'Brien?'

We often have to do it but we don't like it. We like to make our own mess of things, not clear up someone else's.

'No. They sent Fyson in next. He blew his cover.'

'Oh for Christ's sake!'

'Of course I realize –'

'You call this a mission? What kind of –'

'I wasn't directing it when these –'

'That's bloody obvious.'

'Thank you.'

Then we both shut up while he worked out an argument good enough to keep me in the act and I tried to decide

29

how much it was worth shoving my head right down th
barrel just because I'd accepted the mission.

He wiped the sweat off his face with a spotless linen hand
kerchief, not looking at me, and when I knew I couldn't d
anything else about it I asked him:

'Did either of them get any info on the opposition befor
they folded up?'

'Very little.' He was trying to keep the relief out of hi
voice: if I ducked this one he'd have to call someone els
in and there wasn't enough time. 'But at least we know tha
there *is* another party interested in Tango Victor and tha
they'd prefer we didn't go near it.'

'Did Fyson see any sign of their trying to reach the wrec
overland?'

'You can ask him yourself. He's here in the hotel, at you
disposal.'

'Is he still in the operation?'

Slight pause.

'No.'

I looked at him but he was gazing at the map.

'Why not?'

'You prefer working alone. Don't you?'

The bastard was lying but I let it go. When you're workin
alone you can still have a dozen people manning the bas
or the radio or the access-lines and there was some othe
reason why Fyson wouldn't be doing it and Loman wasn
going to tell me and I wasn't going to ask him again.

I didn't like it, anything about it, the whole thing stank, th
activity killed off right in phase 1 and a cover blown withou
any real info coming in and the situation so desperate no
that they'd had to call in a man like Loman to try holdin
the roof up while I ferreted around in the dark.

'You know something, Loman?' He looked up from th
map. 'I think you've lost me.'

He didn't say anything.

I knew half a dozen first-line executives who'd turn th
thing down flat – Simmons, Cockley, Foster, people like tha
– because you don't spend three years in training and th
rest of your time working your way through the elementar
intelligence-assessment fields with a Curtain embassy military
attaché cover to the major assignments at M-Classified lev
and then risk all your experience, all your capability, all you

professional expertise to a chancy job in the dark that someone else has mucked up for you on his way in.

Loman knows this. It takes a long time to rear a good
ferret. So I couldn't understand what the hell they were doing.

'What the hell are they doing?'

'Who?'

'Control.'

'Doing?'

'Throwing us this bloody auction.'

He walked about again while I stood there sweating and
listening to the hot fluttering wind that was hitting the top of
the atrium and shaking the sword-blade leaves, sending them
rattling with a dry dead sound.

Then Loman stopped and stood neatly in front of me with
his hands tucked behind him and his alert bird's head lifted
to look me in the eyes and I knew he was going to keep me
in this operation and work me to death if he had to, or save
my skin if he had to, because there was no choice, because
it was too late to call in someone else, simply because of that.

'I want you to know two things, Quiller.'

Prissy, fussy voice, talked like a bloody schoolmistress.

But I knew he'd get me.

'One is that you can dismiss entirely your fears that we
are engaged on a mission that has started off badly. O'Brien
and Fyson were trying to pick up intelligence and pass it
back to Control, and they failed. But you are not taking over
from them: the original field – Sidi Ben Ali in Algeria – has
been closed from operations and our base will be the oasis-
town of Kaifra in Tunisia. *Our* mission is to examine the
wreck of Tango Victor and report on it. The operation is
exclusively ours, and the task of inspecting the aeroplane
exclusively yours.'

Bird's eyes bright, watching me. Giving me a lecture,
Loman all over, not even trying to talk persuasively because
he didn't have to, all he had to do was work on my weak
point and he knew what it was. Couldn't ever stand the little
tick.

'The second thing is that although our objective for the
mission is a small commercial aircraft forced down in the
desert, and nothing more than that, the importance of the
operation is very great.' He was watching for my reactions
and he knew he wouldn't get any and he wasn't getting any

31

but he went on watching. 'An hour ago I was in the rad room of the British Embassy here, talking to the Prin Minister himself. He wished to inform me personally th your mission is the key to a critical situation of the highe international proportions.' Head on one side, the tone info mative, impersonal. 'I had been told that before, of cours on the highest authority. The fact that they were asking director of my experience to take charge of the operatie confirmed its importance.'

He turned away and took a pace and took a pace bac and stood with his feet neatly together and finished me ot

'This task calls for the highest professional talent. I accepte it on the sole condition that I could have you, Quiller, as n executive in the field.'

Little bastard.

He was in shock.

'You mind if we don't have the lights on?'

This was why Loman had hesitated when I'd asked hi if Fyson was still in the operation.

'It was so bright down there.' I suppose he meant in Si Ben Ali. 'It's done something to my eyes.'

He went and sat down, hurrying a little to reach the chai He sat with his hands on his knees, as if he had to hold h body together, looking straight in front of him. In the du light coming from the bathroom I could see he was shiverin

You see them like this at the Bureau when a missior blown up or they've just been too long in the field; they con in like a rag doll and Tilson says hallo old horse, bit of rough time, was it?

'Just give me the essentials,' I told him, 'then I'll buzz of

'It's all —' it sounded as if he was afraid of stuttering — dunno.' Best he could do, I suppose, for the moment. looked interestedly around the room, print of a fourth-centu tapestry, coloured photo of a mosque, a slight gap in t curtains so I went to fix it and he said Don't! in a kind sob and I left it. He thought I'd been going to open them.

But he couldn't have been tagged here or Loman would have let me contact him. It was just his nerves.

There was a bottle of Scotch on the bedside table and he already hit it for half but it hadn't done anything, he w ice-cold sober. I poured some out and he took it and dra and squeezed his face shut and I got the glass before he dropped it.

'Six months' leave,' I said, 'marvellous, think of the fishing.'

In a minute he made a big effort, jerking a hand out, pointing to the bottle. 'Drink?'

'No, thanks.'

I told him about London so that he'd think of home, lot of tourists in, gawping at the Guards, bloody hot when I left but nothing compared with here of course, nice in the parks, took me damned nearly half an hour before he could straighten out enough to talk properly. He asked me:

'You're not going there? Sidi Ben Ali?'

'No.'

'Loman said it's Kaifra, next.'

'That's right.'

'He wasn't directing me.'

'I know.'

On the sole condition that I could have you, Quiller, as my executive in the field, little bastard, working on my weak point, professional pride – vanity, if you like, what's the difference, but at least he hadn't been lying: if London picked a man like him it was strictly business and if he picked a man like me it meant this op was in the extreme-hazard classification and he'd wanted someone who was in this game for kicks and with nothing to lose.

'They got O'Brien,' he said.

'I know.'

'There's not much I can tell you. We didn't – '

'There's a long gun somewhere, is there?'

Because even in this light I could see there were no marks on the hands or the face and he could hold a glass and walk all right, and he'd been afraid I was going to open the curtains.

'Yes.'

He'd flinched just at the mention of it.

We've all got our little ways: some of the executives can't cope with unarmed combat but they'll fiddle with a bomb till they've got the spring out; others can stand hooding for days on end but touch them with a cigarette-end and they'll break. But none of us like the telescopic rifle: once you know the opposition's hired a crack shot and he's looking for you in the sights it begins to worry you because you can't walk into the sights or get out of your car or move across a

window and it's inhibiting. You start thinking about how t
stay alive instead of how to do the job and every time a doc
slams you miss a breath and in the end you finish up lik
Fyson.

He'd known they were serious, because of O'Brien.

'How long did it take them,' I asked him, 'to blow you?'

'Three days. I know it doesn't sound –'

'Don't worry. Loman says you did bloody well.'

Loman hadn't said anything of the sort.

'Pissing me about.' He managed a faint grin. 'He wouldn
say a thing like that, even if I'd – ' he shrugged with a han
and said – 'but they're very active, you know. I couldn't g
much sleep because we didn't even have a safe-house.'

'They know the plane's there?'

'They know it's in the area, the rough area.'

'Because you were there? You and O'Brien? Or d'you thin
they've got info from the UK?'

From what Loman had told me about the Special Branc
I thought there must have been some arrests, but the lin
with Algeria was plain enough because of Tango Victor
course and there could be some signal lines out.

Fyson had become quiet and I knew I was pushing hi
too hard.

'It doesn't – '

'No, I'm okay.' With another effort he said: 'The Algeria
Air Force did a search about a week ago. Didn't Loman te
you?'

'He hasn't briefed me yet, not fully.'

Loman had made the rdv in Tunis because of the airpor
I knew that. He hadn't been certain of me and it would hav
been quicker to bring someone else in London-Tunis dire
than from down south in Kaifra where there was probabl
only an airstrip. Otherwise he'd have made our rdv in Kaifr
straight away.

'It might have been the sandstorm,' said Fyson. 'It can cov
things in minutes, then uncover them again.'

'Loman can tell me that part of the thing.' I didn't wa
to drain the last of his strength before I'd put the only fe
questions that were important. 'Listen, did you get an actu
sight of the opposition?'

'Nothing recognizable.' He was trying to pour himse
another drink and I did it for him and he bit on to it an

34

ooked better and said: 'There was always that bloody gun,
you see – I kept catching sunlight on it and once I just walked
nto range and he chipped some brickwork away. It slows
ou up, doesn't it?'

'D'you know if –'

Then the phone rang.

It was right next to him and after a kind of jerk he just
lid off the chair and the glass smashed before I could catch
im and try to prop him up and answer the damned thing
t the same time, it was very awkward.

Chapter Four

KAIFRA

At 19.15 I checked out of the Hotel Africa and went across
o where the Chrysler was parked.

It had been Loman on the telephone.

'I have just talked to London and we have another directive
rging us to hurry.'

'The opposition's making progress?'

'That is the inference.'

'Then we'll hurry.'

Now that I'd let him sell me the mission I wanted to bring
off and that sand-covered wreck out there had suddenly
ecome personal to me: Tango Victor was mine.

'It is now 18.51 and I've booked you on Tunis Air Flight
16 to Jerba, depart 19.45, and instructed Avis to have a car
tanding by for you at your ETA, 20.30. I shall take the later
ight at 21.15 to Jerba and proceed independently to Kaifra.
t Kaifra you are booked in at the Hotel Royal Sahara,
oom 37, and I shall telephone you as soon as I arrive. My
TA Jerba is 22.00. In this season the Jerba-Kaifra route
an be driven in five hours and this will be quicker than trying
or air connection to Garaa Tebout, because Tunis Air
on't fly there in any case. Do you have any questions?'

'What are you doing about Fyson?'

'He's been withdrawn from the mission, as I told you.'

'But I mean his nerves are shot.'

'I see. Then I'll send a doctor along.'

We hung up.

So at 19.15 I checked out of the Hotel Africa and wen across to where the Chrysler was parked and they said later a the hospital that the glass had been the worst trouble becaus some very small fragments had got stuck in my face an they'd been difficult to find.

There weren't any bones broken but they were worried b various signs of physiological shock that were still hangin about, and the bruises where I'd been flung across the pave ment. I didn't remember much, but there'd been no actua retrogressive amnesia: I checked on that right away. I wa just walking towards the Chrysler and then the senses wer partially dead through overloading: very bright flash, a lc of noise, smell of burnt aromatic nitro compounds and th feel of the pavement sliding around under me.

They'd made a silly mistake, that was all. They wouldn have risked installing an ignition detonator linkage right ou side in the street: they'd had to put something quick o board and it was probably a rocking activator and a bu had passed close and the slipstream had rocked the Chrysle enough to trigger the thing at the wrong time, three or fou seconds too early.

Loman came as soon as I rang him and found me in th casualty room with bowls and bandages and blood everywher

'Listen, get me out of here and fix another plane.'

Speech sounded a bit sloppy because the mouth had ge cut up by the glass and it had begun puffing.

'Do they want to keep you under observation?'

'Yes, there's the odd bit of glass left in but it'll work itse out, they know that. And for Christ's sake signal Fyson.'

He knew what I meant. There'd been no tags on me sinc I'd left London – every routine check I'd made had come u negative – but when I'd called on Fyson in his room I walked right into a red sector because they'd had him und surveillance and he didn't know and now we'd have to te him.

'They're established agents,' Loman said.

'Of course.'

Because they had a dossier on me. Fyson had blown h cover and thought he'd got clear but they'd tagged him fro Sidi Ben Ali to Tunis and put static surveillance on him a when I'd shown up they'd checked their data and said yes this one's for neutralizing. But they'd only had forty-five minutes to find and fix the car and rig the bang and that could be why they'd mucked it.

The nurse came back with another hypodermic and I said not now and left it to Loman, it was his job, and he was signing some kind of form accepting responsibility when I got my flight-bag and took a taxi and double-checked for ticks all the way along the Khaireddine Pacha because we didn't want any trouble down at our base and I had to get there clean.

The taxi seemed to be swerving a bit down the long perspective of the eucalyptuses, either because of the crosswind or because the driver kept looking at me in the mirror and trying to pluck up the courage to ask me what brand of razor I used because he didn't want one, or maybe it was the hangover from the blast-wave upsetting the semi-circular canals: there was still some head-noise.

But I could focus all right and there were no tags and the airport was negative and at 21.15 I was airborne on Flight 917 with Loman's ticket and the girl was asking me what I wanted to drink.

There was a flight on the board at Jerba scheduled in at 22.35 and I knew Loman would be on that one because of the hurry directive from Control: he wouldn't hang around in Tunis with his executive already homed in at base.

They had a Mercedes 220 lined up and it had an air-conditioner but I didn't switch it on: the day's heat still pressed down on the island from a stifling sky but there wouldn't be any encapsulated environment for me in the desert so I let the organism start adapting as we ran through Houmt Souk and took the causeway to Zarzis.

Starlight and the black plumage of date-palms rushing overhead, the screen pocked and silvered by the death of insects and the heat coming on progressively as the road ran south until I had to start breathing consciously to keep awake.

Hit something once, a bump and the lights swinging and the wheel floating and more difficult, quite a job, much more difficult than I'd thought, than it should be, to keep traction and pull her back straight, worried me and we slowed, of course they'd been perfectly right, twenty-four hours' observation, it was just that those fidgety pimps in London wouldn't give us a break.

Through midnight at Remada and slowing again to seventy-five along the sandy track to Bj Djeneiene to avoid the turn-off at the Libyan frontier, the bruises burning now and the eyes trying to sort out the fast-incoming data without losing focus through fatigue: but the mirror was clear and if Loman didn't pick up a tag we'd have a safe base to jump from in the south.

Kaifra 02.50.

Sandy streets buried among dark massed palms, a few naked bulbs at the crossings, the headlights swinging over the humped shapes of Arabs sleeping below white walls, a mosque with a candle burning, the wind dead and the heat thick on the air and the nerves uncertain, a longing for sleep.

Royal Sahara.

Mais qu'est-ce-que vous avez, m'sieu'?

Rien, un petit accident sur la route.

Il vous faut des soins?

Non, c'est fait. Du sommeil, c'est tout.

In Room 37, air-conditioning, wonderfully cool: I turned it off and opened the window and let the heat in, like opening an oven door, get used to it, be worse out there in Longitude 8°3' by Latitude 30°4', start adapting and don't bloody well gripe.

Sleep.

Loman dragged me out of dreams of flying glass and Corinne swathed in bandages, it's the strain on the arms she was saying.

03.45.

'No. Were you?'

'No.'

He sounded relieved about this because it had been the tags on Fyson that had led to the bomb thing and he didn't want his executive blown from under him before he could mount the op.

'I'm speaking from base. We shall need a little more time to set up the radio, so the next rdv is for 15.00 hours tomorrow at the *Auberge Yasmina, rue des Singes.* Please repeat.'

Straight out of the bloody book, that's Loman for you.

I said I've got that and the thing went dead with a rather pettish click.

The Arab screamed, lurching backwards till he struck the wall and crouched there with his withered brown hands flung out in protection, the scarecrow body shaking under the robes, the old eyes staring in terror and the mouth fixed in the scream that was dying now, its energy exhausted.

Then hideously he began again, the sound shrilling out of him until quick heels came tapping and a needle flashed and he collapsed like a sack of bones, whimpering.

Jbal f-al Sma, u-tēz kbiz lli khal Sams . . .

The nurse tried to lift him and I got up.

'Puis-je vous aider?'

'Okay,' the big man said.

He lifted the Arab and stood with him in his arms.

'There were magnetic storms,' the girl said, 'it is often the way.' She led the big man through the passage and into a room on the other side as footsteps neared, hurrying. The scream had woken the place up.

Mountains in the sky, and great birds darkening the heavens . . .

The driller came back and said: 'Holy cats. Enough to make you knock off the booze!' He sat down, the sweat shining on his big red face and along his arms as he took a packet of Gauloises and offered me one. 'Giving it up?' He scratched a match for himself. 'Magnetic storms my arse — they're checking the bread supplies down at the research station, you know that? Everybody know it's ergot. You been here long, buster?'

'Not long.'

'He ain't the only case, there's others. Six months ago there was an outbreak in Mali, thousand miles south of here. You heard of ergot?'

'Grain fungus.'

'That's it. There was a case in France, remember? Half a village went loco. You with the Petrocombine outfit?'

'Attached.'

'I'm Bob Vickers, South 5.'

'Charles Gage.'

He had a hand like an earth-shovel.

'We've got trouble. Smashed a core-drill on a fault, fou thousand deep.'

The nurse came back and told him to put his cigarette ou and began work on my dressings.

'Okay, dolly. You free tonight?'

Another truck drummed past the building, heading sout] to Camp 4. The windows vibrated and sand flew against th glass. They'd woken me at dawn, the trucks: this was th last oasis-town before the drilling complex nearer the frontier

'What happened to you, Charlie?'

'I ran off the road.'

'Join the club. Mine was a horned viper – see that?'

He showed me the fang-marks.

'Can you pull this sleeve off, please?'

The clinical smell of Dermo-Cuivre.

'You busters hit any oil yet down at South 4?'

'Would I tell you?'

His laugh boomed like a cannon.

'You can relax, Charlie, I'm a godless bum. If my contrac ends before they get that drill out I'm moving right over t Anglo-Belge, okay? Bob Vickers works for the highes bidder.'

He picked up the *Tribune* that lay on top of the pile.

'How long will this take?'

'Perhaps a little time.' Her smile was quick but there wa a flicker to the olive-brown eyes: the Arab had unnerve her. 'There are many pieces of glass.'

They'd been cutting their way out as the organism rejecte them and I'd come here because I didn't want the laceration to start opening up again later when the mission was runnin and the stress came on.

'How long have you got to live?'

'You mean me?'

'With a horned viper bite.'

His laugh boomed again and a spoon tinkled in a beaker

'Holy cats, that was four days ago. I'm just here for th routine blood-test, so take your time.'

She irrigated again and another fragment rang into th enamel bowl. The windows of the Chrysler had been given shrapnel effect by the blast.

At 09.00 this morning on Radio Tunis I'd heard tha Loman had put immediate smoke out. By the sources quote knew he must have reached half a dozen major night-desks in the Embassy signals-room and his story was accepted on the principle that to a jaded night-editor looking for a last-minute flash, one rumour was as good as another.

An 'official enquiry' had 'established' that Mr C. W. Gage, British geophysical consultant on business in Tunis, had narrowly escaped being the innocent victim of an error on the part of 'certain political activists' when the car he was hiring exploded in the street. The enquiry led to the discovery that the man – so far un-named – who had hired the car immediately prior to Mr Gage was a known member of the fanatical United Arab Front organization, and it was there-fore 'confidently believed' that this man had been the intended victim.

It was routine cover.

I don't know what the actual figures are but a big percen-tage of people in my trade finish up at the wrong end of a gun and even the public has an idea that a law-abiding citizen can get into his car quite often without being blasted into Christendom. The classic statement to the press is that 'he didn't have an enemy in the world' and it won't always wash with the public and it won't ever wash with the back-ground monitoring sections of the major intelligence networks because they automatically send for pictures and if they recognize the face they want to know what X was doing in Tunis or Cairo or Bonn and there'll be a directive for some-one to find out.

So today they'd pick up the radio story and tomorrow they'd be looking at my picture in Washington and Moscow and Peking and pressing the buzzer and saying go and see if you can find out what the London lot are doing in North Africa.

The smoke Loman had put out wouldn't provide total cover but it was the best he could do and he'd done it. The only thing that worried me, by its implications, was the fact that today he'd have to do the same thing again because Radio Tunis had also reported that the body of another Englishman had been found floating in the harbour late last night and that his name was Fyson.

The *Auberge Yasmina* was a decaying French Colonial residence with gilded cupolas and a forecourt buried under the

shade of rotting palms where I could hear rats running. Th
sun's rays penetrated only in places, making pools of lig
on the crumbling mosaic floor.

The door hung open and I went inside. After the glare
the street it seemed almost dark in here but I could see
figure, robed in white and motionless in the middle of th
hall.

'Ahlah ou sahlan.'

By the angle of his head I saw that he was looking slight
away from me, and because the stranger's footstep ha
worried him I answered quickly: *Saha. Ala slametek.*
North Africa they are only just beginning to control sandf
trachoma.

He said I should go up and I passed him and then hea
Loman's voice from the stairs.

'All right, Quiller.'

As we climbed, our shoes grating on chips of marble th
had broken away from the mosaic, the hot afternoon lig
blazed through coloured glass so that rainbow patter
flowed across Loman's shoulder as he led the way up.

'They run it as a small hotel, but we're alone here exce
for one or two staff. The heat's too much for the tourists
Kaifra and this is the dead season.'

'What's our cover?'

'Radio liaison with Petrocombine's South 4 camp f
supplies and emergency signals.'

By the time we reached the top floor we were sweatir
hard and he was wiping his face because this wasn't th
Hotel Royal Sahara and there wasn't a lift and there wasr
any air-conditioning. Our weight set the passage vibratir
invisibly and flakes of plaster drifted like orange-blosso
from the frescoed walls.

The radio base was at the end of the building and
followed Loman in. From the size of the domed ceiling v
were now underneath one of the great gilded cupolas I
seen from the street. Faded arabesque screens, cracked mosa
floor and the minimal mod. cons. of a fifth-category packag
deal hotel: bed, washbasin, curtained shower.

'This is Diane Bowman, our radio operator.'

There wasn't anything in his tone.

He made it sound just like a casual introduction. But
didn't look at me: at least he had the grace to look away

e showed me how far things had gone towards perdition,
ow desperately he'd been driven by London to rig up this
mission they'd asked for, to rig the thing up with no time
or selective staffing or initial briefing and no established
ccess facilities and not a hope in hell of doing anything
ore than send this whole operation staggering blindly on
ll it finished both of us.

Tonelessly he said: 'This is Quiller, the executive in the
eld.'

I think she came forward a pace to greet me, I don't
member, and then I supposed stopped, seeing I didn't move.
Fair hair and a young face, the mouth surprised and the
es waiting, uncertain of me, the stance defensive, the bare
ms hanging loose but the hands tensed, a slight girl, a girl
at of a fashion magazine, thin-bodied in a fisherman's vest
d slacks and sandals, this summer's gear for Brighton or
e Broads and all the rage and oh Christ a mission to run
d this child caught in its machinery.

When I could, I looked at Loman.

There was nothing in my tone either; we'd both of us been
ined, long ago, out of our habits; but he knew what was
my mind.

'How long has she been operating on priority missions?'

He stood with his hands tucked neatly behind him, head on
e side but still not looking at me, maybe prepared for me to
ow up in his face and get it over, maybe deciding on policy
t to answer me till I forced him.

'Long enough,' the girl said, 'to know how to do it.'

Her eyes were steady now, no longer uncertain of me. She
od with her arms folded and her chin lifted a fraction.

Loman spoke suddenly. I suppose the anger in her voice
d encouraged him.

'When I direct a mission I choose first-class people and if
s radio operator has my approval then you can have every
nfidence in her.'

He couldn't even make it sound right.

My mind had partially blanked off and I couldn't think of
ything useful to say: he and I both knew what the situation
s and there wasn't anything to talk about. Professional
tinct was still functioning, though, and I crossed the uneven
saic to the window and pulled down the venetian blind
d fixed the catch.

'Keep it shut.'

She said:

'I like the view.'

It was very quiet here: the post-meridian heat of th
August sun was lying like a dead-weight on the town an
we were among the few people who weren't deep in a siest
No sound came from outside this room, no sound at all.

Loman took out his damp silk handkerchief and wiped h
polished face. The sweat trickled on me as the organism trie
to reduce the body-temperature. I didn't move. I was begin
ning to lose the fine-tuned sense of direction, of shape, c
purpose, the thing we call mission-feel that develops t
infinite degrees as we go forward, step by step, into the are
where we have committed ourselves to unknown tasks in th
teeth of unknown hazards: the sense that tells us, at ever
step, that it's now too late to turn back.

This I was beginning to lose.

'Loman. It's no go.'

He made an impatient gesture but said nothing.

I didn't look at the girl. It wasn't her fault.

Under the big dome my voice echoed strangely.

'You'd better signal London. Get some professional staf

He was standing perfectly still, a listening bird, his sma
eyes bright and his neat head tilted. I knew there wasn't an
thing he could say because it was beyond him now: the
wasn't time to get anyone capable from London and it was
his fault but I was getting fed-up.

'I can get killed this way, Loman. We all can. For nothir
Just because those incompetent bastards in London ha
taken on a job that's got to be done so fast that we ca
even hope to survive for as long as it takes to do it. Th
isn't an intelligence operation, it's a suicide pact.'

Loman could think quite fast but he couldn't talk while
was doing it and he didn't talk now so I shut up and let hi
get on with it because this was his pigeon: when the direct
in the field sends the executive in there's got to be a pi
fessional set-up. We didn't have one.

I suppose he'd thought of a dozen angles of attack in tho
few seconds and obviously the one he chose was the one
thought was right and he was wrong.

'I think you're showing an unreasonable bias towards –'

'Is that so?' I was really very fed-up. 'We've been called

by a panic directive to clear up the wreck of an operation
that went off half-cocked and killed one man and blew
another and by a bit of luck I missed a bomb and last night
they picked Fyson out of Tunis harbour and it'd be nice to
think that when they grilled him he didn't break but the last
time I saw him alive his nerve had gone so they wouldn't
have had any trouble. How safe's our base now, Loman?
And all you can do about it is pick a kid out of school who
leaves her radio in direct sight of a building at fifty yards'
optical range even through low-powered glasses and doesn't
pull the blind down because she likes the view.'

In ten seconds he looked at me and said:

'She is an efficient radio operator. Highly efficient.'

When I turned she was watching me, angry because of what
I'd said about her, frightened because of what I'd said about
Fyson.

'All right she's an efficient radio operator but who's going
to look after her if I'm in the desert and you have to leave
base for five minutes?'

Before he could answer she said:

'I can look after myself.'

'How?'

She drew very fast and I hit the thing before she'd finished
and it spun high and chipped plaster off the wall and curved
down and skittered across the mosaic.

'You have to be faster than that.'

Loman said bleakly:

'I would undertake to man the base personally at all times.'

'Good of you.'

I went over and picked the gun up and wiped the plaster off
and checked for damage and gave it back to her, a half-
pound six-shoot .25 standard lightweight, wouldn't stop a
mouse.

'And leave the safety-catch off. There's no point in a fast
draw if the trigger's locked.'

She took it but wouldn't look at me, her eyes were down
and she was breathing fast, the heat and of course the
frustration. I must have bruised her hand but she didn't let
herself nurse it, a point for that but one point wasn't enough
to qualify her for running the radio liaison of a mission with
the death-roll rising before we were even on our marks.

Loman was still thinking but he couldn't find what he

wanted: an argument that could keep me with him. It was too
late now for an easy trap like the one he'd used on me before.

'She was head of signals at the Embassy in Tunis and
monitoring the Egyptian-Israeli frontier-incident reports direct
for London. She has fluent French, Italian and Arabic with
five dialects.'

I looked at the radio, its facia striped by the shadows of
the sunblind. It was a KW 2000CA single-sideband transceiver
with four channels on the dial and an auto-scrambler.

'What's your frequency coverage?'

Her head came up.

'3.0 to 19 mc/s.'

'Channels?'

'Four preset crystal controlled.'

'Receiver sensitivity?'

'Better than one microvolt for one watt output.'

'What frequencies would you use in this area?'

'7 MHz for daytime propagation conditions, 3 MHz at
night.'

'How long have you worked with this type?'

'Over two years.'

'Did you choose it because of that?'

'No. Because it's perfect for the conditions here.'

I nodded and turned away.

Loman was watching me. I felt him watching.

She was all right on the radio and she knew how the thing
worked but if I went out there a hundred miles deep into the
desert I'd be like a diver with a lifeline. My lifeline would
be the radio liaison facility and if it were put out of action
I'd fry out there like a louse. Worse: the mission would end
at the same time and in the same place, *objective unaccom
plished*.

Loman said:

'Arrangements have been made to jump you in rather
soon.'

'How soon?'

'Tonight.'

This was the argument he'd been looking for.

The nearer you get to the brink of a mission the faster you
want to go: it's a kind of target attraction and you don't want
to pull out and the little bastard knew this and now he'd
thrown me the deadline and it was close. In a matter of hours

could be out there in the silence of the sands and alone
vith the objective: the broken-winged smudge on the desert
oor that no one had been closer to than sixty-five thousand
eet.

Tango Victor.

I looked at the girl.

'Did you volunteer for this kind of work.'

'Yes.'

'You know it's dangerous?'

'Yes.'

'What makes you want to do it?'

'The interest. And the danger.'

'Would you say you had a strong sense of survival?'

'Pretty strong, yes. I'd fight like hell.'

I told Loman he could brief me.

Chapter Five

MOHAMED

he hit the set open.

Tango to Embassy.

Loman was restive again, thinking with his feet. He'd got
e to the jump-off point and there weren't any more doubts:
•night the mission would start running.

Tango to Embassy.

'What time,' he asked me, 'did you hear it?'

'09.00 on Radio Tunis.'

Embassy to Tango. Receiving you.

'No details? Just that he was found in the harbour?'

'An Englishman named Fyson. A police enquiry has begun.'

Stand by, please.

She gave him the mike.

*This is for London, Liaison 9. F Freddie absent believe
ther hand believe may pip-squeak first. No: pip-squeak. Near
noke negative please delegate. Q Quaker home on TJ-TK-
1-102 repeat TJ-TK-S1-102. Queries? Tango out.*

I'd spread the map on the bed and he came over and began
·iefing me.

'I told you that after Tango Victor had taken-off from the UK there was a suspected false signature found on a Customs and Excise declaration form. It was discovered that the pilot had knowingly taken-off without proper freight inspection. Twenty-four hours later a report went in to D.I.6 in London that the Algerian Air Force was in the process of mounting a ground-search by five squadrons of its desert-reconnaissance branch along this twenty-kilometre band from Oran here on the Mediterranean coast to Alouef, south of this upland here, the Plateau de Tademaït. It was described as the usual "routine exercise".'

'Was there any monitoring liaison at that stage?'

Customs, Special Branch, D.I.6 and the Bureau were very disparate organizations.

'No. Monitoring liaison began when a telephone call from a Frenchwoman in Tripoli was received at the airfield where Tango Victor's pilot was based – incidentally his name is Holt. The Special Branch was then called in and it was recognized that the twenty-kilometre band on the map here in fact straddled the proposed course of the freighter over land south of the Mediterranean. It seems that Holt diverted his flight to Tripoli without informing anyone, landing for an overnight stop in order to visit an acquaintance who lives there – the woman who telephoned the airfield in the evening of the next day. Evidently he had told her that he was to fly back to the UK after seeing her, and she phoned to make sure he'd arrived safely. It was of course only from that point in time that anyone in London knew that Holt's course across Algeria had been Tripoli-Alouef, not Oran-Alouef.'

The picture was coming up and I did a visual check on the map and saw that a line drawn from Tripoli to Alouef would pass through our target-area: Longitude 8°3′ by Latitude 30°4′

'This was why the Algerian Air Force was unable to find the wreck and why the RAF succeeded. The recent action against O'Brien, Fyson and yourself make it clear that the opposition realizes that we know where the plane is and that they're anxious to reach it before we do.'

'You think they're overlooking the obvious?'

He turned away from the map and walked neatly up and down. 'No. I think they don't rate their chances very high.'

He'd got the point but I didn't expect him to fill anything in for me: this was a briefing session at Local Control, not a planning operation in London. But there was an equation that didn't work out and it worried me: the opposition couldn't have overlooked the obvious point that if they wanted to reach Tango Victor the best thing to do would be to follow us in and make an over-kill on the spot. Loman thought they weren't too sanguine about this and maybe he was right.

There was a theory I liked even less: they could have killed off O'Brien and Fyson and attempted to kill me too *because they knew where Tango Victor was lying.* And we had to be held off while they tried to reach it. This would explain the hurry directive from London.

'What are the chances of another desert-recco exercise?'

He stopped pacing and looked at the wall and I knew this was something that needled him.

'That's quite impossible to deduce.' He was trying to make up his mind whether to block me off here and avoid overloading or cover the situation for me and he couldn't reach a decision standing still so he got into motion again. 'The opposition may conceivably include factions other than Algerian. We shouldn't discount Libya or Egypt or the United Arab Front organization. Nor should we discount the effects of internecine shifts of policy. The lack of a second search by the Algerian Air Force – this time over the target area – does not necessarily indicate that they know where the aeroplane came down: it could be due to a reluctance on the part of the newly-formed government in Algeria to mount an "exercise" so close to the Tunisian and Libyan borders. The assassination of King Hamouda and the seizure of power by the generals has left North African relationships rather delicate for the time being.'

I looked at the map. If we could read it properly it could answer most of the questions.

'What made the opposition think the plane came down near the Tunisian border?'

He looked at me with his shoulders drooping suddenly.

'O'Brien. Then Fyson.'

'Then me.'

'That wasn't your fault.'

'I walked straight into surveillance.'

'You could hardly avoid it.'

'Do you think that our presence in the field is the *only*

49

reason why they believe Tango Victor came down within
hundred miles of Kaifra?'

In a moment he said:

'I would like to.'

I'd never seen Loman like this before: within hours
throwing the mission into gear he was uncertain on maj
aspects that London should have cleared for him befo
sending either of us into the field. Everything about th
operation stank of panic and I didn't like it because I w
the ferret and the ferret's always the first to go when t
whole thing blows apart.

'Who have you got lined up?'

He stopped moving about.

'Lined up?'

'If I come a mucker.'

I felt the girl watching me from near the radio.

'No one,' Loman said.

'With a thing as shaky as this—'

'I anticipate success.' His tone had risen a fraction and
controlled it at once. 'Complete success. You understand
He was wiping his face again. 'Had there been no chance
complete success I would have refused to direct the missio
regardless of pressure. I am asking you to proceed with eve
confidence, both in me and in the constant support we sha
have from London.'

I was learning something about Loman: the higher t
stress the more he talked like a schoolmistress.

'All right. Tell me about access, will you?'

He began moving again at once. I'd pushed the briefir
into the final phase and he wouldn't have to worry any mo
about the background aspects: the area where he w
critically uncertain.

'You will rendezvous with a French pilot tonight as soc
as he contacts me to say he's ready. His name is Gasto
Chirac and he was engaged in combat flying during th
Algerian war. Since then he has flown for the oil-compani
in desert survey work and knows the area thoroughly; he w
also the world sailplane champion three years ago when
raised the altitude record to forty-six thousand feet. There
only one way of sending you into the target area witho
either surveillance or active obstruction and that is by glide

'And parachute?'

50

'And of course parachute. Since this is a night-drop, both will be dull black, to ensure that you go in unseen as well as unheard. The take-off is arranged for 23.00 hours. The rock outcrop you saw on the reconnaissance photographs is approximately five hundred yards from the aeroplane and can be used as a landmark even by starlight; it may also conceivable offer partial shade during the day, though that is less certain. Your equipment will comprise the second transceiver, a 35mm reflex camera with flash, and of course desert-survival gear.'

'What's the estimated duration?'

He'd been pacing towards me and he turned away when I said that and it needn't have meant anything but I thought it did because my nerves were getting into tune as the deadline approached and they could catch vibrations that I'd miss at other times.

'Flexible.' I didn't hear anything in his tone because he'd make bloody sure of that. 'Forty-eight hours at the most: you'll have rations and water for that period, plus reserves. The task itself is not exacting: we are asked for photographs of the plane and its cargo. At the same time you will be reporting in precise detail by radio on what you discover, and your report will go directly on to tape in this room.'

So that if I didn't survive, all they'd lose were the photographs. That was all right.

I left the map and went over to the carved teak table and looked at the second transceiver. There was a recessed button that the other one didn't have.

'Manual destruct?'

'Yes. Ten-second fuse.'

'Acid?'

'Explosive.'

'Safe range?'

'Five yards.'

He paused for a moment and said: 'In any case it's purely refinement: the worst you'll have to contend with in the desert will be the heat. The more difficult phase of this operation is getting you to the jump-off point without attracting surveillance or obstructive action. We must therefore take every possible care.'

Near the edge of the retina an object is invisible: but move-

ment can be seen. At the actual edge of the retina not ev
movement shows itself: but it triggers a reflex and the ey
will turn quickly to bring the moving object into centr
vision for inspection.

Static objects have no automatic interest unless their sha
is significant, but to all animals movement has its ov
primitive significance: it may be signalling the presence
food in the form of prey or of danger in the form of
predator. In man, whose prey is killed and processed for hi
the perception of movement serves as a warning alone, un
the movement can be explained.

Unexplained movement is always suspect.

The rendezvous with Chirac had been fixed for 21.00 hou
at a *redjem* seven kilometres along the road to Garaa Tebo
and I was getting into the Mercedes when the visual refl
was stimulated and I turned my head and looked away aga
and pulled the seat-belt tight and got the engine going a
thought Christ, they didn't even let Fyson die in peace.

Loman had told me he'd got here from Tunis with no ta
and he couldn't have made a mistake about that because
those long straight stretches through the olive groves
would have seen a tag a mile away. I'd got here clean t
and it was nothing to do with the girl because there'd be
no surveillance when I'd gone to our base: that's a trip wh
you treble-check. So it was impossible that anyone knew
holed-up in Kaifra: if you forgot about Fyson.

Fyson had known I was coming here and they would
have had to do very much because his nerves had been s
and he didn't carry a 9-suffix and they'd only had one questi
for him so it was easy and Loman wasn't being funny wh
he said the most difficult stage of this operation was getti
me to the jump-off without someone trying to stop me.

I turned the 220 and drove under the lights of the ho
marquee and looked round to see if there were anythi
coming and took the east road through the tunnel of ov
hanging palms and checked the mirror and kept the spe
steady at thirty, a little more, such a nice evening for a dri

The slipstream didn't cool anything: it just circulated
heat. There were gnats already sticking to the windscre
and I used the wiper jets and the screen went silver a
slowly dark again. The roads in Kaifra are sanded over
places: the *Ghibli* blows it from the south and nobody fe

like sweeping it away so it's left for the wheeled traffic to break up the drifts and scatter the sand towards the edge of the road.

I didn't like the way Loman had said the estimated duration of my work in the target area was 'flexible'. After two seconds he'd put it at forty-eight hours' maximum but that didn't mean anything more than that I'd forced him into an obligatory answer. There are always unknown factors in any target area whether it's the office of the Cuban Minister for Defence or the off-limits research and development section of a Japanese electronics complex under government contract or a square mile of sand in the Sahara, but the director in the field makes a point of mounting a model operation on paper before he sets the real one running: and people like Loman and Egerton and Mildmay do it with a slide-rule and a stop-watch and a blueprint of the area.

That word 'flexible' simply meant that on this operation the director in the field didn't know how long it should take me to do the work once I'd gained access and it pointed to the same thing that all the other features pointed to: those bastards in London were sending me in with almost no preparation and once I was there I'd have to carry the whole of the load. The 'constant support from London' he'd talked about was strict cock because there'd be nothing London could do if I mucked it right in the middle of the job.

Yes of course I must try not to muck it but in a panic directive like this one the chances were a bloody sight higher.

A lovely night, with clear stars and soft shadows. The thing was to do it without bending a wing or anything because of police enquiries later. I didn't want to leave any paint.

He wasn't using his dipped heads but the sidelights were quite bright enough for me: they kept floating into the mirror and out again as we left the avenue of palms and got on to the wide sandy road bordering the desert.

Dark 404, nothing exceptional.

And he was alone. Wearing a fez, someone local. But quite professional, the way he hung back a long way and took a short cut now and then, crossing my bows a hundred yards ahead as if he were someone else. He knew the roads here, the intersections, and after ten minutes I got fed-up because he was so showy: it wasn't going to be easy with this one. So I did a U-turn and took three rights with the lights out

and caught him at an intersection and he had the grace t
swerve and look worried but it didn't make things any bette
because he began hanging on much closer so the only thin
it proved was that I'd done it on my own doorstep.

He was only a tag: there wouldn't be any action unless
did something busy. If they'd wanted to neutralize me they'
have used two men: one with the wheel, one with the gun
the rear tyres first to slow me and then the rear window
picking at the bottom left-hand corner while I couldn't duck
any lower without losing sight of the road.

He only wanted to know where I was going.

The rdv was twelve minutes from now and I didn't want t
turn up late for Chirac so I started a slow routine, using th
sand to slide on and flicking the lights out at the fast end o
a right-angle turn and doubling in the dark and slipping hir
twice before he worked out the score and decided to kee
so close that I could see his eyes in the mirror. No go.

Kaifra isn't a big place and it's surrounded by desert an
that made it difficult for me: there wasn't much choice o
terrain. I suppose he'd got his air-conditioning on and tha
made me fed-up again so I thought I should go and stare hir
out somewhere along the desert road to South 4.

I've only done it twice before and I don't like it becaus
there's a touch of Russian roulette about it and that's incon
sistent: in order to complete a mission you have to stay alive

If Loman had known what I was going to do he woul
have had the shits and I tried not to let this reinforce m
decision to do it. He would have argued that it was the dut
of an executive not only to protect himself against obstructiv
action by the opposition but also to avoid resorting to tactic
that could hazard the mission, so forth.

On the other hand my chances of getting out of the presen
situation alive weren't too high either: the man in the 40
realized that I was going somewhere exclusive because I'
been trying to throw him off. We could keep this up for hal
the night and if we went anywhere near his base he migh
decide to bring in some support to finish me off and if yo
start running with one on the tail and another one closing i
from ahead of you the chances get progressively disappointin
until they move in for the kill.

So I turned left twice and then right and found the roa

hat ran through fifteen miles of dunes to the South 4 camp.
The massed palms blocked most of the starlight but we didn't
go on to heads and he kept coming up very close every time
I jabbed the brakes and when he got used to the rhythm of
the thing I broke it and started drifting across his bows and
he didn't like that either because we couldn't see much on
parking lights and I suppose he didn't want to switch his
heads on because it would have looked so amateur.

Brakes: drift. Another drift and sand flew as the tyres
scattered it. Brakes: oh very close and I cleared it because
I didn't want to leave any paint on him.

Drift. Brake – drift and he got nervous and hit something,
trunk of a palm, and then I gunned up and he spun a lot and
I lost him and swung into the long desert road and went all
the way up through the gears on the automatic and crossed
the hundred mark with the power still coming on, no lights
yet in the mirror but they'd be there soon.

Ravines both sides.

Not deep ones but the engineers had followed the natural
lie of a bedrock *gassi* and then raised the roadway high
enough to stop the south-blowing *Ghibli* from burying it
under permanent drifts of sand.

Coming now, yes.

Faint lights in the mirror. Headlights, faint.

It would be all right out here. The setting was classic: sand,
stars and the highway leaning across the desert to the horizon,
fallen column. There was nothing complicated.

You can do it by first putting a critical amount of distance
between your own car and theirs. You can do this either by
relying on superior acceleration and maximum speed to take
care of the distance-factor or by taking them through a series
of feints and passes to slow them up before you go out for
the kill.

The 220 had the edge on the 404 but it would have taken
twenty miles to build up the degree of distance needed and
I didn't have the time and that was why I'd made a point
of slowing him in phase 1: it had brought the time-factor
right down with a bang and the whole thing would now be
over within the next thirty seconds and if I were still all right
I could go back and keep the Chirac rdv more or less on time.
It was very important not to touch him. Loman could do

quite a lot to keep me out of official trouble because his cov
provided him with the required diplomatic immunity and th
Embassy had been asked to give immediate support in th
event of a signal, but things could get tricky despite pr
cautions and two years ago when Proctor had just finishe
setting up final penetration for a first-class cipher-break
a Curtain-state consulate he blew the mission because he
left his car parked on a pedestrian-crossing and London g
very upset.

Tonight there was going to be an accident and if it wa
the 404's and not mine I wasn't going to report it and ever
thing would be all right so long as there weren't any mar
on the Mercedes.

The power was full on and I left it for five seconds while
worked out the odds. It depended on the kind of man he was
it depended totally on that. And I didn't know him. He coul
drive all right and didn't chuck it in when things got roug
but it didn't tell me much about the one factor that woul
finally decide the issue: his breaking-point.

No data.

It raised the risk but it was a calculated risk and the od
looked fair so I kicked the brakes and watched the need
because in the starlight the swinging parallax of the dun
didn't make for a good enough reference and it was saf
to drive on instruments. Patch of sand and we lost tractio
and I got it back and wrapped the friction round again, slow
through ninety, seventy, fifty with the lights in the mirr
getting brighter as the distance closed.

Fabric getting hot: normal. Maximum deceleration-curv
right out of the book and very effective but now I bega
wondering if I'd allowed the correct distance: all I'd ha
for a reference was the time he'd taken to come back int
the mirror and the brightness of his headlamps when he
turned them on.

Twenty.

Ten.

Zero and I used the last of the momentum to swing th
220 into a fast U that brought us facing the way we'd con
and then I gunned up by leaving my foot just where it wa
and letting the automatic send the needle up progressively.

His headlights seemed rather bright even allowing for th
fact that I was now facing them and I started wonderin

gain whether I'd judged things right but there was a rising
fty on the clock by now and everything was shaping up well
nough; I think it was only the primitive animal brain starting
o worry: the organism didn't like the look of this at all, up
n its back legs and bloody well whining.

Ignore.

Speed now 70.

His estimated speed: 80 plus.

Minimum impact figure if things went wrong: 150.

I didn't put the heads on yet because I wanted to save that
ll later: three or four seconds from now. At the moment
e wouldn't be absolutely sure what I was doing: he would
ave lost my rear-lamps but that could mean I'd simply
urned them off; he would have picked up my parking lights
ut he wouldn't necessarily identify them: with an eye-level
orizon the big North African stars seemed to be floating
n the dunes and this would confuse him.

I had to wait for the instant when he realized that I'd
urned round and was coming at him on a very fast collision-
ourse: then I'd start making him nervous in the final few
econds in the hope that he'd see the point.

Bloody well whining. Brain-think had partially gone and
e organism was snivelling about the risk: we wouldn't be
ere tomorrow, no more women, no more anything, so forth.
is headlights very bright in my eyes, almost blinding. The
unes streaming past, the warm air rushing at the windows.
lock: 85.

Running it close.

Certain areas of the forebrain still functioning: the para-
ount factor was his threshold of fear and that was estab-
shed by personal characteristics: the degree to which he
alued life, the extent of his subservience to the idea of Allah,
e measure of his willingness or otherwise to be beaten in a
are, other things, many other things. Not at all certain this
as in fact forebrain activity: point now reached when self-
ritical capacity very much diminished, sounded more like the
ganism panicking again, trying desperately to raise doubts
d scare me into chucking it.

No go.

It was quite a narrow road. It had been designed to take
e width of two trucks with enough space between to let
em pass. This meant that if you were driving a car the

size of the Mercedes 220 and kept in the middle of the ro
there wouldn't be room for anyone else.

Headlights dazzling now and no means of judging distan
any more, the gap closing at a rising 165 kph and too ris
to leave it later than this so I hit the switch and flooded hi
with light and hit the horns to bring in the scare-factor
the karate yell and sat there staring him out.

I wondered what his name was.

Ahmed Somebody. Mohamed Somebody.

Thirty-four missions and only a few scars and then I met
man named Mohamed, unlikely name for an epitaph, why n
Blenkinsop. My own, yes, my own fault. Not fault exactl
Whole thing was calculated. Miscalculated, thought he'd brea
first.

Light fierce and sight gone, driving blind, eyes shut a
the retinae burning. Sound coming in explosively fast fro
the desert night, he'd been so far away, now so close.

Dark.

Dark and the wind rocking as the slipstream hit a
dragged and set up turbulence, a great cough of sound th
silence.

Brakes.

Eyes watering badly, the road swimming. Dark only co
parative after the blinding light, silence relative to that u
pleasant explosive cough, be interesting one day to t
estimating how close he'd passed, how late he'd left it, ho
far he'd been airborne over the ravine before gravity ov
came momentum, slide-rules and stop-watches, but rea
only one of those things you think are still going to
interesting later. They're not. Christ sake more brakes.

Slowing.

Nearside tyres nibbling at the edge of the road, importa
not to go over, anything could happen if you hit ground
a bad angle and started rolling. Don't spoil it now.

Brakes. Slowing and locking and sliding and bringing
down through fifty, forty, with the ribs pressing into t
seat-belt. Acid in the stomach, various glands performir
a lot of adrenalin, a certain degree of weakness along t
forearms, general feeling of lassitude as the organism tri
to break the tension down, all right you snivelling little ti
I won't do it again.

When the speed was low enough I swung the wheel over a

ned back. There was an orange glow against the sky about
mile away and by the time I got there most of the petrol
d burnt out. I went close enough to make sure what had
ppened and then got back into the car.

Chapter Six

CHIRAC

est bien le numéro 136, que vous m'avez demandé, m'sieur?'
Oui, l'Auberge Yasmina.'
Ca ne répond pas.'
Insistez un peu.'
Mais il ne sonne même pas, m'sieur.'
Pourquoi pas?'
Eh b'en, il est en dérangement. Je vais—'
Vous êtes certaine?'
Absolument. Je vais le signaler. Je regrette, m'sieur.'
  hung up.
The cabin was stifling.
There was still the odd flash, the after-image of his head-
ts: the retinae kept registering the glare. My hands weren't
fectly steady yet: when you do something like that the
anism thinks more about the consequences after you've
ne it than before, because the tension has gone and there's
e for nightmares.
Disregard.
Outside the cabin the terrace of the Oasis Bar was crowded,
stly with oil-men in transit to and from Petrocombine's
th 4 camp. Light from amber lanterns threw shadows
m the trellis screens and the tendrils of tropical creepers;
Malouf Tunisien from overhead speakers was half-drowned
 the voices of the drillers; three young prostitutes were
ng the rounds, formally shaking hands.
Check. Double-check. Negative.
Because I didn't like the thing about the telephone not
rking at the Auberge Yasmina: she'd said it didn't even
g. It's not terribly comfortable to lose communication with
r base two hours before a jump-off. It doesn't steady the

59

hands. It was essential that Loman should know about
404 in case we needed local smoke out: there'd be a po
enquiry because the accident had been fatal and some
might have seen a Mercedes 220 on the South 4 highw
about the time there'd been a glow in the ravine. We do
like police enquiries because it means a lot of questions a
it can hold things up.

Bloody thing didn't even ring and I didn't have any mea
of knowing if it were just a routine breakdown, the he
buckling a conduit, a rat nibbling the cables, or if someo
had cut the lines before they'd gone in for Loman and t
girl with a sub-machine-gun. No means of knowing, at t'
moment, whether the mission was still viable or whether
the arabesque room beneath the gilded dome of the Auber
Yasmina it had been blown to hell.

The whole town had become a red sector: the whole
Kaifra, not just the Yasmina and the Royal Sahara and
Oasis Bar. Because they wouldn't just throw some flowers ov
that burnt-out wreck in the ravine: they were profession
and they had my dossier and they'd know I wouldn't ne
ralize a tag unless I were running close to some kind
deadline.

I left the cabin and went through the terrace and out
the Mercedes and checked and got negative and noted t
trip and took the road north-east to Garaa Tebout and dro
for seven kilometres until I came to the pile of stones.

He broke a pack of Gauloises and lit up.

'Excuse me, do you –'

'No.'

'I am trying to give it up, you know?'

'You won't do it that way.'

He laughed and squinted at me through the smoke, a sm
wiry close-knit man with a hooked nose and stubble a
weathered skin, his eyes permanently narrowed against gla
even here in the starlight.

A Renault stood on the far side of the *redjem* and he l
me across to it and turned on the interior lamps, getting
torch from the glove-pocket. A map was already spread
the rear seat, the same Sheet NH-32 of the Hassi Messao
area that Loman had briefed me with.

'We shall take off an hour late. There was a delay beca

of the work – they have to make hinges on the front edge of the cockpit hood, you know? And they have to make the *trappe* underneath so I can drop the supplies.'

'We take-off at 24.00 hours?'

'*C'est ça.*' He clicked the torch on. 'You know the Sahara?'

'I know the desert.'

'Okay, *c'est la même chose. Alors* – these red marks are the drilling camps in our area: Petrocombine South 4, South 5 and South 6, the Anglo-Belge Roches Brunes A, B and Roches Vertes I and II. The circle here is around the platinum-prospecting complex set up by the Algerians, okay? These we shall use for our bearings.' He looked up at me. 'Of course nothing is certain, you know? It will depend on the winds. If they are right, I can drop you from the *planeur,* but if they are wrong we must come back and I take you out by the airplane – you were told of this?'

'Yes.'

But not precisely. On the second run through the briefing at the Yasmina the subject had only been touched on: Loman knew there were quite enough doubts in my mind without adding to them. He'd just said that Chirac was 'confident'.

'Maybe I can do it, *comprenez*? But only maybe. The winds here are very strange, with freak upcurrents from this range here and dead pockets to the south-east; also the air is cooling very quick after sundown, which is bad. The desert is different from other places, *mon ami.* Y'u know how I learned about the air over this region? From watching the vultures – they are *planeurs,* the vultures, and they smell out the winds. I have watched them. Now I do like them.'

Ash fell and he blew it off the map.

'What are the chances, Chirac?'

'*Hein?*' He flattened his hand, rocking it. 'I cannot say easily. Maybe it is better than fifty-fifty, about that. We will now when we slip the cable and start smelling for the winds, like those birds.'

He moved the torch again. 'These blue marks show the three beacons of the Philips radio relay network that crosses the area where we will go. They carry red warning lamps so we use them too, for our bearings. The drilling-rigs also have lamps at night – there are more airstrips than oases in this region, because everyone looks for the black gold, you see? For the oil. So we have enough landmarks, I think.

After we will slip the cable it is different, a little, because then we are alone and we have to make a straight line south west of the radio tower here. There is nothing else we shall see after this tower.' He shrugged with his hands. 'But maybe it is okay, we will find the winds that we will need.'

I looked at the pattern he'd traced with his torch.

'You mean you're making the final run-in from this tower by dead reckoning?'

'It is the only way, y'u see. There are not any more land marks. But I know the terrain quite well – I fly the geologist all the time and we make aerial survey.'

'Are you familiar with the actual target?'

'*Hein?* Sure I am. It's this outcrop here at 8°3' by 30°4' *n'est-ce pas?*'

Note: Loman hadn't told him about the aeroplane.

'Yes.'

'I do not know the actual rocks, of course – they're very small, and we won't see them anyway in the darkness. But our target is ninety-seven kilometres south-west of the Philip tower, so we have a fix.'

'What's your airspeed going to be?'

'Maybe a hundred, but no more than that, because I must keep the angle of glide at two degrees, or we will not make the distance.'

Fifty-eight minutes for the whole trip, tower to target.

'Will you want me to compute your mean airspeed?'

He laughed and dropped ash on the map again.

'How did you know? I will lend you my Sony.'

He chain-lit another Gauloise, his eagle's face squeezed into a frown over the glow.

'You normally use a pack a minute, Chirac?'

He looked up at me quickly and started to laugh again and then let it go because I obviously knew the score and he didn't think it was worth trying to make it sound funny.

'You know how much I am getting for this trip, *mon ami*? He stamped the butt into the sand. 'A hundred thousand francs in cash, if I can drop you from the *planeur* successfully. And insurance in the amount of five hundred thousand – that's half a million new francs, okay? If I don't get back, my family will be comfortable for quite a few years.' He looked away, thinking for a couple of seconds about what he was saying. He was the kind of man who would keep a photograph of his wife and children on him wherever he went, the gloss of the surface dulling and the corners curling until its very shabbiness told not of neglect but of constancy. 'Anyway I try to get back, *hein?* I am not a fool.'

'How far,' I said, 'will you push it?'

He raised the palms of his hands. 'Listen to me, please. It is nice money, okay, but you know what they say – you can't take it with you. So I will not push it too far, you un'erstand? When I tell you what they pay me, it is just telling you how much is the risk, when they will pay me so high for a few hours' work.' He blew out smoke. 'In a way it is easier for you, my friend, if I can drop you right on the target – because then they will know where you are, and where to find you. But when I turn back for Kaifra, the nearest oasis, I might lose the wind, you see, and I can come down anywhere on the sand, anywhere at all, maybe halfway, that's eighty kilometres from you and from Kaifra – from anywhere, and you now what that means? It means the same as if I have come down in the sea, eighty kilometres from the nearest shore, and try to swim there, you un'erstand?'

Carefully I said: 'But you'll be carrying flares.'

'No.' He squinted at me through the smoke. 'No, *mon ami*, I will not be carrying flares. That is in the contract too, as well as the half-million-franc insurance. If I go down on the sand, I will make no signals to bring people near to your target. I must not do that – I must try to walk out by myself. And like I say, they will be comfortable for a few years.'

A point of light showed in the distance and I watched it.

'And I will keep to my contract,' he said, apparently wanting me to know what kind of a man he was. 'Listen to me, after the Algerian affair I was a mercenary for certain people who I will not mention, some private armies, you now? And I fought like hell, I earned what they pay me. Also I have been forced down in the desert sometimes when there are sandstorms or the motor gives out, so I know what it feels like when you think your life is going, when you have to think about what it is better to do – to shoot yourself or et the thirst send you mad. Oh yes, I have done this. So I now I can keep to my contract if that happens.' He tapped me slowly on the arm. 'The thing is, whatever happens, to remain a man. Do you not think so? Only in such a way can you die in peace.'

They were the lights of a truck coming south from Gar Tebout. I could hear it now.

'Of course,' I said.

'You do not think so?'

'Well, actually I'm a bit wary of last thoughts – it can spo your concentration when you're trying to duck. Would yo say it's normal for a truck to be coming south on this roa about this hour?'

'Hein?' He frowned into the distance. 'Oh sure. The ai field at Garaa Tebout takes bigger planes than Kaifra.' H dragged smoke in and it began fluttering out on his breat as he talked. 'Anyway, we shall try to come back, you an I, from the desert.'

'Yes, fine. Can you douse these lights a minute?'

'Okay.'

He leaned over and turned them off, the torch as well, an I sensed him watching me in the gloom.

'You are expecting some trouble?'

'Not really.'

It was just that the *redjem* wasn't much good as visu cover: a long time ago it had marked a crossing in the path of herdsmen, and near it there was the ruin of a gypsum an mudbrick shelter; this area had once been grazing land fo sheep, I supposed, before the wind from the desert ha smothered it with sand. Chirac had put his Renault on th far side of the shelter but there hadn't been room for th 220 and it wasn't concealed from the road.

It wasn't instinct alone that made me want the lights off we were a hundred and fifty minutes from take-off an London was sending us panic directives and the base phor was dead and this whole region was a red sector and a Chirac could do was add up his life insurance and if there ever been a time when I didn't mind being seen making rd contact along a lonely road it wasn't now.

His face turned silver and our shadows lifted and swur under the roof of the Renault as the light came flooding fror the road.

Heavy diesel. Canvas sides: PETROCOMBINE S-5.

Fine sand falling as the dark came down.

'That is a bum outfit, you know? They don't pay so goo and the air-conditioning is always *en panne,* you should he the drillers talk about that!' He turned the lamps on agai

hen I quit mercenary work I fly mostly for the big
nerican companies here, looking for oil. That is how I come
 know the desert, every square kilometre from Oran to
adamis, and that is why they chose me, your – *associés*.
u want an *aviateur* who knows the Sahara, you send for
irac.'

He dropped the butt of his Gauloise and heeled it out.

I start giving it up now, *hein?*' Without changing his tone
 said: 'You are looking for oil in that place?'

That's right.'

He laughed amiably.

You will be there for maybe three days?'

Maybe.'

He'd been told how much water he'd have to take on board.

That is not long, if you are careful.' He drew the map off
 seat and folded it. 'I will brief you on the actual flight
en we rendezvous with the pilot of the airplane. Is there
thing you would like to know right now?'

Just one thing: where can I get a gun?'

Hein? You don't have one?'

No.'

He leaned into the Renault and slid the map into the glove-
cket, slamming it shut and reaching underneath.

You can borrow this, *mon ami.*'

I took it and found it heavy, a couple of pounds or more,
Colt Official Police .38 six-shot with a six-inch barrel and
quered grips.

When do you want it back?'

When you come back from the desert.'

e twin dark lines were drawn finely across the firmament
m Andromeda through Cygnus to Vega, then they struck
o the black cloud of palm-leaves above my head.

The night was soundless.

Diffused light glowed against the cupolas on the far side of
 trees but I couldn't be sure where it came from. On this
e there was nothing and I moved again, disturbing the
ht of insects below the rotting leaves and moving on as
 as the wall, looking up.

There was no need to examine their whole length, but only
se sections where they could be reached easily and cut.
e hall was unlit and when I passed inside I waited for the

blind man's voice but he wasn't here: that was cert
because he would have challenged me.

I used the pen-torch and found the junction-board w
the connections exposed and thick with dust,. the knur.
knobs green with oxidization, one of them missing and
wire held with a paper-clip. I cleaned the end and the thre
of the terminal and reconnected it. *Mais il ne sonne même p
m'sieur, il est en dérangement.* You don't say.

A sound and I held still and counted a hundred secor
but it didn't come again, one of those unpleasant sounds t
had no particular feature so that you had to identify
according to your fancy: contracting timber or a door in
draught or a distant shot.

A group of wires ran horizontally and then upwar
ending in a hole where loose plaster was plugged. I cros
in the dark to the stairs and used the torch and saw
right ones, tracing them higher and stopping to listen a
climbing again until I came to the top floor. They had
been cut.

She was pointing the bloody thing at me and I said do
do that and she put it down and I shut the door.

– *Hi pry Q Quaker dation minim* –

– *Hold on, Embassy.*

'All right,' I told her.

Repeat please from 'big flash'.

*Hi pry Q Quaker dation minim lady point ops one hund.
proxy point all red vigil out. Do you want to reply?*

She looked at me and I said: 'Tell them to stop be
aching.'

Please send: Understumble point willing relay. Tango out

She cut the switch and stopped the tape and pushed
hair back from her face: it was like an oven in here a
she looked beat.

'Where's Loman?'

'At the hotel.'

'The Royal Sahara?'

'Yes.'

'Why?'

'He wanted to talk to you, but the phone doesn't work

'Try it now.'

Acetone on the air, been doing her nails.

The venetian blind was still down and they'd put the b

66

ansceiver on the other side of the room where it couldn't
e seen from any of the windows even if they weren't covered.
*en' veux pas de numéro. On était en panne ici, mais main-
nant ça marche.'*

I played the tape back to catch the first bit they'd sent but
was only another hurry directive: I'd never known London
et so hysterical, what the hell did they think we were doing
l this time if it wasn't trying to get me to the destination
ith the minimum delay?

I gave her Chirac's .38 and she nearly dropped it because
ompared with her own it weighed a ton.

'Have you had any small-arms training?'

'No. There wasn't time to –'

'D'you know what the phrase means, "to stop a man"?'

'Not exactly.'

'It means to stop him coming towards you. If a man were
inning towards you and you fired that gun of yours at him
e'd just keep on coming, and unless you'd hit him in the
ain or the heart there'd be time for him to kill you or
nash up the radio, or both. But if you use this one you'll
op him short, and at the range from here to the doorway
ou'd actually throw him back.'

'I see.'

God, it was awful: the thing was nearly bigger than she
as.

'Hold it with both hands if you want to, and be ready for
e recoil and the noise. Safety-catch here, load like this,
e, the usual thing, all right?'

'Yes.'

'It gives you six shots, and don't forget to count.'

'All right.'

'Have you got enough drinking-water here?'

'Yes.'

'Salt tablets?'

'Yes.'

I went over to the telephone and picked it up and listened
r bugs, all red vigil yes but we knew that, although I
ppose it was encouraging to know also that Control was
viously monitoring the opposition's movements rather
osely. Say that for London: they were warning us that the
at was on down here before we'd had time to report it.

'J'écoute.'

Negative bugs.

The line's perfectly okay now so will you cancel th
request for repairs, and I'd like 113.

Be awkward if Loman were smack in the thick of a h
signals exchange on the 2000CA and a man called to me
the telephone.

'Yes?'

He'd taken my key and gone up.

'Tango.'

'Quaker, yes?'

I listened for the bugs again.

'There was a tag tonight.'

'What happened?'

'He had an accident.'

'Where are you?'

'That's right.'

'I'll see you.'

'No. Things are getting difficult. I'll spell it out for you,
right? And leave there now, can you?'

He thought about it.

'Very well.' Then he said. 'We'll synchronize.'

'10.17.'

'Thank you.'

I hung up.

It was too dangerous even for us to be seen at the Roy
Sahara at the same time, even if we weren't together, becau
I wouldn't be able to check him for surveillance when he le
there without exposing myself: they'd put one on to me
the hotel already so they knew that part of my travel-patter

I could have waited for him here but he only wanted to
over the briefing again because he'd got the twitters and the
wasn't enough time left. If there'd been anything urgent
tell me he would have insisted on a meeting and he had
done that.

'Tape me, will you?'

She pressed for start.

Quiller to Loman. The tag was in a Peugeot 404 and I
him into a ravine about five kilometres along the road to
Petrocombine South camps. He burned out. I was in
Mercedes 220 so you'll need to monitor the enquiry a
decide if there's any smoke wanted. Further: I'm keeping
rendezvous with Chirac at the Mosque Hamouda Pasha

68

.50 and he'll be taking me to the airstrip. I did this because
want to change the 220 image before I leave the town.
rther: if the telephone here packs up again, check the
nction-board in the entrance hall. *Further*: I recommend
at you remain at base until end of mission if this is possible.
ndon confirms opposition in closest proximity. Quiller out.

She pressed for stop and said:

'You're bleeding.'

'Have you got anything?'

'Yes.'

Since this morning I'd taken off most of the dressings
cause it was bad image security at a time when I was being
nted, but there were still a few places where coagulation
sn't complete. My right shoulder had been stiffening up
 day but there was nothing I could do about that except
pe to Christ I could do the jump without getting the
rness fouled up or anything.

'There's no need to swab it. Haven't you got any plaster?'

I watched her cutting it and wondered who she was, what
d happened at home to make her break loose and work
road and get hijacked into a hit-and-miss undertaking that
dn't proved anything so far except that life was cheap.

'Was it the bomb?'

'That's right.'

Her eyes were serious, concentrating on fixing the thing
aight, a fine dew of sweat above her tender mouth, a strand
 light hair lying curled in the hollow of her shoulder, the
arness of her reminding me of all I stood to lose if tonight
walked into shadows without watching, or made a sound
en silence held the only hope of life.

'Were they trying to kill you?'

'Not very hard.'

Her warm fingers pressed, smoothing it flat.

'Don't you find it odd, to be still alive?'

'I find it quite comfortable.'

She stood back and looked at me steadily, her quiet eyes
occupied with working something out for herself, maybe
 feeling of oddness she expected me to have, because she
dn't know that in my trade the risk of extinction carries its
n anodyne: familiarity. There's always of course the
estion suddenly in the mind when the glass comes fluting
ough the nitro fumes or the headlights burn in your skull

while you sit there staring them out: *is this the one?* F
afterwards, when the shrill of the nerves has quietened, t
only answer is *no, it wasn't the one.*

She looked away and put the reel of Elastoplast back in
the tin, seeing my blood on her fingertips and for a mom
considering it and then doing nothing about it, shutting t
tin and putting it back on the shelf, her movements slo
reflective.

'Where's my gear?'

She turned.

'Your what?'

'The radio and the camera.'

'Oh yes. We had it picked up at a rendezvous. It should
on board by now.'

The time-gap closed with a bang and the mission was th
in front of me, ready to run.

Chapter Seven

MAGNUM

I waited for him.

The street was silent and nothing moved.

Naked bulbs stuck out here and there from the corners
walls, their yellow light defining the perspective of the str
and the turnings from it. The curved fronds of the pa
hung piled against the minarets and the filigree of windo
grilles, their tips burned brown by the heat of never-end
noons; in them I could hear rats rustling.

10.25.

This is the moment, in the last phase of pre-mission activ
when we wonder why we do the things we do: psychologic
the brakes are coming off and we are gathering speed a
soon we shall be pitching headlong into the dark and it's
nerving and we try to busy ourselves while the deadl
closes on us, so that we don't have to think too much. So
uncomfortable to have to sit in a car and do nothing, wl
the last minutes run out. It's not a good time to think.

There was a handbasin in the corner so why the hell di

rinse them there, I didn't like it, the way she'd looked at
em, what was she saying, that it was here on her fingers by
ace of whatever gods had decreed that I shouldn't be too
ose when the thing went off, bloody nonsense, they'd cocked
up that was all, tuned the rocking-mechanism till it was too
nsitive and then a bus had made a draught or something
ke that. It doesn't do, at a time like this, to think you're
eing looked after by some kind of providence: start walking
und ladders and you'll only get run over because survival
egins in the brain, not the navel.

Soft-eyed little philosopher with her downy arms, two
nds to hold the bloody thing and no training for priority
os, Loman ought to be shot.

The street was narrow, running thinly into the dark of
ees at its very end. That was where I would be going soon,
ccelerating through the perspective of the known into the
known dark.

I would wait here another two minutes and then I'd have
take the first of the risks that I must run between now
d the rendezvous. He was very good of course but he
asn't an executive in the field and therefore didn't have the
aining or even the experience: it's a weak point and we
ink it's dangerous and we're always asking the Bureau to
o something about it but you might as well try selling a
ckstrap to a eunuch.

The scent of mimosa was on the air, adrift in the starlight
om blossom I couldn't see from here, and the sky dripped
amonds, Andromeda and Cygnus and Vega and a million
ore, their reflection ablaze in the gilded cupola where she
as, we'll miss a lot of things, oh a lot of things, if we're
t careful.

Sweating like a pig and cursing him now for not coming,
ecking too often – 10.29 – 10.29.15 – 10.29.30 – time you
rned to count without looking all the time at the dial, risk
anyway and if the whole thing blows up you can say it was
s fault, didn't leave me enough time to check him for ticks.
Front-end configuration amorphous, colour dark blue or
rk green in this light, coming rather fast but that was
rmal, Capri, no. Taunus, no, Chrysler 160, the lights dipping
er the sandy hollows, driver alone, the dust flying up in
s wake – 10.30.15 – give him a minute and then go, running
close, blast his eyes.

71

He passed the Yasmina and did a square loop and parke
in the side-street and walked, short neat steps like a bird'
looking from side to side in case he missed anything, the la
time I'd be seeing him for a while or forever if I didι
watch out: and then I found myself admiring the littι
bastard just for still being on his feet because this time they
really blown an egg all over him and for the last forty-eigι
hours he'd been busting a gut to set up an op and he'd doι
it and we were ninety minutes to the off and I suppose yo
could say that was something, you could rank him amoι
the élite: the professionals.

Negative.

Distant throb of a truck on the highway south, somewhe
a starved dog baying. No other sound but the rats among tι
leaves, no movement anywhere along the street's narrowiι
channel.

10.31.15 and still negative.

I got the engine going and the nerves quietened a ι
because he was a director, not an executive, and he cou
have picked up a tag and led him to base without knowiι
and that would have blown it, the lot. But it was all riι
and whatever happened now I'd have the comfort of knowiι
that base had been intact at the moment when the brakι
came off.

The lids of the bins banging back and the tumble of emp
skins and the bones of birds, steam rising and swirling iι
the air-conditioning vents, the boys in bow-ties and the tra
volplaning on their raised hands, the din of cutlery in tι
metal sinks.

'Je m'excuse – je suis trompé de porte!'

'Comment?'

'Je cherche le restaurant!'

'Passez par ici, m'sieur – allez-y!'

The doors swinging and the trays coming back loaded wι
the detritus of *Melon glacé, Canard à l'orange,* the drilleι
dining late so as to get some drinking done first.

The restaurant full, the lobby empty except for a few staι
Check, double-check. Negative.

'M'sieur?'

'Trente-sept.'

Door-boy, desk clerk, telephonist, a man from Hertz.

I used the main stairs. It was possible that I could now be seen through the glass façade above the entrance but the panels were solar-tinted and it had to be risked and in any case there was no alternative route. I'd gone through the kitchens because they were nearer where I'd left the car, below the third lamp from the group of yuccas where I could see it from my room, and if they were watching the main entrance for me they'd draw blank.

10.37.

The estimated schedule was ninety seconds from locking the 220 to reaching the windows of Room 37 and that didn't give them time enough to rig anything.

Loman would have left the shutters closed and the curtains drawn but they wouldn't necessarily be lightproof so I stopped halfway along the corridor and took a bulb out and dropped a 100-millime piece across the contacts and blew the lot and went into 37 without swinging the door too wide.

Total dark, hit a chair, touched the curtains.

The slats of the shutters were angled at forty-five degrees and I couldn't see anything above the horizontal and this was the first floor of a five-floor building so I opened a shutter, taking a full minute to swing it wide enough to let me through on to the balcony.

Check 220: negative.

Above the wax cascade of the yucca-blooms the balconies of the east wing were ranged in unbroken lines. Most of the outside lamps were burning but the rooms were dark: the restaurant was full. The building was in the tourist-Moorish style, an elongated complex of arches and carved screens with two arabesque lamps and a tubbed *orangier* on each balcony and creeper climbing from the lawns below, and he was observing me from the third floor, seventh room from the left.

The lamps were lit on the two balconies on each side of mine but it didn't help because he was using binoculars and their lens-hoods would be cutting out the peripheral glare. There was almost no glint on the lenses and I might have missed them except that he'd forgotten to mask the chrome thumb-screw on the tripod.

It was difficult to judge how much light I was reflecting but the likelihood that he was able to identify me at this range was critically high. Despite this, there was a chance

73

that he hadn't seen me so I moved my head and not my eye because the reflective capacity of the whites is greater than that of the iris and pupil by a factor of more than double and in certain lights it can make the difference between being seen or overlooked, shot dead or only winged.

I was now directly facing the Mercedes 220 and computing the angle and the thing I didn't like was that there was no visual obstruction between the car and his balcony: he'd watched me arrive and unless I could do anything about it he would watch me leave.

Time probably 10.38.30 couldn't look.

It was difficult because I was scheduled to leave here in a minute and a half from now and there wouldn't be time to call up a taxi and I couldn't commandeer the nearest private car I found outside because those drip-nosed Agathas in London have got the whole thing written out under *Public Involvement* (Standing Orders) and if you blot your copybook they'll suspend you from missions and for the next twelve months you'll pass the time breaking hieroglyphs in Codes and Ciphers or standing-in for a sandbag at the thousand-yard range in Norfolk.

He wasn't doing anything, not moving about or anything I couldn't see a barrel coming up but of course there could be two of them and the other one could be inside the room where there was no light to pick up surfaces and my skin began crawling because at this range I wouldn't hear the detonation before the skull was blown.

They were being inconsistent.

Inconsistency is dangerous because it brings in the unpredictable: if you don't know which way the opposition's going to jump you can't tell where they'll land.

They grilled O'Brien and then they killed him.

They surveyed Fyson and then they broke his nerve across a telescopic rifle without firing a shot and they didn't wipe him out before they'd finished with him as a contact control that led to my own exposure.

With me they went straight in for the kill and when they fouled it up they didn't try again: they changed their minds and decided that since I was still alive I was worth tagging and that was so bloody inconsistent that it brought out the sweat on me because at any minute they could change their minds again and I could be standing here against the wall with my forehead coming slowly into the centre of a 3X scope while his finger took up the tension on the spring.

I'd seen all I wanted to out here but I didn't hurry because speed can be fatal if it isn't dictated totally by brain-think and this was stomach-think, this sweat on me and the crawling of the skin, I knew what Fyson had meant, the threat of a long gun can bring you to the pitch when all you can think about is the sudden air-rush, wherever you are, walking in a street or coming down some steps, the silence of the small bright beautifully-turned object as it nears you so fast that the fine tune of its passage is outstripped so that you never hear it, or driving along a road where the buildings are strange to you, their windows open, while the little cylindrical stub of lead and copper-zinc alloy spins towards you, intimately to invade the consciousness and turn it into mindless chemicals, bringing an end to all you ever were.

Slowly, my fingers behind me, finding the varnished wood of the shutter, guiding my feet until the shadow of the terrace screen came to fall across my eyes and I passed inside the room and stood filling the lungs with oxygen for the nerves while the telephone began ringing and I let it go on until I was ready to answer it.

'I am leaving now,' he said.

'All right.'

I hung up.

10.40.

He'd been punctual. It was a help. It is a help, *mon ami*, when you are in a spot and someone demonstrates his reliability. It gives you hope.

I left the shutter as it was, half open: there wasn't any technical advantage in closing it; on the contrary he'd pick up the movement because I didn't have the time to do it slowly. There was a slight advantage in leaving it half open because psychologically it suggested presence: you normally shut things when you leave a place. I left the curtains drawn.

Sound and I froze. Corridor: voices.

The lights, oh yes, they were wondering why they'd fused.

I picked up my flight-bag and went out. It wouldn't be a good idea to go through the kitchens again so I took the swing door to the gardens, going past the swimming-pool on the far side where there was shadow and thinking as fast as I could because the place was a trap: they wouldn't put sur-

75

veillance on me from that direction alone – they'd cover the whole scene.

The hurry wasn't at this end: Chirac would wait for take-off until I was ready to go. But London wanted me to reach Tango Victor soonest possible and that pulled the whole schedule tight and I wasn't going to accept his midnight ETD because with a bit of luck they might finish slapping the dope on before then and we could get off the ground while it was drying.

The path turned left and I took it and kept to the shadow of the oleanders until I was within thirty yards of the 220 and then I stopped because at this point I'd be moving into the surveyed area and even if he didn't recognize me from behind and above he'd know who I was when I got into the car.

I didn't want to do a thing like this without being quite certain there was no other way. Technically it looked like suicide but sometimes it has to be done: we have to move deliberately into known surveyance even when it isn't done to deceive. We have to do it for various reasons: because the schedule of the mission has become critical to the point of jeopardizing it by delay or because the threat to life is so immediate as to justify a lesser risk or because there's a fair chance of dodging mobile surveyance once we've left the immediate area.

Two of these reasons were valid for me now; if I didn't reach the wreck on the sand before anyone else got there the mission would come to nothing and it was therefore at this moment jeopardized and London would agree. There would be mobile surveyance taking over from the man on the balcony because tonight they wanted to know where I was going and the fact that one of them had got killed trying to find out wouldn't deter them since it was now obvious that I was going somewhere interesting, and I had a fair chance of dodging a mobile tag because it was something I'd learned how to do.

10.42.

So I broke cover and the skin began crawling again because it was reasonably certain that on the balcony of the seventh room on the third floor the hooded lenses were now swinging down on the tripod swivel and steadying.

Ignore.

Range sixty yards, angle of fire thirty-five degrees low, target centred.

Ignore and keep on walking and think of other things.

Chirac was rather good material: he'd got the point. After all, he was only helping us out: he wasn't a professional spook and he didn't possess the bruised lopsided sense of loyalty to the Bureau that's always there like a scarecrow wherever we go. Kaifra tonight was a red sector and he was in it and if they got a fix on him and managed to take him and grill him I'd be walking straight into an ambush when I kept the rendezvous at the Mosque Hamouda Pasha.

They knew how to conduct interrogation: they'd operated on O'Brien and got enough out of him to blow a five-star field-executive like Fyson as soon as he'd arrived in Sidi Ben Ali and they'd finished him off in Tunis and got the name of Kaifra out of him or they wouldn't be here now because Loman and I had got here clean. If they did it to Chirac we wouldn't expect him to protect me or the Bureau or his own mother because they were experts, so I'd thrown him the alert and told him to phone me at the Royal Sahara at exactly 10.40 and use four words and those four words precisely unless he was under duress and then he could use any variation he liked: *I am on my way* or *I am starting now*, so forth.

It would give him total protection because it allowed him to keep to the truth: I have arranged to rendezvous with him at the Mosque Hamouda Pasha but he won't go there unless I telephone him to say when I am leaving.

They couldn't blame him if I didn't turn up: I could have caught a cold or something.

Fiat 850, Volkswagen, Peugeot 504, Toyota Land Cruiser with spades strapped on, Citroën DS, nobody in them and nothing else in sight of the 220 so they must have put him round a corner or somewhere in total shadow. He'd moved off when I did but this insistence on concealment at the beginning of our run seemed a bit pointless because he couldn't get on my tail without spreading himself all over the mirror and they knew that. It was another nasty little inconsistency and I didn't like it.

Oleanders, tamarisk, deep cover ten feet from the Mercedes on the other side and I slowed as I walked towards it because they might not like using a rifle in the hotel building – it

would make a lot of noise and people would get inquisitive –
so the best thing would be for the man up there to have
signalled my arrival so they could put someone in cover here
where the noise wouldn't be so loud.

I walked towards it.

If they let me get as far as the car I could stop worrying:
they hadn't had time to rig a bang because I'd kept it under
observation except for the ninety-second period when I'd
gone into the hotel through the kitchens. The timing from
Room 37 to the swing door I'd used as an exit wasn't much
more than half a minute.

Five paces and I reached the 220 and got in and started up,
not looking at the hotel but checking the Vauxhall and the
hardtop GT-6 that had now come into sight from where I
sat, nobody in them, nobody anywhere. No sound of a
starter and I was waiting for it and it didn't happen and I
thought blast their eyes for not playing it by the book: they'd
let me get as far as the car but I still couldn't stop worrying
because they wouldn't just put one isolated observer up there
to log my arrival and departure times at the Royal Sahara.
They knew I was pushing the deadline because they'd already
had a mobile tag on me tonight and now they ought to be
hooking a new one on to me, or a dozen, and they weren't.

There was the bare possibility they were holding off, letting
me run while they could do it without any risk of losing me:
the road from the hotel to the town centre and the main
intersection was approximately 1.5 k's and it was the only
route you could take if you wanted to link up with the major
highway north to Garaa Tebout or south to the complex of
drilling-camps so they'd be virtually certain I'd be using that
stretch. The awkward thing was that I couldn't avoid it. The
Mosque Hamoud Pasha was half a kilometre from the oasis
road and Chirac was on his way there so I shifted the stick
and got rolling because it was the only thing left to do.

The coloured lights of the marquee sent rainbows flowing
across the bonnet of the 220 as I swung past the steps and
took the east road between the overhanging palms, mirror
check negative.

High degree of cognitive dissonance, most unpleasant. I was
expecting lights to come into the mirror and they didn't and
it threw me. Something was missing from the equation and
I couldn't see what it was unless it could simply be that the

were so monumentally disorganized that they didn't know how to operate. It would be nice to think that.

Forty on the clock and I left it there: the road was sandy in places and the crown finished in a ragged edge of macadam within a foot of the palm-trunks. The mirror was hazed over now with the dust I was sending up but if lights moved into it I would see them.

There were buildings at intervals standing back from the road, the small white-domed winter residences of retired merchants and date-farmers, and they vanished as the wind-screen went and I smashed the flat of my hand against the crazed glass and broke a hole in it but I'd been driving blind for two seconds and in those forty yards the Mercedes had drifted off-course and the nearside tyres were over the edge of the macadam and I had to let her go another foot and then bring the wheel round to force the front tyre back across the edge before I could get any kind of stability.

I was slumped low by now and the second shot hit the roof and it banged like a tin drum and I knew the trunks of the palms were getting in his way but there were a lot of gaps in them so I kept low and sighted through the wheel and the hole in the granulated screen but it was very awkward and we began swinging wide again and I suddenly felt cold because if the drifting got worse and I hit a tree and finished up stationary he'd take his time and pick me off when I tried to get out and if I stayed where I was he'd come up close and make it a certainty.

The speed had risen a fraction but it didn't affect things very much: it was just a question of how steady the target was when he lined up the next shot and I didn't like this because if I tried to jazz the thing around to spoil his aim I increased the risk of crashing it and giving him a sitter.

Very close and glass flew and I felt the sudden air-rush from the hole in the windscreen so it was the rear side-window he'd smashed. The two windows on the other side were still all right so he was firing from a position well above the horizontal and the explosive shattering of the glass had covered the noise of the secondary impact on the inside panel of the door.

Almost certain the observer at the Royal Sahara had picked up the telephone when he'd seen me getting back into the 220 but this ambush must have been set up before tonight because it carried communications and it wouldn't have been any use without them: this marksman had been installed as soon as they'd established that my travel-pattern included the only road between the hotel and the major intersection in the town centre, but they'd waited for tonight.

I'd used this route six times since I'd arrived in Kaifra and they'd waited for the seventh and given him the signal that I was just leaving the hotel and he'd gone up to the roof and checked his magazine and the 220 was rocking again as the third shot smashed into the door-pillar and pain stabbed into my scalp but there was no concussion: it was a group of metal splinters and not a ricochet of the shell itself.

This would be the long gun they'd used for the breaking of Fyson's nerve and this time they wanted to kill with it and there wasn't anything I could do except keep all four wheels on the road and hope to survive.

He wasn't an international. He was trained and experienced because the target was now traversing at right-angles at twenty feet per second and the only lighting was back-glare from the headlamps and there were trees at intervals across his field of fire but if he'd been an international the first shot would have neutralized: there's a conceit among the top-flight professionals like Molinari and Kuo and Tomlinson that they only ever use one bullet for each assignment.

This man's *forte* was fast use of the automatic reloader: by the dull thump of the last shell after the ricochet had left it almost inert I'd say he was using something like a .44 Magnum, a brush-country weapon with enough power to drive its ammunition through a six-inch pine tree in full sap, and he'd been firing with a controlled rhythm that had kept him on the target throughout the period of three or four seconds following his first shot. I couldn't tell how long he'd be able to maintain fire and I didn't want to give myself any false hopes because it could be anything up to a twelve-shot rotary magazine and he was working at roughly one per second and if he had nine shells left he'd be using the last one while I was still in murderously close range at a hundred and eighty feet.

A hole appeared in the scuttle three inches forward of the windscreen and both the aural and visual effects resembled those from a blow with a pickaxe and it confirmed what I'd thought about the size of this gun: it was really quite big.

'd overcorrected but this time the error was dangerously
row: the third shell had hit the rear window approximately
ty-eight inches from my head and this one had drilled the
le in the scuttle eighteen inches in front of me and it
uld have worried me but there were so many factors in
y and one of them was the possibility that he hadn't seen
ere the shell had gone in because it hadn't made so much
a mess as the one that had smashed the window.

I could feel him thinking.

We were very close, he and I. Not close friends but close
emies. The total energy of his brain was devoted to the
ricate equations governing our shared situation: speed of
get in traverse, speed and extent of movement laterally as
target wavered, horizontal angle of fire, vertical angle of
and the incomputable factors presented by the con-
uration of the palm-trees and the movement of the light
m the headlamps, so forth. And the result of this mental
rgy was being expressed by the flight of the cylindrical
jects whose accuracy was linking us closer and closer
ether, moving us nearer the point at which there would
ne profound personal involvement as the intention in this
n's brain exploded in my own.

*The more difficult phase of this operation is getting you to
jump-off point without attracting surveillance or obstruc-
action.*

Put it like a schoolmistress but when it came to the crunch
terms were simpler: flesh and blood and a bullet, the will
live and the urge to kill, the moment of truth.

Oh Christ he was close and I felt the air-wave across my
s and the force smashed the facia and sent splinters
ining past my face as we drifted badly because of the
ck and I tried to pull her straight and for the first time
sed him, being afraid and needing to diminish him by
nes. The trees swung and the lights sent their shadows
ching as the tyres lost their hold on the sandy surface and
back end broke away and I brought it straight and used
throttle for traction and got it and piled it on.

Five.

He'd brought down the error from forty-eight inches to less
n one and he'd done it in two shots and I sat waiting for
listening to the whistle of the wind through the gap in the
een and watching the dips and hollows of the road as the

81

lights pooled shadows there and then swept them away,
image in my mind, a dark face pressed to the gun, its e
brilliant in the light on the road ahead of me that was gathe
by the telescopic lens and focused on the pupil, thrown
the screen of the retina for interpretation by the brai
higher and to the right – fire.

Six and the impact and a ricochet and fine glass fragme
shivering in the air from the instruments and then a should
blow as the shell doubled and I took the last of its iner
and the wheel jerked and I lost it, the lot, spinning once ov
the loose sand and rocking across the edge of the macad
with the vibration shaking the granules from the frame of
screen and the windrush sending them past me in a strea
of flying hail as the flank of the 220 struck across a tree-tru
and we pitched the other way and found the road and bound
there with a tyre bursting and a headlight blacking out.

Lost it again and we spun with the last of the screen fr
ments shaking away and falling across me while I dragg
the manual into low to kill off the rest of the speed but
front end wouldn't respond and a palm-trunk ripped a whe
panel off and left the front fender creased backwards a
howling on the tyre with its shrill note rising as I got tracti
in low and brought her back on to the road and shifted
lever and took the speed up again through the early ra
with the stink of heated rubber fouling the air.

The howling noise was very loud, marking my passa
through the night, but if I slowed he'd take his time and
up the final shot and I kept up the speed, drifting crabw
with the burst tyre dragging and the one headlight slant
away from the road. Something important was trying to
my attention but brain-think was at a discount and the oa
road came up before I realized that it was a six-shot and
was changing magazines.

Half a kilometre from the Mosque Hamoud Pasha
front tyre melted through and burst and a lot of the howl
stopped but the steering was very awkward now and it
really a question of how long it would take him to get i
his car and come up on me with a full magazine.

The dark oblong shape of the Renault was standing un
the palms, glow of a Gauloise, threw my flight-bag in
pulled the door shut.

'Go very fast, will you?'

Chapter Eight

AIRBORNE

et the door-lock and got the belt adjusted.

He glanced at me.

'*Ca va?*'

'*Ca va.*'

I suppose I was bleeding again.

He swung through the main intersection and accelerated rd along the South 4 highway and I pulled down the ssenger visor and angled it to line up the mirror, negative. Chirac flicked the stub through the window.

'I heard some shots just now.'

'So did I.'

He laughed cannily and shut the window and pushed the nts open and there wasn't so much noise.

Do you expect we shall be followed?'

'It's on the cards.'

'*Comment?*'

'*C'est possible.*'

Two of the stars on the south horizon were beginning to w red and I watched them.

'Do I go fast enough?'

'Not if you can go any faster.' There was 140 kph on the ck and the engine was running at peak with valve-bounce eping in. 'How long will it take to reach the airstrip?'

'Maybe ten minutes, a little more.'

London was panicking but I didn't have to try cutting tual seconds off the schedule: it was just that if the man th the gun had got into his car he might have seen the nault when we'd left the Mosque.

Mirror negative.

I could see now that the two red lights were stationary ead of us and if it was some kind of breakdown I hoped wasn't blocking the road because we wanted a clear run. ere were three lights now and when I'd considered all the her possible explanations I voted for the idea that there re two vehicles halted on the road about a mile in front us: a few seconds ago I'd felt my weight shifting slightly

to one side and my elbow had been pressed gently again
the door panel so we must have taken an almost indefinab
curve and the visual effect had been to reveal one of th
second vehicle's rear-lamps by parallax.

'Is that a truck?'

'I would expect so, yes.'

'If it's a breakdown, just keep on going.'

'Okay.'

We were coming up on the lights very fast and he beg.
flickering the heads as a warning and I wondered wheth
he'd be able to judge how much room there was to go pa
at this speed before it was too late to do anything about
Chirac was all right but there was a bit too much garlic-an
Gauloises philosophy about him, the thing is to die like
man, so forth, absolute balls because whether you die li
a man or the back end of a pantomime horse you're goi
to stop breathing when it happens.

There were some other lights, white ones, moving arou
in the ravine below the road and then I got it and stopp
worrying and sat back and watched him put the Rena
through the gap between the edge of the road and the poli
car and ambulance standing on the other side. Nobody tr
to slow us: they were all busy down in the ravine, two
them carrying a stretcher.

'There was an accident,' Chirac said.

'It looks like it.'

He reached for the blue packet and manœuvred a cigare
out one-handed. 'Some people drive too fast, *mon ami.*'

It looked like a false sunrise as we topped the dunes a m
from South 4 camp, the brilliance of the derrick-lamps lifti
into the sky and flaring there among the stars.

We were already running parallel with a wire guard-fer
hung at intervals with notices: *Défense d'Entrer – Défe*
de Fumer – Danger du Mort. Trucks moved beyond the fen
unloading sections of piping, and the derrick lamps sho
down on storage tanks and a fleet of jeeps and half-tracks

'The drill is down to four thousand metres,' Chirac said
we, began slowing, 'and last week they make a core-drill
and bring up oil in the sandstone, so it will be not long n
before they strike. But like I tell you, they are a lousy ou
so maybe the oil will be lousy too.'

The two guards checked our papers with the gates still
sed, then gave us passes and let us through and Chirac
ve at the regulation 20 kph past the living-quarters to the
th end of the airstrip where the windsock was hanging
p a hundred yards from the hangar. From here the
nediate skyline was a frieze of pumping-units, rigs, hut-
nts and vehicles, with the towering derrick and radio masts
ng behind them. The steady drone of the diesels sounded
m the rotary table half a mile away but here it was
atively quiet and I could hear voices from inside the
urity-zone where the first stages of the pipeline were being
up.

The hangar was a single-span stressed-iron unit, an item of
war stock with the original camouflage design showing
ntly through the silver heat-reflecting paint. There weren't
ny lamps burning inside and for a moment I didn't see
glider because its matt night-blue finish gave it the same
e as the shadows on the corrugated walls.

Chirac put his hands on his hips.

Et voilà! Mais quelle vache, hein? What a cow! But it will
very well, and that is what we need.'

Much bigger than I'd expected: a three-seater pod-and-
om design, shoulder-wing, straight dihedral, very large
ord, ugly to look at because of the lump at the front end
l the almost black paint.

Have you flown this type?'

Mon Dieu, there isn't another like this! The Algerians
d it for radio-observer drops during the war, then the
téo converted it for research on thermal currents, then
glo-Belge put different mainplanes on it for low-altitude
veys, and now look what we do, we make *trappe* beneath
cabin and paint it like this! *Tout simplement,* he is a
v! But I can fly anything, *mon ami,* even a cow, so we
ll go well up there, don't worry please.'

He fished for his Gauloises and lit up and remembered
fire-risk and said *merde* and scuffed the thing out. I
hed he were a degree less nervy.

'd expected a lot of interest from the drilling-crews but the
y people in the hangar were the three riggers doping the
ric of the new trap-door and a man in flying-gear coming
oss to us from the far end.

What's our cover-story for this flight, Chirac?'

85

'Comment?'

'What's the official reason for our using this glider?'

'Oh yes, I will tell you that. It was being flown for An[g]
Belge on a magnetic-rock survey a few days before, but
wind becomes too low, you see, so it was force-landed on
nearest airstrip, which was this place. Now we are going
take it back to Anglo.'

'Why at night?'

'The wind is good right now.'

'Why the blue paint?'

'Ecoutez, mon ami, who the hell asks to know a thing l[ike]
this?' He jerked a thumb towards the main camp. 'That d[rill]
does not stop, never, day and night, you see, unless it bre[aks]
or it strikes oil, and then they are even more busy than alwa[ys]
you un'erstand? When they work they have no time to th[ink]
of different things, and when they stop work they are [too]
damn fatigué to do anything but sleep. They do not wish [to]
ask about the planeur.' He turned as the man in the flyi[ng]
gear came up. 'Pierre, je te présente Monsieur Gage, l'Ang[lais]
dont je t'ai parlé. This is Pierre Batagnier, who will fly [the]
airplane that will tow us.'

Small compact man, more flesh on him than Chirac, m[uch]
less nervy about the eyes. We shook hands and he went o[ver]
to the riggers.

'Alors, Michel, tu es prêt?'

Ten minutes, the man said, and it would take longer th[an]
that to warm his engines.

Chirac got the map and spread it across a crate and [the]
pilot joined us. 'Okay, now listen please. Pierre will tow us [to]
the north-east of here until three thousand metres of altitu[de]
and that will bring us somewhere by the third Philips ra[dio]
beacon at this blue mark here. This is because it is a norm[al]
route made by airplanes across the drilling-complex fr[om]
South 4 to the Anglo-Belge Roches Vertes II, so nobody [will]
think it strange to hear us go that way, you see? After [that]
point we will slip the cable, and Pierre will return here alo[ne]

I kept thinking of base.

'Now we shall be for ourselves, and we will make a ci[rcle]
to bring us east of the Algerian platinum-prospecting ca[mp]
right here, and then we will go down maybe a hundred me[tres]
at a fifteen-degree angle of glide to make a good speed [for]
our final run to the target area, you un'erstand?'

Kept thinking of the arabesque room below the dome,
me kind of association, mustn't ignore, think later.

'And now we will cross the No. 2 Philips radio tower, the
ue mark here, at maybe a hundred kph of airspeed, using
ese red marks for our bearings. They are Petrocombine
uth 5, South 6 and the Anglo Roches Brunes B drilling-
mps, and we shall see their lights on the derricks. We will
in the target area maybe sixty minutes from when we have
gun, here at the radio tower. So it is at this point you must
art to make the figures for dead-reckoning on the *ordinateur*
ny, you un'erstand?'

'What's this distance here: Philips tower to target?'

'Ninety-seven kilometres. Of course we will go a little more
r than this in actual air-distance, because of our angle of
ide, but that will depend of the winds we will find as we
ake our approach.'

The arabesque room and the way she'd been holding the
n at me when I'd gone in. Some kind of association. Im-
rtant? Something overlooked?

'Now please tell me if there is anything you will wish me to
peat, about this thing.'

'You've made it clear enough. The wind-factor governs the
tuation at both ends of the flight, is that it?'

Cellulose. Dope – nail-varnish. Sense of smell strongly
sociative. Dismiss.

'*C'est ça.* If there is no wind when we will make the circle
ver this complex here, we must make a less big angle of
ide, not to lose too much altitude. And if there is no wind
ar the end of our approach to the target area, I must stay
uch higher so that I have my chance to get back here, or
yway so that I come down somewhere not far from any
ater and people, you know?' He began folding the map.
f course when I tell you "no wind" like that, I mean any
ind that is not good enough to go higher. *B'en, je crois que
st tout.*'

Batagnier straightened up.

'*Allons-y?*'

'*Allons-y.*'

The pilot went back through the hangar, shouting for some
ound-staff, and one of the riggers trotted after him. A
inute later a Koffman starter banged and the engine took
er, then the second one fired.

I checked the time: 23.51.

'My stuff's already on board?'

'You can see it from inside the cabin, not through 1 *trappe*.'

I climbed in and checked the set-up. They'd taken out 1 centrally-disposed third seat and made the drop-trap in 1 floor below it, accommodating the 'chute immediately forwa of the polyester container to keep the loads balanced: I wou be sitting beside the pilot and the weight of a third man v transferred to the supplies and transceiver. The ripcord v linked to the fuselage by a tension breakaway for automa opening and release, so that all the pilot had to do was dr the trap and the rest of the operation would go into sequen

The hangar had begun drumming and I saw a tow-tru moving across and turning and backing up. Chirac was calli to me above the noise and I pulled the hook-release ring let them link up the cable.

I climbed out and they tilted the mainplane horizontal a began towing. The pod design formed a sound-box and t noise was like an empty crate being trundled on roller-skat and the whole structure flexed so badly that Chirac had keep shouting orders to the driver of the truck to break the periodicity. A gust of sand stung our faces as Batagnie twin-engined Fauconnet gunned up and swung its tail, rolli towards the airstrip. The tow-truck made a diagonal li across its wake and left the glider in position fifty yar behind it.

Watching Chirac as he directed the preliminaries to tal off it occurred to me that he was the key man in the Burea attempt to have Tango Victor's cargo examined at first han and to a certain extent Loman had been justified in persuadi me that we weren't taking over a wrecked operation w orders to clean up the mess, but were setting up our ov mission with a specified objective.

Someone in London had said: we want a mercenary fi to do us a night-drop in the Sahara, someone who'll keep his contract, a man who doesn't mind risking a stray sl if the money's right.

It wouldn't have been difficult to find a man like Chir in a region where there were more airstrips than oases a where working-conditions were tough and the pay comme surate, but when they saw his record and learned that

was an ex-champion sailplane pilot they seized the chance
and refined the mission and bumped up his insurance to half
a million francs to cover the increased risk and told him to
get himself a glider.

The access had been revamped in a big way and the fact
that the Minister had decided to sting the Treasury for that
amount of loot made it clear that the Bureau had told him
it had a chance of paying off. From this data I was certain
of two things: the opposition was monitoring all aircraft
movement in this area by every means including listening-
posts, and they were doing it in the hope of tracking me in
to the target area and neutralizing me at the site of the
objective.

Priority requirement: silence. The silence of these wings
across the starlit dunes, our passage leaving no trace on the
screens of the acoustic scanners dispersed among the oases
between Sid Ben Ali and Kaifra and the complex of drilling-
camps.

Strict hush.

The sand blew back from the Fauconnet as Batagnier ran
up the revs and tested for mag-drop and the ground-crews
by the glider turned their backs to it, hanging on to the
wing-tips. Then the roaring died and the props idled and I
saw Chirac turn and look in my direction, lifting a hand.

Give it to London then, give them a bit of credit. They'd
been prepared to drop someone in from a powered aircraft
and risk the opposition picking it up and going in for a kill
in the final phase of the penetration: a crude and bloody
business that always costs more lives for fewer results whenever they're driven to mounting this kind of operation with
the opposition already in the field. They do it on the principle
that when the objective is high priority and there's even a
ten per cent chance of the executive's coming out alive with
the stuff they want it's worth this brand of brute frontal
attack on the target that might offer a chance of knocking
out the opposition in the target area itself. They do it when
they're desperate.

They'd been desperate but they'd seen Chirac as the key
to something more controlled and they'd worked on it and
come up with a design that at least made sense on paper
and the delay in planning had brought them right up against
the clock and they'd had to shake the whole network with

89

panic directives but give them this: they'd got a bit of elegance into the mission at last, a bit of class, sent for a top kick like Loman and told him to pick his own executive for the field and set the thing up and make it succeed, bring off a classic.

I anticipate success. Complete success. You understand?

All right you little bastard we'll give it a go.

They'd turned the glider to line up with the runway and walked into the carbon-monoxide airstream that was coming from the Fauconnet. Chirac was getting into his parachute and one of the ground-crew was holding mine ready for me and when I was settled into it Chirac passed me some goggles.

'You will need these, if there will be a sandstorm.'

I slung them round my neck. The rigger was helping me to adjust the 'chute-harness and we pulled it too tight and a flash of pain burned in the nerves of my shoulder where the ricochet of the sixth bullet had left bruising.

'Ca va, mon ami?'

'Oui.'

I dropped my flight-bag into the cabin and climbed aboard and buckled the restraint-belt. Chirac called something to the ground-crew, I didn't catch what, then he followed me in and settled his feet on the rudder-bar and checked the four instruments: airspeed-indicator, spirit cross-level, compass and variometer.

He raised his hand.

'Allons-y!'

The rigger stood away and lifted both arms in a signal to Batagnier and then walked to the wing-tip, waiting. The rev went up and the airstream began fluttering at the hood of the glider as the Fauconnet rolled cautiously, taking up the slack in the towline. A jerk came as it tautened.

Chirac was peeling some silver paper.

'You want some gum?'

I shook my head and he put the strip into his mouth and flicked the paper into the air current and slid the hood shut as the Fauconnet gunned up and we began rolling. A haze of sand came flying against the Perspex and the man at the wing-tip broke his run and fell away as the speed rose and the vibration hammered under our seats and Chirac felt the resistance coming into the controls and brought the stick back

90

gently, feeling his way, gently again until the vibration died
out and the sand-haze cleared and the mission was airborne.

The first derrick-light came into view on the starboard side.
Chirac couldn't see it from his seat but he noticed me
watching the light and said above the windrush:

'South 5.'

He'd clipped a chart on the facia but never looked at it.

When the light came abreast of us north-east I checked the
time at 00.13 hours. The silver-painted storage tanks were
distinct and I could see a truck on the move.

Ahead of us we could see the navigation lights of the
Fauconnet and the short bright flames from its exhaust-stubs.
Its engine noise was steady, drumming at the hood above us,
and the smell of exhaust gas had seeped into the cabin.

South 6.

00.27.

Altitude 1300 metres.

The detail was less distinct: the ash-grey sheen to the west
of the drilling-tower could have been storage tanks or the
semi-domed roofs of the living-quarters. We were now
picking up No. 2 Philips radio beacon, its red warning-lamp
shifting slowly across the desert floor as we overflew it.

The air was cool.

Monoxide and spearmint and above our heads the stars in
their millions flowing peacefully across the curve of the Per-
pex. Course north-east.

Overflying the Roches Vertes drilling-camps at two thousand
metres I thought I heard a change in the Fauconnet's engine-
noise: a slight increase in volume and pitch. I waited for
Chirac to remark on it but he said nothing and I looked at
the instruments.

Airspeed unchanged at 110.

Angle of climb unchanged at 18°.

They were the only two that would reflect the altered note
of the Fauconnet ahead of us but they remained constant.
Batagnier hadn't increased his speed and he hadn't pushed
up his angle of climb and I didn't like it.

Red light moving below, very distant on the starboard side.
No. 3 Philips tower.

Impossible to tell whether a new sound had come into the

immediate area. There should only be one source: the 100CV twin-engined Fauconnet.

No mirrors, either inside the cabin or outrigged in nacelles

The blindspot rearwards of this pod-and-boom design was rather large. The air was cold now but I was beginning to sweat because London had done their best but it might not be good enough, not quite good enough. If their decision to charter a glider for final access to the target area meant that the opposition had set up listening-posts to monitor aircraft movement in this region, then the sound of the Fauconnet was at this moment being registered on their scanners. There hadn't been anything we could do about that: Chirac had ordered this course north-east from South 4 because it was an established airlane across the drilling-complex and if we'd made any kind of circuit to avoid the camps our sound would still have been picked up and we would have been immediately suspect.

The probability that they were picking us up now was all right because they wouldn't investigate every aircraft move ment across this region provided it followed a routine pattern: what they were listening for was unusual traffic and especially an unscheduled flight from any of the strips near Kaifra in the direction of the open desert. Each post would essentially have its own facility for the immediate investigation of sus pect aircraft movement: a machine standing by with its engine warmed and a pilot ready for take-off.

The danger wasn't there. It was in the possibility that our own operation had been penetrated without our knowledge It had been necessary to engage people outside our own cell and although Chirac and Batagnier must have been screened it wouldn't have been advisable to let the ground-staff at South 4 know that this flight had a clandestine aspect, even though there had been no secrecy about the take-off.

London had done its best but if the change in the engine note of the tow-plane was in fact an illusion created by the additional noise of another aircraft flying behind us the mission would end here, two thousand metres above the desert and a hundred kilometres from the target: Tango Victor.

The aft structure of the glider provided a blindspot big enough to conceal a bomber. The glider itself provided a blind spot for the Fauconnet even if it carried outside mirrors. I

here were a third aircraft now flying a north-east course
owards No. 3 Philips tower only the pilot of that aircraft
would know.

'Chirac.'

'J'écoute.'

'Have you noticed any change in the engine-note?'

'When?'

'A minute ago.'

'Oh yes – he went into coarser pitch.'

'He's got variable props?'

'But yes. And we are quite high now.'

'I see. Have you got any spare gum?'

Altitude 3000.

Chirac watched the instruments.

Thirty seconds later the Fauconnet began levelling off.

I couldn't see the No. 3 tower light any more from starboard: over the past ten minutes it had been drifting slowly
out of sight towards our midline as Batagnier changed course
o overfly it directly.

The engine-noise was flattening to a steady drone as he
hrottled back to compensate for the increase of speed at
level flight.

It was now very cold in the cockpit.

'You will please check your seat-belt.'

He went on watching the instruments.

I checked and reported.

'Very well.'

He pulled the release and the cable snaked away and the
orce of the deceleration thrust me hard against the belt as
he nose went down. I caught sight of the tow-plane once
more, quite small as it wheeled against the horizon to retrace
ts course, then we were drifting, alone in the night sky.

Chapter Nine

DROP

There was only the wind's sound.

Sometimes it changed, subtly or grossly, as Chirac searche
the heights for their currents. The air rushed inaudibly ove
the wings and the sound was not from there but from im
perfections in the streamlining of the cabin: the landing-gea
housing, the flanges of the hood-runners, the edge of th
drop-trap.

A sibilance came from them, a whistling through the teeth
then as we swung to meet the wind and headed into it th
sound changed to a low fluting, eerie and musical, then die
to a whisper as we drifted across the current, the long wing
lying against it.

'South-west,' said Chirac, listening to the sounds. 'Mayb
ten knots.'

A head-wind for our flight-path. That was why we'd com
here. But he could have been wrong about the prevailing air
movement and it was reassuring to have his forecast con
firmed.

'We can go straight in?'

'Not yet. In a little time. I want to know more.'

He sat listening, touching the controls a degree and bringin
them back, feeling the air as sensitively as if his hands wer
spread open against it, his fingers sifting it for informatior
Below us the landmarks turned slowly, the lights of the thre
camps revolving inside the greater orbit of the radio tower.

00.46.

Nerves all right but a thought insisting, a reminder of th
margin of error that no one had wanted to talk about, neithe
Loman nor Chirac nor I myself.

I'd asked Loman about the duration and he'd said flexibl
and I'd asked Chirac what the chances were and he'd sai
fifty-fifty, and it meant the same thing: with the target a
this distance and the run-in made by dead-reckoning th
margin of error for dropping me with accuracy was criticall
wide and the break-off point was anywhere on the invisibl
circle drawn around the mission objective where I couldn'

survive long enough to do any good.

Ignore.

The wind whispered past the Perspex hood and above us the starfields turned, their vastness diminishing us, making of us a mote of dust adrift in the dark.

Altitude 2900, must keep to facts.

Keep to the facts, in any case, that don't add up to despair: it's too soon for that.

The starboard wing lifting and our weight shifting and the air desolate in its crying, the sound the winter wind makes under the doors. The nose going down and a scream coming into the sky, dying away as we climb suddenly, the squab seat pressing up and the harness creaking, a shelf of air where we hover and then slide away, circling, the wind plaintive, its voice the voice of the mad Arab, whimpering . . . *mountains in the sky . . . and great birds darkening the heavens . . .*

The air cold, a blade of it cutting across my face from the crack in the hood-runner. My whole body cold, and stiff with its bruises and in no mood shortly to be hurled from its minuscule shelter among the stars.

'Very well.'

A certain philosophy in his tone, a note of fatalism, no time left for the little Gallic ironies, none of the *mon ami* as we swung through the figures on the compass scale towards the south-west, our final flight-line.

'Are you going in?'

He said yes and I unzipped the case of the Sony.

Weight shifting as he began flattening the curve.

Still visible No. 3 tower. Coming into view: No. 2 tower and the white-light markers of South 5, South 6 and the Roches Brunes camps.

'You will begin to compute when we will pass over the No. 2 radio beacon, you know?'

'Understand. I want your value for the head-wind.'

'Eight knots.'

Noted.

Also noted: eight knots estimated average and not re-assuring to spell it out like that but this was the main factor in the margin error, his inability to know to what extent our airspeed would be true and to what extent it would be expressed by the wind in the pitot-head. From his experience of this region he could say that in this season and at the hour a ten-knot wind at three thousand metres above the platinum camps would indicate a wind of eight knots average along our course to the target area but what he couldn't say was that this indication was reliable enough to let him drop me within the prescribed limits of the objective.

If we flew into this precise degree of head-wind he would drop me right in the centre of the ring but if there were an error of two kph on either side he'd drop me so wide that there wouldn't be a hope of locating Tango Victor before my supplies ran out.

The harness creaked as he moved the control-column and I watched the angle of glide go down to fifteen degrees. The soft rushing of the air rose until the sound was like the hissing of a steam-valve and the whole of the airframe began shivering as the stringers took the strain.

Altitude 2850 – 2840 – 2830.

Airspeed 95 – 105 – 115.

Time 00.51.

No. 2 beacon dead ahead of us, a crimson glow.

I turned my watch to the underside of my wrist and used the left hand to steady the Sony on my knees, the right hand to operate it.

Speed still rising through 140 – 145 – 150.

Airstream very loud, a lot of vibration.

The light on the tower was moving slowly towards the edge of the blindspot below us and he couldn't leave it much longer.

'Be ready, please.'

'Ready.'

Angle of glide fourteen degrees: he was anticipating and realized it and corrected to fifteen.

'Listen now, please. I am going to trim the angle to two degrees in a few seconds. Then I will tell you when we will pass over the tower. It is then you must begin computing.'

'Understood.'

He brought the column back and the red light vanished.

Quite a lot of pressure from the seat.

Wind-noise decreased.

Angle 2°.

Compass: 225°.

Begin computing.'

Her name is Monique.'

'I expect she's pretty.'

'Oh yes, I think.'

The inconsistency still on my mind.

In Tunis they'd rigged a bang and got it wrong and didn't try again. In Kaifra they'd set up observation and put a tag on me to find out where I was going and that was all they'd wanted to do because if they'd meant to neutralize they'd have used two men instead of one. To this extent I could penetrate their thinking because they had my dossier and therefore they were professionals and would follow procedures known to me. Then they'd tried to kill again, this time with a long gun, and that was inconsistent.

'Also I have two children, you know? They are boys.'

'How old are they?'

'Jean-Paul has five year old, and Georges has seven.'

I hadn't been able to give it to London to work out so I'd have to tell him as soon as I called up base. He didn't now I'd been shot up but someone might have found the Mercedes by now and half the town would know about it and he'd pick it up before very long and then I suppose he'd just wet himself and assume they'd junked my cadaver and he wouldn't be able to phone the airstrip staff at South 4 because of the strict hush conditions so now he'd be hopping up and down in front of the base transceiver desperate for a signal and crossing himself at thirty-second intervals.

'I have got a snapshot, you know, of those three, that I made a long time before. But I can not fetch it now.'

He couldn't move, couldn't move even a hand to get to his pocket, hadn't moved for twenty-nine minutes, just sat with the control-column watching the angle of glide and the compass while I punched the Sony for him every time the second and passed the top of the dial.

Airstream steady.

'Sixty-four.'

'Okay.'

Two theories: the opposition had an undisciplined cell or their signals were inefficient and the inconsistency was by accident and not design, or there were two cells operating

and they were in conflict on the question of policy. In either
case it indicated pressure: their Controls were putting out
panic directives as fast as London.

01.31.

Dropping in nineteen minutes.

'I will tell you of something quite amusing. It was on the
same day when I make the altitude record that Georges is
born, you know that? The flight for my *planeur* had been
arranged, and I went up after I come from the hospital to
see my new son. I feel so light, you know, so happy, that I
always think it is that fact which helps me go so high up.'

'You felt inspired.'

'*C'est exactement ça!* I find the thunder cloud at one
thousand metres and I fly up with it until twelve thousand
and then find the wave lift waiting for me, and the sky is the
limit! The feeling was quite like anoxia, you know, but of
course I had the mask on a long time before. So I wanted
to have him christened "Icare", you see, but my wife say
"Georges" is more convenient, because she has an uncle of
this name.'

01.42.

Eight minutes to the drop.

Of course it was just conceivable that Control had picked
up a trace of the marksman. There was a ten-tenths flap on
in London so they'd have alerted the whole network for data
monitoring and there must have been signals coming in from
both hemispheres for analysis.

There aren't many telescopic rifles among the European
intelligence networks because it's a device used specifically
for assassination and there's not nearly so much fuss caused
with a little cyanide in the toothpaste. The long gun demands
a relatively sophisticated set-up and a couple of years ago
when Parkis had directed the *modus operandi* of a neutrali-
zation thing it had taken him three weeks to line it all up
including requisition of premises, covert communication
channels, access and egress, target movement monitoring and
the technical demands of the gun itself in terms of range,
angles of fire, appropriate ammunition, so forth. But if it's
a special case and there's enough time for these preliminaries
and the eye at the scope has been trained into the international
class there's an overwhelming advantage because the terminal
act can be performed impersonally and without the risk of

...iation: once the instructions have been confirmed by
...ontrol or even Local Control the target has only to pass
...rough the selected point in his travel pattern and he knows
...othing more.

Parkis had used Tomlinson for that one, winkled him out
...f a duck shoot on Lord Kenfield's estate and put him into
...a executive jet at Gatwick with a Remington .410 across
...s knees and a street map of Kronstadt to read. He had a
...tten cold but it didn't affect his performance, just the one
...ot, and it broke up a cell we'd been trying to get at for
...arly three years.

01.45.

Five minutes.

The thing was that if our overseas units picked up anything
...out a known marksman last seen with a ticket for Tunis
... Jerba and passed it for routine analysis in London there'd
... an immediate hit when London told them I'd been under
... gun. They'd know it was almost certainly the same one
...at had worried Fyson in Sidi Ben Ali but even a random
...gnal with some new information in it could link up with
...isting data and put a name to the man and there's a saying
... the Bureau that stands up rather well: *once you can blow
...e man you can blow the cell.*

Four.

Airstream variable and therefore unpleasant because wind-
...eed variation could make a mess of what I was doing on
...e Sony and I could come down anywhere.

'Now, please?'

'Seventy-six.'

He wanted to count up for distance and I wanted to count
...wn for time which was a bit more logical but he'd stuck
...s heels in about it and said he didn't feel comfortable
...orking backwards' so I let it go.

Three.

'Ninety-one point eight-five.'

He watched the instruments.

'Repeat the briefing, please.'

His voice had gone dull suddenly.

'Free the belt. Slide back the hood. Wait for the order.
...mp and look out for the leading edge.'

'Very well.'

Didn't really seem necessary but he'd dropped people before

and he knew his onions: at the last minute when yo
thinking about the imminent free fall you can cock the who
thing up by getting your feet caught in the belt or bashir
your head on the hood you forget to open, do it by numbe
and it's fool-proof.

'Where shall I put this thing?'

'Leave it on the seat.'

Dull, toneless, because she was pretty and one was fiv
the other seven.

01.48.

'Ninety-three point six-five kilometres.'

'Bien.'

Two minutes.

I didn't have anyone, *nothing of value, no next of kin*, b
that kind of comfort's really an intellectual pursuit becau
we've all got a skin and that's what the organism says we'
got to save, yelling its bloody head off, couldn't care le
about the insurance.

'Ninety-five point six-seven.'

'Okay.'

One minute.

The night seemed vast.

The stars gave a sense of orientation but only in one pla
and all they did was show which way was down and th
was where I was going, down through the dark to the en
less night-lying waves of sand, of silence.

The 8 looks so like a 9 and they're side by side.

Slipshod maintenance, dead flies in the pitot-head.

A change in the wind.

Ignore.

'Ninety-six point two.'

'Very well.'

Twenty-eight seconds.

The old feeling that we were arriving somewhere. Difficu
here where the night was as vast as it had been before a
the dark as featureless, to understand that our journey togeth
was over. No control tower or platform or jetty or gat
nothing to mark a junction or a terminal, only the dark a
the delicate pointer going its rounds.

Tick-tick-tick.

'Ninety-six point five.'

'So. Be ready then.'

He brought the column back just a little.
Level flight.
Ten seconds.
We had agreed that at this point I would stop computing.
Ten seconds represented a quarter of a kilometre and that
such distance could be critical if I dropped wide but if I
went on computing to zero as a refinement it wouldn't allow
for the time I needed for getting out.
Tick-tick-tick.
French keen on shaking hands, frustrating for him, control-
column too sensitive, no go the niceties.
I hit the belt clip.
Tick-tick.
Hood back and a blast of air roaring.
Leave the Sony on the seat.
Altitude 75 metres.
Tick.
Good luck Chirac.
Adieu!
Free fall.

Chapter Ten

TANGO

One, two, three.
Blood in the head and the stars swinging below me.
Less horizontal buffeting, more vertical.
Four, five, six.
Free fall velocity rising very fast.
Air less cold.
Seven, eight, nine.
Pull it.
Crack of the pilot 'chute.
Then the jerk and the drag and oh Christ —
Blackout.

Swinging gĕntly.
Couldn't quite relate anything yet.

Nearly did it again and thought I'm not going to and ↓
pain didn't stop but at least I stayed conscious. It had be←
the shoulders, that was all, the bruising on the pavement
Tunis and then the ricochet of the .44 tonight and then tl
awful wrenching from the harness because I'd been mo
or less upside down when the main canopy had filled a⊓
the fall velocity had been braked from more than a hundr←
kph to less than fifteen and the pain had overcharged tl
nerve channels and that was that.

Still very uncomfortable, feeling of being on fire, inabili
to concentrate on other things but the forebrain functionir
well enough to alert the organism and I began looking dow
wards so that I'd see the sand coming up and have a chan
of relaxing the muscles because if I hit it the wrong way I
pass out again and I had a lot to do.

No particular visual definition yet: a certain lightne
below, with darker areas, but could be illusory.

I could make out the figures on the dial of my wat←
without needing the phosphorescence, not much point
wanting to know the time but it helped me to feel I w
getting back into some kind of control over things. Time w
important: ask London.

There was something I ought to be checking on but
didn't matter for the moment, couldn't be expected to lo←
after everything when there was this Godawful sensati←
across my shoulders. Be easier when the harness was o
Swinging gently, the rhythm soothing, the night air s⊂
against my face.

It does matter.

Bloody well wake up and have a look, can't see it, do⊓
panic, use your suspension lines, pivot full circle, none t
easy, monkey on a string, now keep looking because it's ve
important indeed.

Couldn't see the bloody thing anywhere.

Rest. Relax. Watch the ground.

The whisper of wind in the shrouds.

He couldn't have forgotten to pull the release. You think
such extraordinary things when your life's on the teeter,
course he'd pulled it, he was an experienced flyer and h←
dropped people before. But he'd had to give me five secon
to get clear so that the 'chutes wouldn't find each other a
I couldn't see it because it would be above me and t

opy was in the way, thirty feet across and right over my
ad, what the hell would you expect.

A lot of pain, it wouldn't go.

Then bloody well shut up about it.

Nothing below with any definition: it just didn't look like
pty sky, that was all, the desert was there all right.

If I hadn't punched an 8 instead of a 9 and if some slip-
d instrument-basher hadn't left enough dead flies in the
ot-head to affect the airspeed reading and if the wind
dn't changed I was now floating above the only point on
 surface of the earth describable as Long. 8°3′ by Lat. 30°4′
d it was less than forty-eight hours since they'd put on the
w for me.

Run it back, will you?

Stop.

Back another fraction.

Stop.

Yes, that's the one. I've got it now.

An ash-grey smudge on the photograph.

Tango Victor.

Somewhere below me now but very difficult to believe
ause Loman had said flexible and Chirac had said fifty-
y and that meant the margin of error was horribly wide
d although the wreck of the twin-prop short-haul freighter
s certainly within a few kilometres of the point where I
s due to come down I might never reach it, never see it,
ause this was the desert.

ook, they don't do this to you without thinking about it
t: even those arthritic old tarts in London aren't as bad
 that. When they send a ferret down the hole they don't
 him much but they've done it with me so often that I've
naged to pick up the odd clue about the way they think.
wasn't lack of planning in the advanced pre-briefing phases
t had left us with a critical margin of error at the access
nt, and it wasn't indifference to the question of my sur-
al or otherwise that had let them send me out here where
 chance of life was small. They just had to do what they
ld.

This was the *best* they could do, not the worst. This was
 they could do, instead of nothing.

They hadn't been able to turn this one down. I think they'd
bably tried but the pressure had been too great and they'd

been forced to set up the op. I'd only known it to hap
twice before since I'd been at the Bureau and in each ca
the decision-making had been at Prime Minister level.

He wished to inform me personally that your mission is t
key to a critical situation of the highest international pr
portions.

If he didn't talk like a bloody schoolmistress he could ha
put it rather more concisely. *This one's shit-or-bust.*

We call it a one-shot mission and it means if you don't pu
it off the first time you don't get another go. You can refu
it if you like but if you accept it you've got to play it the
way and put up with panic directives and dodgy communica
tions and makeshift access lines and do what you can wit
what you've got and somehow get in there and do the jo
and bring back the goods. It means more than just th
increased risk of your losing your life: it means that if yc
can't complete the mission it's the last chance anyone's goir
to get. There are various factors governing this but the mo
common one is time.

Time governed the Tango mission. In London they'd bee
pushed for time but they'd set it running as best they coul
and provided superlative access lines right into the targ
area: my final approach to the objective was being mac
invisibly and in perfect silence. The margin of error wa
deadly but if they'd narrowed it the invisibility and the silenc
would have had to go: we would have brought a powere
aircraft and searched the area with flares and landing-ligh
and made a direct drop on to the target but I wouldn't ha
had five minutes to work in before the opposition arrived.

The margin of error had been unavoidable. That didr
make it any narrower: but it made it more acceptable.

Air spilling from the canopy. Its dark fabric was sprea
above me, filling the sky. I couldn't see the supply 'chu
but I believed it was there, following me down, had
believe it was there because if it wasn't I would already ha
begun to die.

The senses were coming back and I had the impressic
that each swing was taking me more and more to one sid
the canopy was restless and I could hear the rising sibilan
of the airstream through the suspension lines. There was
lateral force operating and this must be the south wind, t
Ghibli, that Chirac said he hoped to find blowing when

his attempt to reach the South 4 strip. It didn't feel
ry strong; I wished for him that it would be enough.

Warmth was touching my face and I looked down. The
at of the sands was rising and I reached for the lines and
ld them, waiting, seeing nothing but knowing that land was
ar.

Important to remain conscious.

The chances were that I'd hit sand and the impact would
cushioned but if Chirac's dead-reckoning had been accurate
ough to bring me down on a radius of five hundred yards
om the centre of the target area I could hit the rock out-
op and if a spur caught one of my shoulders I'd flake out
ain and that would be dangerous.

The canopy above me had been blocking my view and when
it ground and the nylon collapsed I must get an immediate
sual fix on the supply 'chute. I would be able to see it
ile it was still airborne because when I'd baled out the
speed had been 99 kph and Chirac was going to wait five
conds before he released and with a wind-factor common
both drops the supply 'chute would come down approxi-
ately a hundred and fifty metres from where I landed. But
I didn't see it before it struck ground and the canopy
llapsed it would be hidden by the dunes: and I wouldn't
ow its direction.

With our bearing of 225° from the radio tower we'd flown
th Pegasus directly ahead and I could see the constellation
w but Chirac had made a right-hand bank when I'd
mped and I didn't know if he'd resumed his course before
elling up to make the second drop or if he'd simply pulled
t of the turn and levelled at a tangent. If I didn't see
ere the supply 'chute came down it would mean a search
the dark among the dunes with no certainty of ever finding

Warm air against my skin.

The lines whispering: I could feel their fine vibration.

Sudden inundation of optical stimuli and the world filled
th contrasts – the far horizon-line where the stars met the
m of the earth and the rising undulations of the dunes
otting it out as I pulled on the lines to break the impact
d then went limp and rolled once on my shoulder with
e harness wrenching, dragged the release and tried to get
, couldn't.

Everything kaleidoscopic and the pain like a furnace ro
in my bones, try to see where it is, most important, the hi
stars sliding down the wall of night and sand in my mou
get up, not really important yes *very,* spitting the sand o
a dark shape moving over there where there's nothing, nothi
to mark it, the canopy lowering, lowering, yes *got* it, t
roaring and the red of stars flying, fall this way then, *t*
way, fall with your head towards it and remember, rememb
when you wake, your *head is towards* it, the black sa
bursting against my face.

Pale fire.

Blue, pale blue fire before my eyes.

A ring of it, a rosary, an annulus of luminescent blue.

The two pointers at right-angles, their blue, it doesn't ta
their blue light trisecting the ring of fire, take long for t
brain to seize when it wakes on what it can find, famil
things to facilitate recall, twelve and three, the underside
my wrist lying turned towards my eyes, three o'clock.

Your head is towards it.

Over there. It came down over there.

Three o'clock and all's well, we have the means to survi

Got up and it happened again and I became very frustrat
and spat out the sand, hanging on all fours like a dog a
thinking this won't do at all, where's your dignity, now
up and stay there and *don't turn.*

Over there.

Note carefully. The high dune to the left, curving to t
unequal sided V where it joins the next, the lower one, a
the bright star five degrees above it to the right. Obser
and absorb.

I had a reference. The gap in the dunes and a star. It w
the only known shape here where I was a stranger: it wa
kind of temporary home.

It took time to get there. Over an hour. It was more l
three hundred metres instead of a hundred and fifty and
directional error was ten degrees and the dunes were da
I took the parachute with me because later it would ma
extra shade and I couldn't leave it behind, the idea was
actually to litter the desert with landmarks, but it took a
of dragging. I couldn't fold it and the sand kept getting i
but it did a good enough job wiping out my tracks.

There was a light wind blowing, blowing from Diphda in the south, is it enough for your needs, *mon ami*? It had blown sand already against the container on that side and the chute was almost covered. The desert hides things from you: beware.

A rip-string and I pulled it, opening the polyester like a sardine-tin, putting the lid on its back and scooping sand in before the wind could lift it. The 2000CA was on top and I took it out and stood it on the lid and pulled up the telescopic aerial, not hurrying, just a routine movement of the hands and perfectly confident, Loman was experienced and the only time he'd ever lost a base was in Bangkok and we weren't there when it was blown and besides she had a gun, the big Colt that Chirac had lent me, hold it with both hands if you want to and be ready for the recoil. And anyway I'd asked Loman not to leave base because one gun wouldn't be enough if she were alone and they raided the place, feet on the stairs and the door kicked open and the first one going down but after that she'd lose her head and just go on pumping the thing wild with her eyes shut and they'd reach her before the sixth.

Chrome of the aerial shining, the low wind moving its tip.

3 MHz.

Channel 2.

Mike.

Tango.

It sounded strange, a human voice in so desolate a place.

Tango. Tango.

The same stars, these same stars, would be there above the gilded cupolas where the rats ran among the rotting palms. The town would be asleep.

Eyes closing and I opened them again quickly and took a breath, steadying. Fifty-six hours ago I'd got off the plane from Tokyo and the metabolic clock was still trying to get the time right, a feeling of not quite being here, of not being anywhere, just afloat on some kind of tide.

Tango. Tango.

A domed ceiling and a cracked mosaic floor, three faded arabesque screens and the shabby appurtenances of a fifth-class hotel.

The other end of the lifeline.

What frequencies would you use in this area?

7 MHz for daytime propagation conditions, 3 MHz at nigh
Tango. Tango.

The sand blown by the wind, its fine grains hitting the sid
of the polyester box with a dry whispering, the only answer.

Already in the past hour the sand had almost covered th
spread of nylon: in the starlight I could just make out the fe
dark folds that remained. Soon it would cover the harnes
then the box, and then if I went on sitting here like this, lik
a man in prayer, it would cover me as well, a desiccate
mendicant forgotten by his gods as he intoned for their de:
ears the mystic word, until he was buried, grain upon grair
beneath his sins.

Tango. Tango.

One of them would be there. Loman might have had t
leave base to contact Chirac or use a phone if the wire ha
come adrift again on the junction-board or he could hav
gone down there to the hall to fix it but in that case Dian
would be manning the transceiver, and would answer.

The wind gusted, scattering the sand.

A faint gleam on the aerial and the chrome rims of th
dials. It was a good-looking set: a matt-black case with
neutral grille and the controls tapered and finely-knurled, th
on-off switch recessed so that a chance movement wouldn
activate it. The illuminated dials were dark.

No adequate excuses. Flight-disorientation, the blast-wav
the general wear-and-tear of getting here alive. Not reall
adequate.

I put the switch to the 'on' position and checked the fre
quency again at 3 MHz.

Tango.

Tango. Base receiving.

A good signal, loud and clear.

I'm down.

Are you in the target area?

I don't know.

He waited and I didn't say anything so he came in agai

Do you have any problem?

Not really.

He waited again.

I wasn't being very communicative. You're supposed
volunteer a bit of information, not leave your director
tease it out of you. Thing was, I wanted to go to sleep now.

108

Was the drop made successfully as concerns bearings?

Oh yes. Put the little bastard out of his misery or he'll keep *you* talking all bloody night. *On Chirac's reckoning I'm some-where near the target, but it's too dark here to see anything. There aren't any rocks on the skyline. Going to take a dekko in the morning.*

Silence again.

Are you perfectly fit?

What?

Are you in a fit physical condition?

Of course I am.

Bloody sauce. Resented that. I told him:

Listen: there's a telescopic rifle in Kaifra. Christ sake watch out for it. And the Mercedes is a write-off.

He was thinking about this.

We heard some shots.

Kaifra was a small-oasis town and you'd hear the stuff coming out of .44 Magnum wherever you were.

They were the ones.

You are not wounded?

No. Another thing is that I think there's more than one net-work trying to penetrate our operation. Been working a few things out and there's one or two inconsistencies.

He considered this.

You're talking about their apparent indecisiveness during the pre-jump phase?

Their inconsistency.

Yes. This has already been the subject of signals with Control but we're glad to have you confirm.

A pat on the head for a good little ferret, dear Lord you banish me unto the wilderness and the only company you can find for me is Loman's.

One star, the bright star that had guided me here, was going on and off at intervals and I took note of it.

When will you start looking for the objective?

At dawn.

Not before?

Rather quick.

It's too dark. Instructions?

On, off. On, off.

It wasn't the star doing it. I was doing it myself. The star was lying exactly on the horizon and my head kept going down, fatigue, reaction setting in, so the star looked as it were going on and off.

Silence. He was sulking.

No instructions.

Tango out.

Quick fade of the image: the dome and the arabesqu screens.

Mike back into the recessed clip and the switch down an next time don't forget to turn the bloody thing on when yo want to call up base, save a lot of worry, I thought they had it, both of them, thought we'd all had it.

Loman could do the worrying now. He'd got his executi into the field but the bearings were all to hell and we'd g to cool our heels for another three hours before we cou get moving again and in three hours the opposition cou make up a lot of ground. There'd been no security blacko for the take-off from the South 4 strip: London could ha sent in a unit of screened ground-staff with a pre-arrange access to facilities but even then there would have been peop at South 4 who knew that a glider had gone up, and sho of requesting Petrocombine's co-operation in treating th event as a para-military secret it would have been impossib to keep the thing hush. The opposition cells would be routine combing the area for items of intelligence and if they picke up the news that a glider had been towed airborne they'd wa to know where it had landed and if they drew blank at the local airstrips they'd assume there'd been a desert dr and they'd send for a direction-finding unit, fully urge because radio would be the only means of communicatio between the field and base.

Once the opposition set up a D/Fing operation in a tov as small as Kaifra I'd give our base twenty-four hours befo it was blown.

There was a sleeping-bag in the container and I unroll it and threw it down but it was no go: I'd have to make effort, some kind of effort, to find out if I'd come dov anywhere near the target. This before I could sleep.

Even if there were only a thin chance of locating th freighter's wreckage before first light it was worth having go because in the night's cool the sweat-loss and water-inta would be less than a tenth of the quantities produced by th day's heat.

110

There was another thing: psychologically I'd been homing-
on the target since they'd shown me the picture of it in
London. The smudge on the photograph had become the
object of intellectual attraction and I felt its influence on
me now, stronger than before because it was closer.

It was impossible to judge how far I stood from the nearest
dune: I could only see it in two dimensions, its dark spine
humped against the stars and breaking the distant skyline. It
was less than a thousand yards away but the desert is like the
ocean: the chance of death by isolation is immeasurably
greater, and values become changed. Go a thousand yards in
the dark and you may never come back.

There was a torch among the supplies, with some spare
batteries, but I wouldn't use light for a marker: you learn
to conserve, to know the sudden pricelessness of ordinary
things. There was a tin mug and I put it upside down on the
top of the aerial and waited for the wind to send it ringing;
then I walked to the dune and climbed it.

In the photographs, taken from the near-vertical, the
definition of the shale upthrust had been vague, but I would
expect a stratified configuration at ground-level in this region,
like the rocks near Kaifra, sharp and broken and sloping,
distinct from the curvilinear dunes. But I saw nothing like
that, though I twice turned full circle. The skyline was uni-
formly smooth.

Then I began shouting and turned again, my voice going
into the distant dark and dying there. Twenty or thirty feet
high, the squadron-leader had said, so there'd be an echo
from them if they weren't too far away.

Tang-o . . . Tang-o Vic-tor . . .

My feet burying deeper as I turned.

My eyes closed so that I could listen better.

Shouting, turning under the dome of stars.

Tang-o . . . Vic-tor . . .

Dying away.

All I could see from the height where I stood, all I could
hear, was the margin of error, wide as the endless dunes.

Chapter Eleven

SIGNAL

A sense of frightening exposure.

Last night there had been the stars, their names known an
their order long ago established by the ancients. Now ther
was nothing. A map had been replaced by a blank sheet
paper. In the dark it had been possible to believe that whe
morning came I might see familiar shapes, however far away
buildings or trees. Morning had come and I saw nothing.

For another minute I lay with my eyes open, pinned to th
earth's surface in infinite solitude. It was the sameness
this terrain that appalled: if there had been a range of high
dunes within sight, or a rock or a tree, any kind of featu
to break the facelessness here, I could have related with
and arrived at some kind of orientation: I could have note
that it was on my left or on my right, in front of me
behind; and there could have been the idea that if I set o
to reach it I might find other features becoming visib
beyond it as I approached.

There was nothing.

Nothing to see, nothing to hear. The silence was absolut

During the night the low wind had died, and my sleepin
bag was only half-covered by drifts of sand; but my trac
to and from the high dune had disappeared. This was th
desert, and if a man chose to disturb the perfection of the
primeval sands, let it be shown that his passing shall leav
no trace.

I drank from one of the five-litre *bidons* and pressed t
sides before screwing the cap on. The sun was a diamet
above the horizon and I thought of opening for reception b
Loman would only order a change of frequency for daytim
conditions and ask if I'd sighted the objective and that wasn
a question I wanted to hear put into words.

I hadn't been delaying things since first light but there w
a marked reluctance to go and find out the worst: and
could do that by going to the dune over there and climbi
it. We don't mind if London's policy is to send us in wi
only a minimum of data but we always know that at any sta

112

an operation it can take us beyond the point of no return:
nd that point could already be behind me now.

Edwards had been in this position eighteen months ago in
ugoslavia: in the thick of a direct Control-to-field signals
xchange in the final phase of the mission he'd found out by
ccident that if he failed to reach the objective he'd auto-
natically become expendable – and he'd kicked. We didn't
xpect to see him back in London for at least ten years if he
vere lucky but he'd infiltrated a CIA courier line and did a
ast deal with a batch of strict shut documentation and got
flight out of Zagreb with a party of chess-players on a
ultural exchange and asked to see Parkis the minute he
eached the Bureau and Parkis had flayed him alive and then
red him.

The point Edwards had been trying to make was that it's
ll right if an executive fouls up a job and Control throws
im to the dogs before he can do any more damage, but it's
ot all right for the Bureau to send him out on a Curtain
ning without telling him there's a high risk of his becoming
xpendable *automatically* because the mission's been planned
ke that.

There's no middle line we can take on this one. The com-
lexities of an intelligence operation don't even have a static
esign: its pattern shifts as the mission progresses, and values
re changed hourly. Control can put a man in the field on a
outine bugging stint at a pre-summit convention and the
hole thing can suddenly hot up and he's out there trying to
andle something so big that if he drops it he won't survive
nd all you can blame the Bureau for is not pulling him out
or the sake of his own skin.

But that isn't what the Bureau is for.

Parkis had given us the picture after he'd fired Edwards:
arkis doesn't like unrest among the ferrets. During the
nd-phase of the mission it had been decided that the only
ay to get Edwards right through to the objective was by
utting him off from most of his escape lines and letting the
pposition think that no one would attempt this brand of
e impossible unless he were a lunatic. To an extent it came
ff because they withdrew a lot of surveillance and Edwards
ot through to the signals room of the Hungarian Embassy
nd was closing on the objective – his actual mission was a
pher-bust near the centre of the Jugoslavian network – when

he'd seen what London had done to his escape lines a.. panicked and got out.

We don't like Parkis but we thought he was right. All w ask is that the Bureau doesn't plan a mission that *depend* on an expendable executive. That, in certain cases, woul amount to murder.

In my case there was a fact among the unknown back ground data that I knew must exist and that I had tacitl accepted when Loman had given me final briefing at th Yasmina. It was obvious, and it was this: if I failed to reach Tango Victor I couldn't expect to be pulled out of the area The entry in the book wouldn't read *Mission Failed* bu *Executive Deceased*. In most cases it comes to the same thing but there's a technical nuance because the failure of a bi operation creates a lot of depression at the Bureau and i makes the whole thing look a bit better if it can be show that the executive lost his life in the attempt: it means tha no one can say he wasn't trying hard enough.

London wanted me to find an aeroplane and examine it cargo and if I couldn't do it they'd want to make it ver difficult for anyone else to do it. They'd taken great pain to put me down here in strict hush and if I couldn't find th objective they wouldn't allow Loman to make any nois pulling me out.

Understood and accepted.

But it seemed a long way to the top of the dune.

They were Zeiss 22-50's but I didn't use them until I' turned full-circle and looked for the freighter with the nake eye because if I had to use a 22 magnification to pick it u it would mean it was a day's march distant and the sun wa already hot on my skin.

From the low area among the dunes I had looked and see nothing and from this height I looked and saw nothing but i was infinitely worse: down there the piled waves of sand ha limited my range of vision but from here I could see for fifty miles in every direction and *still* there was nothing. It was dun-brown seascape, an area so vast that it had no end unti it met the sky itself. The silence of it alone was diminishin to the spirit, adding lifelessness to endlessness: the semblanc of a seascape, because of this, was only partial; there was n sound here of the wave's leap or the hiss of spindrift. Silenc and stillness together cast the mind beyond the thought o

...ath and held it in awe of this place where life itself had
ever been.

My shadow alone moved, turning as I turned, its giant
pointer lying curved across the dunes.

An instant's hesitation of the hands, fear of confirming the
negative findings of the naked eye, then I raised the binoculars
and adjusted the focus to infinity. The red of the spectrum
refracted at the edge of the field to leave a glowing ring, and
through it passed the flow of images, repeated until they
became meaningless: one sand-dune looked like another, and
here they were spread in their millions.

After two minutes I had to lower the glasses, mesmerized.
The agoraphobia still played in my senses, a hovering dread
of exposure that I couldn't quite keep away as I stood here
in the middle of the empty earth beneath the empty sky, a
goose-flesh feeling of vulnerability: I was a creature without
shelter, without a hiding-place, caught in a trap where the
vastness of freedom itself imprisoned me.

I prefer the more natural haunts of my kind, the sooty
warrens of the city streets, to this cosmic waste where the
grains of sand are unimaginably many.

I turned twice more, full-circle.

At least there would be no more effort needed, now that
this point was reached. The reckoning had been wrong, that
was all. Somewhere between the Philips tower and the zeros
lining up on the computer there had been a mistake made in
the figures. The margin of error, *mon ami*, is even larger than
we'd thought.

There was no point in organizing a day's march: by the law
of averages I would be as likely to move away from the
wreck of the freighter as towards it. I had a compass but I
didn't know the bearing. If I set off at random the odds
against success were precisely three hundred and sixty to one.
Onset of lassitude, euphoria almost. Pain coming back,
normal reaction, nothing important to do, can concentrate on
the discomfort, crouched on the sand with my back to the
heat and the light, here endeth the mission, you can't win
them all. A vague sense of wonder that the sun was perfectly
silent, sending this degree of heat over so much distance,
you'd expect to hear a roaring, however faint, here where
silence could be broken by a grain of sand hitting the side
of a box.

My shadow humped before me, an insubstantial Buddha.

Try again I've tried then bloody well try again.

Lurching about, it's the sand, you can't ever get your balance. The red ring flaring at the edge of the field and the dunes flowing through, full-circle. Negative. Take a rest.

A kind of sleep, timeless and with no dream-element recalled, teeming images but so disconnected as to have no significance, then on my feet again and wandering about, feeling stronger physically but not really determined about anything, the organism taking care of itself, getting the wind up because the box down there wasn't very big, forty-eight hours plus reserves and that's our lot.

Kept bumping my forehead against the eyepieces, sweat running down, awareness of sand in the boots and a thirst beginning, a certain amount of cerebration continuing: the parallax factor critically important because a near dune could block medium-field gaps, be an interesting thing to work out – given a man of certain height standing upon a dune of certain height and given a million dunes, the nearest of them concealing the gaps between those more distant, what proportion of the terrain can he actually observe, and what proportion is hidden from him?

To hell with academic problems: concentrate on the one thing that could just conceivably drag the mission back on its feet and yes, you snivelling little perisher, save our skin.

Parallax.

By lateral movement the observer exposes to view the gaps between distant dunes hitherto concealed by those in the foreground. By bodily rotation he increases this extension of view a hundredfold. Put it like that and it looks fair enough but the wreck isn't necessarily visible in one of the gaps, it can be lying on its belly full-square behind the highest dune of them all and you can practise your lateral movement and bodily rotation till the heat knocks you flat on your face.

The red ring flaring, the sand flowing through. The shadow changing as I turned from the sun through the south to the west. The sun hanging there in its roaring silence and pouring the sky ablaze across the eastern wastes of the earth until its tide lapped about me, burning.

They are there, the gaps you couldn't see before: you're looking at them now but can you tell which they are? You expect to find any difference between one thing and another

116

this region of the damned where the sun and the wind have
driven away identity?

Turn. Keep turning.

Of course this wasn't the only dune in the Sahara and I got
off it and tried another one because a kind of madness was
setting in and although I knew about it I decided to ignore it
because the organism had taken over a long time ago but it
was going to be hard work: it was saying if we don't find
the wreck and finish this job they won't ever pull us out and
we'll die here so we're going to climb every dune in the
desert till we see it, come on.

Climbed one of them twice, found my own tracks still there,
getting rather dodgy, four times down there for a drink of
water, not very slaking because it was warm.

The sands flowing like opaque flood-water through the
vision-field, the gaps dipping like the lines on an electro-
cardiograph.

Turn. Keep turning.

Stop.

21°.

Now go down, go down and drink. And open up.

Tango.

Tango receiving.

I want to confirm that I am in fact in the target area.

You've seen the plane?

*No. But I've sighted a rock. It should be the shale outcrop.
According to the RAF people there's no other rock visible
within seven miles of the objective and even on dead-reckoning
Chirac couldn't have dropped me so wide.*

He considered.

I would agree. How far away are you?

*It's difficult to tell because the air's so clear. I'd say about
two miles: it looks like one but I've doubled it.*

What bearing is it?

Twenty-one degrees.

He was looking at the photograph and its annotations.

*Then you should find the aeroplane almost directly in your
path when you head for the outcrop. Its bearing from there
two hundred degrees.*

I'll make my heading twenty. Change frequency?

Yes, to 7 MHz. Please repeat.

I repeated and asked for twin-synchro and we ended.

Then I did what I knew I would do: I went to the top
the dune and put up the Zeiss and looked again at th
distant tip of rock. My life had depended on sighting th
single landmark, and I wanted to be sure I hadn't dreamed u
a mirage.

Their mass had been thrust upwards from the earth's cru
to leave them standing reared and angular against the sk
their strata sloping at twenty or so degrees from the hor
zontal and their base littered with brittle fragments that ha
broken off. In several places a whole shoulder of rock ha
foundered, making an angled arch and giving shade, and und
one of these I made my camp.

The flooring was the canopy of the supply 'chute and th
roof was provided by my own, propped and draped wit
the help of the telescopic tubing that was part of the surviv
gear.

Lizards had run from the area of shade, skittering so fa
across the sand that they seemed to float on its surface.
watched them, encouraged by the evidence of life in th
region where I'd thought that nothing could hope to live.

For an hour I slept, in the heat of the noon. The distanc
had been nearer two miles than one and I'd had to mak
two trips, each time bringing a parachute and half the gea
and provisions: four hours' work including rests in the shad
of the rocks before I set up camp. Earlier, even when it ha
been cooler, this degree of effort would have been beyon
me: it had been the sight of the tip of rock, the knowledg
that it was there, that had given me the strength.

At 12.34 hours I made a signal.

He had to be told, before I decided what kind of effo
was needed. Effort used up water and it used it up very fas
He had to be told, although there wasn't much he could d
about it. The first thing was to get him to believe it.

*Can I have that bearing again, from the rocks to th
freighter?*

Two hundred.

I checked the compass. The bearing was lined up directl
with the tracks I'd left.

What's the distance from the rocks to the plane?

Four hundred and eighty-five yards.

He wasn't going to like it.

...oman, I'm at the rock outcrop now. I've pitched camp.

I had to wait for him to re-check the annotations on the photograph. No change of tone.

Your heading was twenty degrees?

Yes.

You must have passed close to the aeroplane.

Not close enough to see it.

Then the poor bastard shut up for a bit.

I looked across the blazing sands to the point where my tracks vanished. There were big areas between the dunes and they didn't have the regular formation I'd seen at the point of drop: the rocks would deflect the wind here, setting up turbulence. But I had a clear view for more than five hundred yards and the bearing was correct and I ought to be looking straight at the wreck of the freighter. I was looking at an unbroken waste of sand.

Loman came in.

Quiller.

Hear you.

Do these rocks show any signs of ferrous oxidization?

He was dead scared but he didn't show it in his voice. He showed it in his thinking: he'd got the blown-up photograph in front of him with the distances marked and he should have worked this one out for himself and instead of that he was panicking. I told him:

No. And it wouldn't make any difference, Loman. The compass could be affected up to fifteen degrees and I'd still be able to see a twin-engined freighter less than five hundred yards away.

Pause.

You are quite sure.

Christ, d'you think I'm just guessing?

I was bloody annoyed because they'd said it was a picture of a plane that had crash-landed at Longitude 8°3′ by Latitude 4°4′ and now I was here on the spot and I couldn't help thinking how much effort we'd all made just to prove they were wrong.

Even Loman was thrown.

I don't understand.

Join the club.

After a while he said: *How was the drop?*

Routine.

I knew what he was driving at but I wasn't in the ﹍ to give him any help: let him stay on this tack and I'd bla﹍ his head off, that was all.

Did you bring all your provisions with you from the poi﹍ of drop?

Yes.

And both parachutes?

Yes.

It was exhausting work.

A bit thirst-making.

There's been no kind of accident? No water-spillage?

No.

He saw I wasn't going to co-operate so he just put it o﹍ the line, didn't like having to do it, wasn't his way.

How would you describe your general condition, physic﹍ and mental?

Not too bad. Bit of sunburn.

His tone went dull: over-correction.

I would appreciate a more precise answer.

So I thought he ought to have one.

Listen, Loman, the drop was a right bastard and I've ju﹍ shifted a hundred and seventy kilos through two miles ﹍ soft sand in the direct sun but if you think I'm too far go﹍ to be able to see a whole bloody aeroplane against a neutre﹍ background at five hundred yards you're wasting your tim﹍ Who was the executive you were running last – Dewhurst ﹍ someone?

Quite a long time went by. I don't think he was sulking o﹍ anything: he'd got a damn sight too much on his plate an﹍ he was going to have a lot more unless he could do somethin﹍ about it and that didn't leave any time for making ment﹍ notes to the Bureau to the effect that certain executive﹍ appeared to require supplementary refresher courses in No﹍ folk.

Quiller.

Hear you.

Can you give me an approximate configuration?

Of these rocks?

Yes.

Stand by.

I switched off to save the batteries.

He'd begun thinking straight but it was going to be a nas﹍

. minutes because there weren't many answers to the
estion and this was the one with the built-in dead-end to
e mission.

The compass gave 14° – 194° for the elongation and I noted
and took the pad with me and it was like walking out of
e shade into a molten gold wall. This was the eastern face
d a lot of heat was coming off it because of seven or eight
urs' pre-zenith absorption. I could feel the sweat drying on
e as fast it came through the pores: there was no moisture
en I passed a hand across my face.

I made my way clockwise.

Lizards scuttled across the broken shale on the ground:
ey were quite big, a foot long, one of the *Iguanidae,* and
ey didn't go far from where I passed, but froze with their
gular heads lifted to watch me. Possibly they had never
en man before and their caution was primitively learned,
e mistrust of an alien creature so large that it blotted out
e sun.

South face and turning west.

The general configuration was oblong and the angles were
arly defined: the material was so hard that erosion hadn't
unded it. The sun and the night frosts had loosened the
ata into laminations and the wind had worked at the result;
places the weathering force had left horizontal necks and
e weight of the unsupported rock had brought it down so
at now it leaned on the main structure in irregular but-
sses, making shade. In these areas there were more lizards
an nearer the open and I supposed their one enemy was
e vulture.

No. 2 Fighter-Reconnaissance had said there weren't any
her rocks within seven miles of this group. I thought about
at for a minute and then gave it up.

West to north.

They watched me with their gold-ringed eyes. A pair of
em turned their heads slowly as I passed, only one of them
shing into the crevice behind them with its long tail scatter-
g the group of snail-shells in the hollow where they fed.
: night there would sometimes be moisture here.

I thought: seven miles.

If Loman got the precise bearing from the RAF we might
ork out the chances but they were almost nil: from this
orning's trek the immediate reckoning was a minimum of

121

fourteen hours by day, leaving out the factor of dimin...
energy in terms of progressive fatigue. And the thing was se...
cancelling because the more water I carried the more I'd u...
up.

North to camp.

My hand reached for the beaker and I stopped it and l...
it to the transceiver switch.

Tango.

Tango receiving.

Pencil ready?

Yes.

*Overall shape: oblong. Elongation 14° – 194°. Directi...
clockwise. Five paces. Right-angle to left. Seven paces. Righ...
angle to right.*

Pauses while he drew the shape.

Could you, mon ami, have made an error of seven mile...

*Twenty-one paces. Oblique angle right: one-four-oh degree...
Six paces.*

Two bastions of rock seven miles apart. Near one of the...
a crashed plane.

*Oblique angle right: one-two-oh degrees. Sixteen pace...
Angle eight-oh. Fourteen paces.*

A crashed plane confidently assumed to be visible at a di...
tance of four hundred and eighty-five yards in a directi...
precisely established by air photograph.

*Angle left: one-six-oh. Ten paces. Angle right: one-five-o...
Six paces.*

Question: why is the plane not visible?

Make a straight-line return to the starting-point.

Bit of bad luck, mon ami. We not only missed the targ...
by seven miles but we made the drop so close to the wro...
group of rocks that I naturally thought they –

Six paces?

What? I made it seven.

All right. The join isn't precise but no matter.

He loved things on paper. Loman loved things on pap...
Also he loved things being precise. He loved to get thin...
exact and it tended to blind him to reality and he didn't ev...
give a thought to the fact that if you have to pace out a ro...
configuration with your boots kicking through rubble a...
the heat trying to knock you down and the sand giving w...
when you need to measure your paces correctly you wo...

ish up exactly where you started. You'd do it here, all right,
ut you wouldn't necessarily do it on paper. And that was
here it really counted. Bloody Loman would tell you that.

Steady. Anger – heat – sweat – thirst. Don't forget where
ou are.

Not his fault. I was having to wait, that was all. He was
ooking at the photograph now, looking at the sketch and
en at the photograph. Taking his time.

Christ I can't go seven miles.

Fourteen hours' minimum through that blinding furnace
nd finish up delirious and the last drop gone.

The definition on the air photograph wasn't too clear
ecause they'd blown it up to the point where the grain
ould start fogging so he probably wouldn't be able to match
e narrow end of the formation where the pacing went six
nd six and five, all short runs, but the overall shape ought
give him an answer.

Sweat in my eyes. In the shade here it wasn't evaporating
fast. Pronounced heart-beat: quite regular and perfectly
ormal in these conditions. Thud-thud-thud.

Looking at the photograph, then at the sketch. The girl
atching him. I didn't know if he'd got juxtaposed stills of
e terrain surrounding the target area and I wasn't going to
sk him because that'd be another nasty one if both outcrops
ad much the same shape at this degree of blow-up. The girl
atching him.

You there, Diane?

Yes.

How's tricks?

All right.

Lovely day, isn't it?

Yes.

Tried to say it with a smile, couldn't make it. Nerves in her
oice, nothing explicit, just a tenseness. I suppose she knew
e score, worked out what we were doing, didn't like it, none
f us did. Rotten having to wait.

He said:

Those are the right ones.

Shut my eyes and said:

Oh that's good.

I'm going to ask those people to confirm everything for us,
e scale, orientation, and particularly the distance and

bearing of Tango Victor from the rocks. Someone might n̄
made a slip.

Just what we need.

It's a possibility we have to consider.

How long will it take, Loman?

Perhaps thirty minutes.

Kaifra – Tunis – Crowborough – London. No delay at a
from Kaifra to the Embassy because he'd use the radio an
the signals room in Tunis would use their own. Crowboroug
– London was the slow bit, by normal telephone.

I want to be out there longer than that.

He still hadn't told me to get moving and I didn't like it
he sounded too bloody relaxed. The panic had gone becaus
we knew now that we were at least in the target area but h
still ought to be worried because the aeroplane had dis
appeared.

You're camped in the shade at present?

Yes.

I want you to stay there for the moment. I'm in signals an
London is monitoring.

Didn't like it all and the sweat was running into my eyes
what was he in signals for at this phase?

For Christ sake fill me in, Loman.

I just want you to stay at your base so that I can call yo
immediately if I need to. I take it you'd prefer not to carr
the transceiver about in the full sun.

I know that bit.

Five-second pause.

Chirac has reported.

He all right?

Oh yes. But he didn't find the wind he needed, so he had t
circle for several hours to gain enough height to make a fina
run-in through dead air. He came down in a gassi twent
kilometres from South 5 and they picked him up in a half
track.

Oh Christ, there'd been some kind of security leak, sme
it a mile off. He wasn't relaxed at all, he was just over
correcting again.

Did he report by phone?

Yes. He hadn't been able to begin his final run-in unt
shortly after dawn, and he says he was observed by an aircra
at considerably higher altitude.

orse than I'd thought.

What area, Loman?

Quite a long pause. Didn't want to worry his executive.
All the worrying was meant to be done at Local Control.

*Not far from the point of drop. He puts it at something
like fifteen kilometres from there. He was flying in the dark
for most of the time and couldn't even see the No. 1 Philips
tower or the Roches Brunes derrick.*

I couldn't see why Loman had to get into signals with
Control. And I was beginning to think I didn't want to know.
You don't bring in London on a local security leak unless
the whole thing's been bust wide open.

What was the aircraft registration?

He couldn't read it.

Too high?

Yes.

I had to think how exactly to say it.

Loman, have we still got a mission?

It was a bloody awful thing to ask your director in the
field and I knew that but I wanted the answer.

Let us hope so.

There was a faint crackling noise somewhere. Not from the
set. I looked past the edge of the canopy.

Quiller.

Hear you.

What is that noise?

Lizard, cracking a snail open.

He didn't bother to answer.

I looked out from the canopy across the blaze of sand, for
an instant seeing it, then seeing it vanish.

Loman, I want to go out there.

Not yet.

*While I'm fresh. Let me go and look for the bloody thing.
It must be there somewhere.*

Certainly it must. But we have to wait for London.

Bloody London, gets on your tits.

Switching off transmit.

Very well, but stay open to receive.

Had to drink some water, then I lay on my back and
decided not to think about the aircraft that had been observing
Chirac only fifteen kilometres from the point of drop,
Loman's headache, not mine, though of course when the

crunch came I'd be right in it, like that poor bloody sn⸎

Slept.

Tango.

Check: 13.19. Switch.

Tango receiving.

I have London's signal. Monitoring liaison with Algie⸎ informs that five squadrons of desert-reconnaissance hel⸎ copters are to search a prescribed area of which your ow⸎ position is approximately the centre.

I watched the lizard. It had found another one and th⸎ crackling noise began.

When do they start?

They are already airborne.

Chapter Twelve

SANDSTORM

I stood watching them.

They were quite high, about five hundred feet, but the⸎ shape and their flight were unmistakable: they drifted ⸎ circles, their wings held like black hoods to trap the ai⸎ From this distance I couldn't see their heads but they wer⸎ watching me: despite their feigned disinterest I was the foc⸎ point of their circling.

I hadn't noticed them before but they'd probably bee⸎ somewhere overhead since early this morning, attracted b⸎ the movement of the dot that had been making its laboriou⸎ way among the dunes towards the rock outcrop. Their patie⸎ observation heightened my feeling of vulnerability and I ha⸎ the urge to go back to the refuge that thirty minutes ago I'⸎ been sharing with the lizards.

Nobody likes being watched, and this was particularly u⸎ pleasant because I was being assessed as potential carrion.

I moved again, trying not to drag my feet and leave track⸎ The heat of the sun was like a weight on my back, pushir⸎ me down rather than forward, and its light struck upwar⸎ against my face, reflecting from the sand. I knew that th⸎ water-flask was still a quarter full and was tempted to drin⸎

126

when I'd broken camp and pushed everything into the
shade I'd noticed that one of the *bidons* was already empty.
In the last ten hours I'd used half the water-supply, pouring
it into my body as you pour water on a fire.

The desert is not like other places. The slaking of the
increased thirst puts back only fifty per cent of the water
lost in the cooling process, and in this degree of heat my
cooling process was breaking down because the sweat was
being evaporated the instant it reached the skin. In one hour
I was generating seven or eight hundred calories and my
sweat was ridding me of less than five.

Sometimes their shadows drifted near me as they crossed
the sun.

At the four hundred and eighty-fifth pace I stopped.

Long. 8°3′ by Lat. 30°4′.

The sands were smooth.

Loman hadn't received confirmation from No. 2 Fighter-
Reconnaissance before I'd left camp: I'd told him I wanted
last chance to find Tango Victor before the helicopters got
here. But I knew now that I should have waited, because give
or take a few yards I was standing where the smudge had
been on the photograph. Somewhere they'd made an error:
the scale had lost a nought or the bearing had been inverted
and this wasn't where the smudge was at all.

The wreck of Tango Victor was across the dunes there, or
a thousand yards the other side of the rocks, not far away,
ten minutes on foot in normal conditions. Here the conditions
weren't normal and it could take me an hour or five hours
to find it because the dunes were higher than I was and in
some places I couldn't see more than a hundred yards: I was
moving through a maze.

A bird's-eye view was the only way and five squadrons had
been mustered and refuelled at the nearest airfield to these
rocks: Fort Thiriet was a hundred and thirty kilometres
distant and the helicopters had been deployed in a sweep
formation of sixty aircraft on a twenty-five kilometre front
to the immediate north of the Areg Tinrhalès and they were
heading this way while I stood and cursed some stupid bloody
clerk in uniform who'd finished the mission for us before it
began.

The pressure was finally on and there was nothing I could
do about it. There was data streaming in so fast that I

couldn't deal with it: the overall picture they never like g⸱⸱⸱
us was coming up under the hypo. The Chirac security lea⸱
had been bad luck and not his fault but it had revealed th⸱
importance of the objective in the eyes of the opposition
all they'd been informed was that a camouflaged sailplan⸱
had been observed over the open desert at dawn today, bu⸱
an entire arm of the Algerian Air Force had been assemble⸱
across the country and deployed from Fort Thiriet, an ai⸱
field right on the Libyan border.

There'd been no time to put out even a token announcemen⸱
of a 'routine exercise' and this fact alone meant either tha⸱
Libyan Intelligence was fully aware of the situation or tha⸱
the Algerian government was so anxious to locate Tang⸱
Victor that it had risked embarrassment at high level betwee⸱
the two countries.

In addition to this was the indication that it was their la⸱
throw and that they were confident of locating the objectiv⸱
before anyone else: because if they failed, and if an opposin⸱
network succeeded, they would have made it obvious tha⸱
their search had been for the crashed freighter, whose carg⸱
was so politically explosive that the armed forces of tw⸱
countries had been called in to assist the intelligence service⸱

The Bureau itself was intensely active and within a matte⸱
of days had brought its support communications to the pitc⸱
where half an hour ago Local Control could give me fu⸱
details on the desert-reconnaissance operation including th⸱
precise area and width of sweep. At the same time the entir⸱
network was under general monitoring and if Analysis Sectio⸱
thought I'd be interested to know that an attempt had bee⸱
made to assassinate General Chen Piao or that a missile-to⸱
missile device had just come off the drawing-boards i⸱
Smolensk or that the Brazilian Minister for the Interior ha⸱
handed in his resignation three weeks after accepting the po⸱
they'd pass it to Control for Local Control and the executiv⸱
in the field and I'd get it almost as fast as a phone-call fro⸱
London to Crowborough on the priority line.

I wouldn't get it in so many words. The original data woul⸱
go through filters until the essence was extracted and mad⸱
available. Even if support communications hadn't bee⸱
energized then general monitoring would have reported sudde⸱
air movement in Algeria by desert-reconnaissance units an⸱
Analysis would have jumped on it straight away because the⸱

ad Algeria as the *locale* of one of the listed ops currently
unning.

Behind me, as I stood here isolated in the desert wastes,
vas an organization striving to inform, direct and support
1e as I went deeper into the mission and closer to the target
rea; but now that I was here there was nothing they could
.o for me, and nothing I could do for them.

Loman had predicted a forty-five minute deadline for the
rrival of the Algerian squadrons in this area and there were
fteen minutes to go in terms of their ETA. In terms of the
ctual mission my time ran out to zero as I stood here
stening for their rotors, because even if I climbed the nearest
une and saw Tango Victor dead in front of me it was no go.
ondon wanted photographs and a full radioed report of the
reighter's cargo and fifteen minutes wasn't long enough for
1e to go back for the transceiver and bring it here.

The sands were quiet.

My shadow lay prone, a spirit felled by the heat.

Something in my mind was trying to attract my attention
nd I was aware of it but unable to read its significance: it
as like a sound heard but not identified. I let all thought
ubside, leaving the way open, while my body and its senses
emained where they were as my mind ranged, released,
nding images for me: the low wind and the pattering of
1e sand on the side of the box, the folds of the parachute
alf-covered, and the unexpected word in my head – *beware*
- without either reason or coherence.

Drawn blank.

I turned back towards the rock outcrop and the sand hissed
aintly across my boots. Halfway there I stopped and drank
1e rest of the water and left the cap of the flask dangling
n its lanyard. Then the sky became gradually filled with
ifinitesimal vibrations, so faint that I thought the sound was
nly in my head, but as it strengthened I began moving
aster and when I was certain what it was I broke into a
umsy run through the sand's obstructive softness, worried
ow that I'd left it too late to reach shelter before they came.

There seemed to be no particular direction to the sound:
was a steady thrumming under the sky as if the air itself
ad started to vibrate, to shake with some kind of cosmic
isturbance. The vultures had broken their circling flight and
ere drifting southwards, driven away by the noise. It was

T.B. — E

loudening quickly now and for a moment I didn't see t..
helicopters because I'd been looking for them too high. The
were detaching themselves from the skyline and growin
bigger and I went into the niche I'd made for myself amon
the stowed 'chute canopies and lay flat with my legs draw
up, and waited.

Once they'd seen the freighter and landed near it I wouldn
be so exposed, but while they were still airborne they'd b
checking this outcrop and for the moment I wanted t
remain unseen. I didn't know what kind of orders Loma
would give me when our mission ended a few minutes fror
now: it was just possible he'd ask me to observe the activitie
of the opposition at the site of their objective in case ther
was anything we could usefully tell London.

He would probably leave it to me, when the time came, t
decide whether I should expose my presence and hope to liv
as long as the first implemented interrogation or crawl fror
here to the open desert and cut a vein. All London woul
require was that the opposition shouldn't learn anything fror
me and that was easy enough to arrange.

The noise was very loud now and the rocks were trappin
the echoes. I pulled my legs up a bit more and managed t
crawl another inch into the narrowing gap. Something was i
here with me but I didn't know what: something alive an
I suppose sheltering as I was from the throbbing sky outsid
Telepathy at its lowest level is emotional and I was awar
of fear, not my own but another creature's. There wasn't any
thing more for me to fear because neither I nor the missio
were any longer under attack.

The camouflage was highly-developed and only the glint c
a gold-ringed eye gave it away. It was about two feet in fror
of me and almost on a level with my face: probably I'
driven it in here unknowingly when I'd stowed the canopie
and provisions and it had been afraid to clamber across th
strange terrain they'd formed on the rocky floor. Its forefee
were splayed on each side of the scaly bulk of its body an
its head was lifted to watch me, the black iris glistenin
within the ring of gold. It kept utterly still, afraid of m
because visually I menaced it gigantically, almost filling th
niche, and possibly afraid of the helicopters: it had no sens
of hearing but it was probably picking up the vibrations i
the rock.

130

—I had positioned the transceiver so that I could use it if I wanted to, and I ought to tell Loman the situation even though he couldn't do anything about it.

Tango.

The form of the pointed head was prehistoric: it was a descendant of the lizards that had been here before man.

Tango. Tango.

The motors chopped heavily at the air and I was tempted to move my head and take a look but there wasn't any point; they were military desert-reconnaissance aircraft making an area sweep at low altitude and there wouldn't be anything in their shape or colour that could tell us anything we didn't already know. The chance of their catching the movement of I turned my head was one in a thousand but I might just as well not risk it.

Teach me, my small and ancient friend, how to keep still.

I didn't call up base again because it was obvious now that Loman had decided to keep radio silence. I got a lot of squawk and tried two channels and came back and found them quite close at 6 MHz.

113: *ihtafidou bi kasdikoum i-la mitine oua sabina degré.*

The volume of sound from their rotors was making the frame of the transceiver vibrate and I could feel it under my fingers. Shadows swept across the mouth of the niche where was lying, and the lizard appeared to move slightly but I knew it hadn't: it was just the shift of the light-contrasts as the shadow passed over us.

120 – 121 – 122: *an-zi-lou mina oulou-ouikoum hata miyate nitra.*

They obviously had a group captain above and to the rear of the line keeping them in order. It occurred to me that I was being gratuitously masochistic about this because at any moment the observer in the machine nearest these rocks and the site of Tango Victor was going to call up and report seeing the freighter. That would be the precise instant, if we wanted to be particular about it, when the mission would end. But I couldn't resist listening-in because I always like to know what people are doing.

Ali: ha-l'-laka a-ne toufahissa hadihi a sokhr mini djhatika?
Ta-ya-b.

Dust began blowing in: their rotors were creating a wave of turbulence across a twenty-five kilometre front, whirling

a cloud of pulverized quartz into the air and letting it fa...
they passed. The light became amber-tinted and the colou...
of the lizard deepened.

104: *sahihou al kasd.*

The stink of kerosene.

Head lifted, a golden eye staring.

If the vultures eat the lizards and the lizards eat the snail...
what do the snails eat?

The note of their engines held steady.

I waited for one of them to break the line and land nea...
the freighter. The others would follow, gathering in a swarm...
It was going to be very noisy here.

It had been the weather that had beaten us: the wind...
There hadn't been enough for Chirac so he'd been forced t...
circle for height till after dawn and they'd seen him and i...
wasn't anyone's fault and for a moment I felt sorry fo...
Loman because the little bastard had done his best, put hi...
ferret into the field and set up a makeshift base with a...
operator to man the set even though the poor little bitc...
couldn't hold a gun and he'd seen me through the acces...
lines and kept me in touch with London, done all he coul...
and now the whole thing had gone grinding into the dust an...
he wasn't a man to take a failed mission in his stride, n...
Loman.

The note of their engines was steady.

And quieter now.

Kerosene.

Kerosene and the dust settling and the brightness comin...
back into the light while I lay prone watching the reflectior...
in the dark unwinking eye, while I lay surprised and not quit...
understanding, listening to the thrum of the rotors passin...
towards the west, while I lay with weakness flooding into m...
as the tension came off and the nerves lost their tone, th...
sound from the sky dying away until, as I lay listenin...
silence came.

Switch.

Tango.

Can get quite worked up when your base won't answer the...
I remembered and spun it back to 7 and called him agai...
Still wouldn't bloody well answer. They've been off the a...
for over two minutes now well don't panic there's no actio...

eeded but why don't they answer they're my base and this
s my lifeline.

Tango – Tango.

It was her voice, soft and precise.

I said:

Where the hell have you been?

Loman hates that: he likes you to make a point of replying
vith the code for the mission, not his day today, the sweat
unning into my eyes because we'd confirmed these were the
ight rocks and the freighter must be near them and they'd
ut sixty choppers across the area and they hadn't seen it so
: couldn't be here after all.

I'm sorry. We were monitoring the helicopters.

So was I.

Then Loman came on.

Tone rather light, rather correct.

Quiller.

Hear you.

Where are the aircraft at present?

They've gone.

They overflew your position?

It wasn't really a question. Diane spoke Arabic and she'd
monitored their frequency so she'd heard them telling each
ther to 'check those rocks' and she would have told Loman
o he knew bloody well they'd overflown my position. He
ust didn't understand it and I knew what that meant: he'd
ot confirmation from London.

I was still lying prone and there wasn't any more need so
crawled backwards out of the niche but stayed in the shade,
ay shoulders against the rockface. There was a scuttling
ound and I turned my head and saw it had gone. Then I
hut my eyes because the panic was over and I wanted to
hink.

Did they overfly your position?

I ought to be helping the poor little sod.

*Yes. Slow speed, low altitude, took their time, couldn't
miss it. You've had confirmation from No. 2 Fighter-Recco,
s that it?*

Pause.

Yes. There has been no error of any kind.

Didn't make sense.

There must have been, Loman.

You and I have confirmed that the rock outcrop where yo
are now is in fact the rock outcrop in the photograph. Th
RAF has just confirmed by signal that the object in the photo
graph is a crashed aeroplane and that it is lying on the san
at a distance of four hundred and eighty-five yards — fou
eight five — from the outcrop with a bearing of two hundre
degrees — two-double-oh.

Vaguely I thought no wonder he's been worrying abou
my mental condition but he can think again now because
hundred and twenty men of the Algerian Air Force couldn
see the thing either.

You do it for me then, Loman. You work it out. That
what you're for.

After a bit he said:

Stay on receive.

I shut my eyes again.

There wasn't anything he could do anyway. Get a penc
and paper but there weren't any figures, no way of checkin
Talk to the girl but what could she do? Any of us do?

Beware.

Not quite a word: the shape of a thought. The fine grair
hitting the side of the box in the low wind. More scuttlin
now, maybe I was stuck right outside one of their dens an
they couldn't get home. It had sounded like the sand whe
it had pattered against the polyester box in the low wind, wit
the folds of the 'chute canopy still showing where the san
hadn't yet drifted. I'd made a mental note at the time, warnin
myself that the desert wasn't like other places.

Of course he'd go straight into signals again with Londo
and ten minutes from now they'd have a full-scale emergenc
meeting in session at the Bureau and I hoped it'd keep fir
for them.

No one else could have got here first. We knew there wer
at least two other networks with a crash-priority interest i
Tango Victor but there hadn't been time for them to get her
and anyway we'd have had a flash about it from Control
if the opposition beats another cell to the post in the en
phase of a mission then everyone gets to know about it, don
worry. And they couldn't have taken the wreck away, eve
by a concerted chopper lift, without making so much noi
and leaving so much mess that the rest of us would have ju

aken a look and gone off home.

Scuttering. They were quite big things, heavy when they
ran although they ran like a flash. They bothered me, wouldn't
et me alone, the sound of the sand pattering against the side
of the box, the low wind slowly covering the nylon 'chute,
a mental note, the desert hides things, beware.

Someone was saying oh . . . my . . . Christ . . . in a kind
of measured tone, perhaps not aloud, just inside my head,
and I opened my eyes and looked through the scratched
sunglasses to the blaze of the dunes out there. Then I hit the
ransmit.

Tango.

She answered straight away so I knew he couldn't be in
signals with London and I suppose it made sense because this
problem wasn't for Control, it was strictly local. He'd been
using his time thinking.

He came on and I said:

*Can you get hold of a met.-record for this area covering
the last three days?*

He didn't ask why, so perhaps he'd been thinking on much
the same lines as I had. He just said he'd contact the airfield
at Kaifra. The phone was obviously working now because he
was back in a few minutes and said yes, there'd been a sandstorm two days ago, particularly severe.

Chapter Thirteen

OBJECTIVE

The tube went in and I pushed, leaning on it.

When I pulled it out the sand ran into the hole it had
made, filling it. There wasn't anything pointed I could use:
the end of the tube was blunt and therefore not very efficient
as a boring tool but it was all I had. It was one of the
sections of telescopic tubing among the survival gear, meant
to hold up fabric and make it a shelter.

I pushed it in again, six feet away, and leaned on it.

Skin perfectly dry. Cooling had stopped.

I'd have to watch that because heat stroke develops quite

rapidly: the body temperature starts rising soon after th
stage where the sweat evaporates without having time t
cool the skin. Quickened pulse, loss of consciousness, death

I drank again to replace some of the sweat but the wate
was hot and gave no sensation of quenching the thirst: it wa
just liquid going into the organism. I was having to calculat
now and we were running it close: one more litre was le
for working with, and one reserve litre for staying aliv
during sleep. I could go another ninety minutes at this rat
on a litre but that didn't have anything to do with it becaus
the heat explosion would begin a long time before then unles
I could take some rest.

They had come back and their shadows drifted across th
flank of the dune as I pushed the tube in and struck nothin,

Pull it out. Two paces and try again.

It must be this one, this dune, or the one on the far sid
of my No. 2 camp. I'd brought a canopy and three length
of tubing to make shade, and the 2000CA had been left o
receive. In the last two hours I'd taken four equally-spaced
rest periods of fifteen minutes. Loman had come on the a
to tell me 1: that the Algerian squadrons would refuel wes
of here and disperse to their home stations without makin
a return sweep and 2: that Chirac had confirmed that eve
a medium sandstorm could bury an aircraft the size of Tang
Victor.

Chirac had pointed out that the freighter had probably h
the sand with the undercarriage up to avoid flipping over an
in any case would have gouged a deep trough until the aero
foil had started planing. This would leave the tip of th
rudder only two metres or so from the ground and the mai
structure considerably lower. The 35mm Nikons hadn't bee
able to register this because they'd been almost vertical
above, but from ground level it couldn't have been easy to se
even before the sandstorm had blotted it out.

Probe and try again, two paces.

The chance of hitting the rudder or the aerial mast wa
remote. According to Chirac's reckoning the mainplanes, tai
plane and fuselage would be at least two metres from th
surface. I'd once been in Arizona when the wind had reache
seventy and the whole desert had got up and blown acro
the sky and it had taken us a day to dig out the half-track

Push and lean and pull out.

didn't know anything about falling over till my shoulder
gan blazing. I couldn't seem to get up because the whole
ight of the sky was pressing on me. Heart hammering a lot,
obbing behind my eyes, get in the shade, crawl there if
all you can do, but get there.

and in the teeth, gritty, and my hands burning, using them
forefeet, clumsy, going too slow, have to hurry, pool of
de, prone.

He called up at 16.31 hours, waking me.

No, I said.

Slight moisture on the skin and the pulse back to normal
t I knew it'd start again within ten minutes of going back
o that furnace.

He wanted details.

I'm using a metal probe, area focus the same as before.
It seemed to have taken me a long time to say it and now
was out of breath. He didn't answer straight away.

How much longer can you go on working there?

I don't know.

My hand just reached for the flask: I hadn't actually
cided to drink.

I am only asking for an approximate idea, of course.

He had to say it again before I registered.

*There's water for about an hour's work. But I'm starting
– starting to get – heat stroke symptoms.*

Quite a long pause.

Would you be able to remain under shade until nightfall?

My head swung up suddenly and my eyes opened.

You mean you could drop more provisions?

No.

The pulse had quickened and there was an almost immedi-
increase in sweating. But he'd said no and it was the first
ae it had actually been admitted that this was a strictly
it-ended mission unless I could find the objective.

I propped the mike on my knee, heavy to hold, cost water.

*Take all – it'd take all the water I've got, waiting till dark.
't would be cooler then. You could work –*

No go. Thing is to press on. Tango out.

Only way to shut him up. Not a thing he could do, not
n drop more water. He'd have to signal Control and tell
m the score: the executive in the field has a limited number
hours to live, am I to abandon?

I got up and went out and the slam of the direct heat nea
knocked me down and I staggered a bit and then got so
kind of rhythm going. The tube was stuck in the sand whe
I'd left it, too hot now, blister your hand, so I kicked it ov
and got hold of the other end and began walking to the pa
of the dune where I'd halted operations. About halfway the
I tripped over his foot.

It took a little time because he might be able to tell me thin
by the way he was lying, face down and with his feet towar
the end of the dune. I worked slowly, trying to get all t
data the situation could provide. My tracks had a slight cur
in them: I'd made a detour on my way from the cano
without meaning to, and this was why I hadn't tripped ov
him when I'd gone in to rest. I turned him over.

He had died in terror.

The hands flung out as he'd fallen, perhaps running t
hard, running like hell away from the wreck of the freight
running in terror. His face showed that much. He had di
screaming.

Not far away there was something black showing in t
sand: my feet had brought it to the surface; it lay at the ed
of my tracks. It was plumage and as I pulled it upwards t
wing rose, scattering sand, and then the gross black body w
its bald head dangling, the hooked beak agape. The bird, li
the man, had died screaming.

There was another, so near the man that in moving t
body, turning it over, I had exposed part of its wing. T
heat didn't seem so bad now and I was moving more quick
a sense of purpose reviving the organism. I made a dir
line to the end of the dune where his feet had pointed, a
tripped again, dislodging a peaked cap from a man's hea
His body was in the same attitude: he'd been running aw
from the freighter. His face had the same expression.

A third vulture was lying at the foot of the dune. I w
kicking into the thing before I knew it. I didn't stop
examine it because the renewed strength in me was pushi
me onwards and the fourth time I drove the tube into t
sand it struck metal.

Distance 485 yards. Bearing 200°. Longitude 8° 3'
Latitude 30°4'.

Tango Victor.

used the tubing like an oar, bringing the sand away but
y enough to guide me. This was the leading edge of the
plane and I moved across the flank of the dune and began
bing again. It was already clear that the bodies had been
ng only just below the surface because they were to the
th of the freighter, in the lee of the dune: it had been the
th wind that had done this, the *Ghibli*.

The sand fell away as I worked at the area aft of the
iling edge, port mainplane. It was where the door of the
in was likely to be. For a while I missed it because it had
n left wide open and I was actually digging through the
ft of sand that had formed in the cabin itself between the
t's compartment and the freight section. The heat was
nse because the fuselage had become a quartz-coated oven
I gave it a couple of minutes and came away.

t seemed twice as far to the canopy and I drank some
ter and dropped prone and let the muscles go but the
mmering didn't stop, must do better than this, body had
keep going because there was work for the mind, still had
mission running and we'd found the objective, not long
w. The hammering shook me, colours throbbing behind the
s and the skin perfectly dry, rather worrying, the bout of
ewed energy had been dangerous, keep still, just keep still.

Tango.

didn't answer, didn't move, you want to live, you've got
keep still. Breathing difficult, the weight of the shoulders
npressing the lungs, roll over, over and lie still, a thin
kling from somewhere, unearthly sound, coming again, a
h cackling above the canopy, they'd seen the two bodies.

Tango.

Don't move. Don't even think, brain function heat-pro-
ctive.

The spread nylon bluish above me and motionless, the air
ally calm, my arms melting into the sand, my legs dis-
ving, the nerves inert, the pain of the bruises ebbing, the
dy cradled in euphoria, control it, stay just this side of
consciousness, the hammering fainter and less insistent, the
gs filling of their own accord, the healing process taking
r from the stress syndrome, lie still and all will be well.

Moisture gathering on the skin, the skin cooling, the heart-
rthm slowing, the colours receding from the optic nerve,
er restored.

139

Tango.

I opened up the transmit.

Hear you.

A sound from someone farther away, obviously Diane,
soft intake of breath. I suppose they'd been getting ed
because I hadn't answered for a while.

Loman asked:

Have you a problem?

Not now. I've found the plane.

Three or four seconds.

Congratulations.

Poor little bastard, saved by the bell, the whole bloo
mission back in his hands, quite overcome. He was asking
for a report.

*I can't tell you much yet, I've only just started. Thin
covered with sand. Both crew were running away from
when they died.*

Please take photographs.

I'm going to. Oh you mean of the crew?

Yes.

I thought for a bit.

I've moved them.

That doesn't matter. Photograph their faces.

I didn't like it at all.

Loman, have you any idea what's inside that plane?

No. I am merely passing on instructions from London.

I believed him because there couldn't be any reason
him to withhold information at this stage: his executive w
going into a hazardous area and wanted all the help he co
get. The blackout on this cargo was so total that Cont
wouldn't even tell the director in the field, a man of Loma
status.

Play it by the book for a change and consider demandi
information from London before proceeding. Loman wo
have to signal if I asked him: executive requests details as
type of hazard, so forth. It wouldn't be unreasonable beca
commercial aircrews are not timorous men and these two I
run clear of Tango Victor with the fear of Christ in th
and I was expected to go in there and find out why.

Loman.

Hear you.

Have you any idea of the risk, I mean how big?

140

He thought about that.

*No. You say the crew were running away from the aero-
plane when they died. Do they look as if they were frightened?
Terrified.*

It was perfectly clear to us both that London had an idea
what had killed Holt and his navigator: the instructions had
been for me to take photographs of their expressions.

Do you want me to signal Control about this?

I thought that was rather civil of him.

Because he didn't fancy it at all. He'd got his ferret right
up against the quarry and ready for the kill and he didn't
want to disturb it. The moment I went off the air he'd switch
channels and send to London through the Embassy in Tunis:
Quaker now destin objiv point. It's the only signal that
makes any kind of bang throughout the departments concerned with the specific mission and it would give Loman a lot
of joy to send it. To ask for additional information would
just cause delay and he knew we couldn't afford it but he
was still ready to do it if I insisted.

From here I could see the dark hole in the dune and all I
had to do was walk over there and go inside and complete
the mission: all they wanted was a batch of pictures and a
bred report on Tango Victor's cargo and it probably wouldn't
take more than half an hour and then Loman could pull me
out and we'd go home, a crash-priority operation at PM
level completed inside seventy-two hours of Tilson's briefing
me in London.

Not really the time to tell them the executive in the field
had got gooseflesh.

Loman.

Hear you.

They realize this cargo could be dangerous.

Yes.

They probably know what it is.

Yes.

*Why would they decide to keep us uninformed on this, even
though it's going to wreck the whole mission if I'm killed?*

He answered almost at once and I knew he'd been waiting
for this question and had prepared the reply.

*I can only think that the area is so sensitive that the risk
might be greater if their knowledge were passed on to us.*

I'd expected that.

You're talking about implemented interrogation.

Yes.

At any phase?

At every phase, including this one.

I was going to ask him how he worked that one out bu
was simple enough when I gave it a second thought and I
suitably warned: brain function wasn't satisfactory, the
and everything, and the worry about what was inside
black hole over there. What he meant was that in Kaifra
was exposed to the risk of capture and interrogation by
opposition cell and that if it was implemented by the us
pain-stimulus methods he would probably give them inf
mation. The info he already possessed was lethal if it
into the wrong hands but without it he couldn't have ta
over as director: it was just that London was scared of add
to it unless they had to.

They'd know, as soon as he told them, that I was n
within minutes of going into the freighter and if they co
signal me direct there wouldn't be any problem: out here
isolation there was no risk of anyone raiding me and si
I was on the point of moving into hazard they'd be prepa
to warn me on the type of difficulties I'd be faced with.
they couldn't do it.

They'd have to advise me through Crowborough, Tunis a
Kaifra, exposing the signal to switchboard staff, cipher cle
and people in the same room with them. They could thr
out a preliminary signal carrying a selected code struct
and then follow up with the encoded material for me to br
up but it still wouldn't be safe because the clerks in
Embassy cipher room could read it for themselves.

Bloody nuisance but there it was.

They were cackling again and my scalp got up. Bad si
bag of nerves just when there was something important to

*All right, Loman. Tell London they can go and stuff the
selves. I'm going in.*

Quite a long pause.

Very well. Please take all precautions.

How the hell can I when I don't know what's in there?

Not at all good, nasty show of nerves. Couldn't look av
from the hole in the dune, getting obsessive, best thing wo
be to finish the job quickly.

Loman, what stage are you going to start running the ta

s soon as you enter the aircraft.

hey gave you an auto-destruct?

Of course.

hey'd had to. They're not entirely witless in London:
y'd narrowed the risk down to a matter of minutes. They
ldn't signal me any advice because nobody had to know
ut this cargo, not even Loman, but in a few minutes from
w I'd be telling him and in precise detail and they'd
ered the situation in the only way they could: the moment
report was finished he'd be putting the tape into an auto-
truct container and once he'd shut it and set the fuse the
would be over because if anyone else tried to open it
y'd just blow it up.

he precisely-detailed information on Tango Victor's cargo
ld remain only in Loman's head, and until now I hadn't
lized that in one respect this was a shut-ended mission for
too. For her own sake he'd send Diane out of the room
en I started reporting: she couldn't reveal what she didn't
w, and most trained interrogators can tell whether you're
g or not when you say you've no information for them.

Loman would remain at risk and if the opposition located
base and raided it and went to work on him the auto-
truct thing wouldn't be a lot of use.

o this was a 6-K mission.

Not many of them are. It's mostly left to the discretion of
director and executive in the field because they're placed
ter than anyone else to decide what ought to be done, but
etimes an operation comes up where the area's so sensitive
t they like you to sign one of their buff-coloured forms
ore they brief you. Of course you can refuse, just as you
refuse any specific mission for any of a dozen reasons,
once you've agreed to sign Form 6-K you're issued with
et of capsules and it's up to you to make sure they're
ersed among your gear so that if you've put one in your
ht-bag and you leave the thing on a bus you've still got a
re in your pocket.

hey can't force you to do what you've signed for: it's
that your professional pride has been brought into things
as far as I know they've never had anyone let them down.
at gives us a giggle is that these capsules are issued to us
Firearms, it seems so bloody appropriate.

ome of us have pulled in a 9-suffix to our code name and

they don't bother to make us sign anything: we've pro
we can't be broken this side of unconsciousness, so we do
carry capsules on this kind of mission unless we've actua
asked for some, to avoid possible unpleasantness during
operation. Not many directors have the 9 because they
far less exposed in the field than their executives and I kn
Loman hadn't got one because there's a list and we kn
who's on it.

So he must have signed the form on this trip. There'd
no point in ordering him to put the tape in a bang-box if
was liable to get snatched and grilled. They're usually brigh
coloured with a distinctive pattern, so people don't conf
them with indigestion pills or anything.

Perhaps that was why he'd been so nervous. We all ge
bit ragged towards the end-phase and this time we w
having to cope with the heat as well.

The sweat was coming freely now and the pulse was ab
right so I told him I was ready to go.

Very well. We shall be off the air for a few minutes.

Going to signal Control, tell them we'd found the pla
three jolly cheers. I picked up the set and the camera a
walked into the sun.

The first one had a thin moustache, rather well trimm
bit of a lady's man and hardly the type who'd want to
into the album looking like this. Three shots from three ang
and don't ask me why they wanted actual pictures, there v
something important I was missing but there wasn't time
worry it out. The second one had either been pecked
caught his face on something sharp when he'd flung hims
out of the cabin. A couple of close-ups of the dead vultu
and one shot of the doorway making a hole in the dune.

A lot of dry cackling again, I suppose they were frustra
because I wouldn't let them get at the two cadavers. But th
shadows were bigger and I looked up and saw they'd co
quite a bit lower: their heads were turning on their lo
gristly necks to keep me in sight as they circled.

Then I had to wait, squatting by the transceiver a
covering my neck against the sun, thinking of nothing
particular, how hot it was, what the hell did the snails e
the way she'd looked at her fingertips.

Tango.

Hear you.

I'll be keeping open for you from now on.

All right. I'm immediately outside the freighter and I'm going to leave the set here and take the mike inside on the extension.

Understood. Will you —

Then there was a quick fade, as if he'd suddenly put a hand over the mike, and I thought the last two words had probably been spoken to Diane as he asked her to leave the radio-room before I began reporting for the tape.

Onset of chill, the hairs lifting on my forearms. The bodily changes due to the heat were being modified by the psychic unease aroused when I'd turned them over and looked at their faces.

Aircrews are practical men with a high threshold of fear and the durable brand of philosophy that is learned by living with the elements and acknowledging their infinite power. I would expect them, as the mountainside loomed through the fog or the explosion shook the airframe, to show natural and momentary fear before they concentrated on whatever action remained open to them. I would expect to find, on the faces of men who had died in a plane crash, an expression of anguish, fear, or resignation. Not of terror.

The brain is concerned with practical considerations: facts and figures, the interplay of kinetics and mechanical forces involved in high-speed collision. The psyche is more subtly concerned with abstracts ranging from ecstasy to nightmare, including terror. The raised scalp, the trickle along the spine are induced by things strange to us, or abhorrent: the silence of a slowly-winding snake, a leaping shadow, a howl in the deep of night.

I could think of nothing like this that could have struck terror in these two men before they died. But our people in London could. *Photograph their faces,* Loman had said. *I am merely passing on instructions from London.*

The birds cackled above me, wheeling lower, perhaps because I'd stopped moving. I wondered if I ought to go over and do something to protect the two bodies: Holt and his navigator wouldn't know what was happening but I didn't want to have a thing like that on my mind as well. In the end I did nothing because there wasn't anything to throw over them and even if I buried them the birds knew now that they were there.

Loman.
Receiving.
Your voice faded out on that last signal.
Yes, I covered the microphone.
Telling her to go?
Yes.
Just checking.
Understood.

I disconnected the microphone-lead and coupled it to the coiled extension, reconnecting.

Testing.
Receiving you.
I'm going inside.

Chapter Fourteen

FRENZY

Silence.

Heat.

Darkness.

A faint smell: the rubber casing of the torch. I slid the switch and light hit the skeleton framework of the fuselage. I went forward and stopped in the next second and stood off-balance listening to the steady hiss from somewhere below. Forebrain desperate for explanation: a stream of images out of sequence. The sound becoming fainter.

Sand. Sand dislodged by my feet from the drift the wind had brought in and pouring on to the metal trough of the mid-section here between the pilot's deck and the freight compartment.

Pulse slowing again. Rhodospin was concentrating and my eyes were adapting to scotopic vision, the torchlight growing brighter. Other senses finely adjusting, hyper-receptive to stimuli: heat on the skin, marked absence of motion or even vibration as my weight shifted on to the floor of the pilot's deck. The entombing sand was deadening the motion normally set up by people entering a vehicle with sprung mass and pneumatic tyres.

The door to the freight section was ajar and I moved the torch beam through the four-inch gap in a vertical sweep but it lit nothing except the ribbed wall of the fuselage. The urge was to go in there first, kick the door wide open and go in ready for anything, so I moved in the opposite direction because the urge was emotional: I was afraid of going in there and wanted to get it over. It was safer to follow the instincts and reason.

London wanted to know things.

Loman.

Receiving you.

I'm now in the pilot's compartment. Throttle closed, under-carriage control in the raised position, flaps at full. Fuel reserve at one quarter, all lamp switches in the off position. Instruments and controls compatible with a forced-landing situation by daylight. The crew got out of their 'chute harness, the 'chutes still on their seats. Radio is switched to 6 MHz, one set of headphones on the floor and an earpiece smashed: evidence of impact effects or possible haste to leave the plane.

The torch beam went on moving, sometimes reflecting from polished surfaces. Pair of worn flying-gloves, photo of a Eurasian woman tucked into a panel over the left-hand seat, packet of chewing-gum sticking out of the map-pocket.

Can you see anything not normally found in the cabin of an aircraft?

This was obviously the first question on a list they'd given him. I spent a full minute on it with the torch.

No. One or two personal effects: pair of tennis shoes in an open locker, carved teakwood statuette in one of them, copy of Playboy. Nothing else.

Thank you.

Do you want pictures?

No.

It was the cargo they were more interested in.

The extension lead got caught on a seat strut and I freed it and moved back towards the freight section, my boots grinding on the loose sand across the floor. I didn't hurry because there were a lot of questions crowding in, one of them worrying me. If it was something in the cargo that had driven the two men out of here with the fear of Christ in them I couldn't see why the door was no more than ajar; the

147

four-inch gap seemed too narrow to allow anything to atta.
through it, and obviously they wouldn't have stopped to pu'
the door shut after them.

It worried me also to think that the vultures had died wit!
them, as if something had followed them out of the plan
to kill anything that lived.

I looped the extension lead across one shoulder to stop i
fouling and opened the Pentax, setting it for flash and keepin
it slung in front of me so that I could operate it with on
hand. There was a chance that if anything happened whe
I went in there I could get a picture of it and if one da
someone thought of processing the film they'd see what ha
finished me off.

Loman. I'm going into the freight section.

His voice was more distant now because the 2000CA wa
standing outside on the sand.

Understood.

I sent the torch beam through the gap and swung the doo
wider by one inch, stopping and listening, the nerves reactin
again and the scalp tightening. Kept seeing their faces, an
the gaping beaks of the birds. Another inch and stop an
listen and take a grip and bloody well think with the brai
instead of the plexus.

But it was difficult because the organism was aware o
danger and preparing its defences, draining the blood from th
surface to the internal organs, increasing the breathing-rhythm
to feed more oxygen to the muscles, dilating the pupils t
admit more light and refining the nerves until they reache
the state where they could be activated by stimuli below th
normal threshold of sensitivity. The brain was being by-passe
by the nervous system, the automatic defence mechanism tha
snatches the hand from a hot object, that snaps the eyes shu
as a spark flies, without the aid of the brain.

Another inch and stop and listen. Nothing. The beam o
light shifting in a calculated zig-zag from high to low: th
ribbed wall of the fuselage and alloy racks, an emergency
hatchet clipped to a bracket alongside an extinguisher.

A depth of silence I couldn't remember having experience
ever before; the silence of the desert, of the dead.

Quiller.

The sound of his voice explosive.

Wait. Release the breath.

Hear you.

Is there any problem?

No problem.

I'd been off the air for more than a minute and he was having to sweat it out, couldn't see what I was doing, couldn't hear.

Swing it another inch and stop and listen.

Faint metallic clicking.

Not perfectly regular.

Quite close and below me.

It stopped when I held my breath and began again when I breathed. Satisfactory: the Pentax was slung from the neck and the case buckle was intermittently registering my heart-beat when my diaphragm expanded and contracted in breathing.

Trickle of sweat into the corner of one eye, stinging a little. Shielded from the intense direct sunshine, the skin was releasing through the pores. The heat in here was of a different quality: it oppressed, stifling.

Another inch and the beam passed over a cylinder standing erect, clamped to the alloy rack, and I shut my eyes before I triggered the flash to minimize the effect on the dark-adaptation process but even so the torch beam looked almost yellow when I opened them again.

Loman. First picture: a cylinder, compressed-air type, four feet high, clamped vertically.

Only one?

So far. There may be others.

Forebrain thinking was becoming clearer: the psyche had been too dominant, concerning itself with occult responses, indulging in a sick belief in fiends, in spectral fantasy, dwelling on creaturehood rather than inanimation.

Nothing had moved, even when the flash had gone off. Nothing in here was alive. Logic found no case for a rigged trap of any kind: they wouldn't have left one themselves and nobody had been here since they'd died.

I swung the door at right-angles and took two shots.

General scene: freight compartment. Two frames.

Thank you.

They looked like people.

Some stood in a group, two or three of them leaning one against the other; about a half-dozen had fallen, either to the

floor or piled against the end of the rack at varying ang..
They looked like people because at the top of each cylinder
was a round protective shield fixed over the nozzle, and below
it was the neck widening into shoulders. Scotopic vision had
been affected by the last use of the flash and I couldn't see
any details.

Two shots to allow for panorama montage.

Thank you.

*There are about twenty more cylinders, same size, and the
impact broke some of them away from their anchorage. It
looks as if they were all stowed vertically between buffers of
foam plastic. The nozzles have got protective caps. Three
shots, close-up.*

Blinding light and I waited, shutting my eyes and switching
off the torch. First theories at random: the crew had known
what they were transporting on this trip and they knew it was
lethal and perhaps explosive in terms of chemical expansion
or in terms of gas compression sensitive to release. Possible
risk of fire or gross reactive burning without flame, nitric
acid, so forth. But I wouldn't have thought this kind of hazard
would have induced actual terror in reasonable men.

Slid the switch, the beam less yellow now.

There were four racks, two on each side, padded with
shock-resistant material and fitted with straps and clamps. For
some reason the cylinders couldn't be shipped horizontally
or in crates and their stowage precautions had been quite
good to have left some of them still in place after the high
deceleration loads of the forced landing. Five oblong crates
filled the space between the racks, hard against the rear bulk-
head, and they had been protected with a matt black liquid
material with rapid hardening qualities: Bostik or a thermal
sealing product. Two domed canisters were stowed one each
side of the compartment with restraint bands and protective
jacketing. A red label was common to every crate, cylinder
and canister, with the words *Flashpoint Zero:* the Lloyds
designation for dangerous cargo.

I gave Loman a general picture and began on the individual
labels, starting with the containers that were easy to reach
without clambering across the disorder.

*Cylinder. Matt grey, three parallel red bands, metal tabs
reading: PH/18179/M – Cat. IX. Next cylinder same markings, tab reading PH/18180/M – Cat. IX. Next cylinder*

_nted matt green with four yellow bands. Tab: ZRG/635/2
– Cat. XII._

There were thirteen in one group, three in another, with
markings that tied with one of the domed canisters. The crates
contained identical material, all tabs the same.

His voice came faintly from outside.

Have you a problem?

What?

Have you a problem?

He meant was everything all right and I got annoyed
because I'd only taken half a minute's respite: the heat was
coming mainly from overhead and sweating was profuse. The
need for concentrating on the labels was inducing nausea, the
beam of the torch wavering, sensation of extreme fatigue.

No problem.

I'd been in this bloody oven for twenty minutes and I didn't
want him to poke me to see if I was done.

_Matt blue, two white bands. Tab says: OTJ/487/A – Cat.
V._

And somewhere in the background the failure to understand the urgency, _he wished to inform me personally that
your mission is the key to a critical situation of the highest
international proportions_, a top echelon director sent in with
his signature on a 6-K form and the death-pill in his pocket,
a shut-ended crash-priority mission with the final phase now
running, and nothing going on to the tape except these hieroglyphs. Cylinders of BCW gas or something newer than that,
something more lethal, but surely it didn't matter any more
how destructive a weapon was or what it was made of:
within a given hour today or tomorrow the cities of New
York and Moscow and Peking could effortlessly be laid waste
and the present concern at the conference tables was how to
dismantle, piece by piece, the structure of the kill and over-
kill. I didn't understand why I was here.

_Matt red with black bands. Tab: YCJ/2829/E. There's no
reference to any category on this one._

They wanted my report on the cargo of Tango Victor and
they were getting it and it wasn't my concern to ask why. I
was a ferret and this was the rabbit and my teeth were in its
neck.

_GF/A-9/Cat. XII. A point is that 'Cat.' might stand for
catalyst', not for 'category'._

Noted.

I began work on the cylinders that had broken out of their clamps and were lying askew on the cabin floor. The nearest of them had smashed its protective cap and the brass nozzle had been snapped off at the neck, and this I reported to Loman. The metal tab was edge-on and I had to kneel between two of the other cylinders to read it. The torch beam centred on it and I struck out blindly to force the thing away but it screamed and I hit a shoulder and crashed across the loose sand with the blaze of the sun bursting over me as the wind came howling and threw me whirling over the roaring dunes and I spun dying, drifting and spinning, falling.

The world burning and the whirl of dunes rising as high as mountains round the dizzying horizon, dwarfing me and dominating, looming over me in darkness while the giant birds came screaming as they gathered for the carrion, red of eye and enraged and swooping on me, scream of the mad Arab in my skull repeating, repeating, *mountains in the sky, and great birds darkening the heavens,* their long necks stretching and reaching and the first strike of a beak and my hands too feeble, the terror trickling in the blood as the sun burst and I fell again and lay sand-drowned.

Sharp pain finger, hit again, hideous, the beak hooked, hooking and a talon tugging, horror and their red eyes raging and the foul wind of their wings beating at the air and the sand flying up, pain again and tugging and my living hand for carrion *they will not* and quicker and snatching at a wing with cunning, pulling and the gross black body closer, *I refuse* and my fingers stronger, pulling again and now the talons hooking in a frenzy and my red blood running but a killing to be made, the bald head turning on the gristly neck, my hands closing and twisting on the last thin scream from the beak and the others fainter now, their cackling farther away, my legs buckling but up again and I stood with it, a dead weight dangling from the broken neck and I swung it, turning, swinging the heavy scarecrow body in a circle till the dead wings caught the air and flapped open and I let it go, you red-eyed bastards, show you, fall and breath knocked out and lying numbed, the sand bloodied and the night-coming waves soundlessly breaking drowning.

Tango.

Lightheadedness: the mind hollow as a shell but the few
oughts lucid and of an extreme simplicity, diamond-bright
d surrealistic, a return to pre-maturity, A is for Apple,
his Little Boy has Killed a Bird.

Ague, the limbs jerking, I would like to be somewhere
arm, I am so cold here, S is for Snow but this is Sand. The
g birds had attacked me and tried to eat me but I won.

The sand reddish, the spots becoming brown in the sun,
e finger a curious shape and the white of bone shining,
ck-peck yes I remember.

Remember all right, the memory functioning satisfactorily,
mewhere the forebrain trying to seize on facts, desperate
know and to act but blocked, frustrating.

Tango.

They were circling, as they had been before. I thought I
ard them making sounds like chickens, but the brain was
busy that it wouldn't let me listen properly to anything. It
anted to know the facts. Obviously psychochemicals but not
lated to mescaline or lysergic acid, not Sarin or the Soman-
abun group although there was this jerking of the muscles
t no paralysis yet. Vision unimpaired, on the contrary, the
ltures had the exaggerated 3-D effect you see in stereo-
opes, the outline of their moving wings very sharp against
e sky.

Acetylcholinesterase, the memory super-clear like the vision,
e GF, GE and VX group destroying this substance and thus
ocking the nerve signals to prevent resetting, my legs jerking
orse than my arms, nothing definite.

Blackout sensations, possible onset of coma, try to keep
rebration clear and coherent: the gas was heavier than air
d the residue had stayed in the fuselage, pooling in the
ough of the freight section, and that was why I'd been all
ght till I'd had to crouch over the fallen cylinders to read
e tabs. The initial psycho-shock had made me think of a
eature, something that had to be fought off, classic reaction:
rror is ancient and animistic, fear of a predator, of being
ten.

Check time I'd been unconscious between ten and thirteen
inutes blackout still threatening, secondary stage of the syn-
rome in some nerve-target agents is coma: muscular trem-
ing, coma, death. Finger not good, bone exposed, *how can
tell extent of blood loss and its contribution to syndrome,*

other injuries, the thing had pecked at lot, the dunes beg
ning to float and the dark aeroplane increasing at the ri
of the vision-field and I got up because they were driftir
lower and I didn't want that again, couldn't stand that agai
the surrealistic clarity darkening now and things becomir
confused and the memory going, what was tango, who w
tango, *get up and hide, can't stay out here.* The dunes begir
ning to roar and I was running, falling, running again.

Tango. Tango.

Voice faint whose voice get up or they'll have you, ey
out.

It was different this time because the terror was less. Th
maelstrom was whirling round me and the birds grew mor
strous, cackling overhead and one of them making a dive a
me and going away and trying again, but the coma wa
blunting the nightmare and there was room for an area c
almost rational thought: I was trying to run as far as th
group of rocks because if I fell again and couldn't get u
they'd come and squabble over me.

The rocks grew enormous and I thought I'd reached the
but they floated away and I had to run in a curve because th
desert was a vortex, circling round me, then one of the bir
was suddenly right against my face with its hooked bea
screeching and I felt the draught of its wings and caught th
acrid farmyard stench of the thing as it came for me re
eyed with the talons spread from the stiffened legs and th
screeching didn't stop but when my hands went into th
storm of feathers it beat frantically and there was blue-blac
plumage in my clenched fingers as it rose out of my reacl
my legs trying to buckle but I stopped them because I ha
to run, go on running, the sky was murderous.

Rocks loomed again and I tripped and crashed down ar
slid across loose shale, really here, really home, a dark clou
floating under me, the spread of fabric rumpling into fol
as I crawled deeper, deeper into the niche where the lizar
lived, where I would live, safe from the cackling sky.

But they came nearer and I couldn't move any more, the
wings thundering close as they hooked and pecked and I trie
to move but they knew I couldn't, the ether smell and the pai
digging, I don't know, I haven't met this kind of a thing i
Europe, their green gowns and the flutter of their hands, we
just hope for luck, I guess, and she said yes. They didn

...eech any more, where are they, where are what, leaning
...ver me, wanting to hear what I was saying.

'It's very fast-acting.'

Some of them had gone away and the smell of ether was
...rong. I hadn't seen him before. I tried to say Diane.

'Diane.'

Her head turned to look down at me and she said my God,
...hat *is* that stuff?

'The brand name is Theratal and I gave him 30mg IM, a
...t more than the normal dose. I've used it for pulling kids
...t of trips, though not with a dose that size.' He was putting
...me instruments away. 'This is nothing to do with ergot, you
...ow – he'd be dead by this time.'

My left hand felt like a boxing-glove and I told them to
...ke the stuff off but he just leaned over me again and lifted
...y eye-lids in turn, nodding to her.

'Get this stuff off my hand.'

'You feeling okay now?'

'I want to use my hand.'

'You have the other one, don't you?'

He looked at her and laughed comfortably, pressing the
...o brass locks and picking up the bag. She seemed worried
...y this.

'Are you going now?'

'There isn't anything else I can do until tomorrow. He just
...s to rest and I'll leave instructions with the ward nurse:
...ey have Diazon-3 here and it's the same thing with a Belgian
...and name. He'll be okay.'

She went to the door with him and I'd got half the bandage
...f by the time she came back and tried to stop me. She was
...earing a zipped windcheater and her hair was in some kind
... bandeau.

'Is it night?'

She said it was.

There seemed to be odd periods of blackout between periods
... lucidity but they didn't worry me. I wanted to know things
...d she could tell me, and the lucid periods lasted longer
...an the blanks.

'Is base intact?'

'Yes.'

'Chirac pull me out?'

'What?'

'Did Chirac pull me out?'

'Yes.'

There was still three cylinders I hadn't reported on b
London must have got enough or they wouldn't have order
Loman to pull me out. He'd sent Chirac with a helicopter, t'
only way: that was why I'd heard their wings thundering.

'Get this off, will you?'

She said it had to stay like that and I told her to shut u
and get it done. I don't like being one-handed even wh
there's nothing particular to do. She fetched one of the nurs
who'd been here before. The nurse said the bandage had
stay on and I managed to swing my legs off the bed and
up, nearly flaked out again and said to Diane *listen I mean*
and she talked some persuasive French, the *m'sieur* was feelir
very frustrated because of his accident and it would be bett
to do what he asked, so forth, worked in the end because
any case I was in a rotten mood and they could see I w
going to tear the bloody thing off if they didn't co-operat
But the whole wall kept coming and going and I had to
still for a minute while it stopped.

Finger looked a mess. I told them how I wanted thing
just a No. 1 dressing on it and the others left free, especial
the thumb, lose three fingers and you can still grip thing
lose the thumb and all you've got left is a hook and a hamm

'How is the mad Arab?'

'Comment?'

'*L'Arabe fou, comment va-t-il?*'

She spoke English perfectly well: she was the girl who
fixed me up here yesterday and she'd talked to Vickers, t
big oil-driller; but she was annoyed because I wanted n
hand done differently.

'*Je ne comprends pas, m'sieur. Ecartez les doigts, s'il vo
plaît.*'

And she didn't want to talk about the mad Arab, eith
That was all right but there were one or two things beginni
to needle me and I didn't like it: the American said just n
that it wasn't anything to do with ergot and I could belie
him. They were checking the bread supplies as a formal
while a more specialized medical team was trying to find c
the real cause of the trouble. There'd been other Ara
Vickers had told me, and what I wanted to know is how the
got anywhere near that aeroplane without first knowing

as there, and how they'd survived and reached Kaifra with-
ut broadcasting the fact, because even in delirium they'd
rely mention the plane, and that would have initiated an
mmediate air search.

But it hadn't. The Arab had been here in Kaifra at 15.00
ours yesterday raving about the 'mountains' and 'great birds'
ut there but he couldn't have mentioned the freighter or the
lgerian squadrons would have overflown the area much
ooner.

Blank period and someone held me suddenly, tried hard to
urface, no go. Memory throwing images for me but no
quence, the dazzle of the headlights blinding and fading
ad the trays on the waiters' hands and the storm of dark
umage against my face, keeping me upright, holding me
eady, could hear my breathing, its rhythm slowing, a cold
ompress on my forehead, her eyes worried, Diane's, poor
ttle bitch, been sitting prettily in the British Embassy ordering
uns for the Queen's Birthday and then the bastards had
anghaied her and now she was having to wet-nurse some-
ing the vultures had left, not at all nice.

'All right.'

They still kept a hold on me and I had to say it again *I'm
'l right* till they'd let me go, difficult patient, yes, I grant you,
ut don't like being held up, demoralizing.

When the nurse had gone off I said:

'Go and tell them.'

'Tell them what?'

She thought I hadn't been listening. The nurse had finally
ad enough of me and she was going to bring help and get
e undressed and into a bed.

'If they try anything I'm going to smash the place up so
ake sure they understand because it'll save a lot of noise.'

She went off a bit impatiently and I had five minutes to
raighten out, steady deep breaths, muscles relaxed, one or
vo questions, why wasn't Loman here, he must be packing
s up at base, the Arab could have been working in strict
ush for the opposition yes but in delirium he'd have broken
own, shouted aeroplane all over the place, something didn't
uite add up in this area.

Opened my eyes and she was there again, her eyes worried,
aiting for me to start collapsing but I wasn't going to any
ore, didn't intend to, the organism was trying to take over

and I was going to let it.

'You tell them?'

'Yes.' She stuck her small hands into the windcheater ▮
she was obviously ready to pull them out fast to do someth▮
if I keeled over again and that annoyed me and I got off ▮
bed and went a couple of paces and leaned on the wall a▮
she had more sense than to help me, could see my face.

Very good being on the feet again. Therapeutic.

'Who was the doctor?'

'He's visiting the American camps.'

'Where did Chirac land me?'

'At South 6.'

'And brought the doctor along with me?'

'He'll be able to shoot that stuff into the Arabs now.'

'Yes.'

'The last one died in the night.'

Turned away as she said it and turned back when I did
answer. She looked quietly furious, not a bit worried now
said:

'Getting on your nerves, is it, all this?'

Surprise, comprehension, frustration: she had wonderf▮
eyes and you could read everything in them and that was w▮
they'd been such bastards to use her, reaction-concealme▮
capacity sub-zero and her hands too small to lift a gun.

'Do you always go on till you drop?'

'Oh Christ,' I said, 'don't you start.' I leaned off the w▮
and tried walking about, not too bad, no pratt-fall. 'List▮
they were in poor condition anyway, what d'you expect,
diet of dates all their life, or they inhaled more of it th▮
I did. You'll have to find something better than me to wor▮
about.'

I walked some more, a few steps to the window and bac▮
did it again and felt the hallucination thing starting up a▮
their high cackling screech and the fourth one smashing in▮
the instrument-panel and stood and didn't do anything, hu▮
limp, remarkable efficacy of total muscular relaxation, ve▮
old ferret, an instinct now, the wall steadier but I had to sl▮
the breathing consciously, I didn't think she'd moved to h▮
me, learned fast.

'We have do –' try again and get the slur out while you'▮
at it, 'Do we have a rendezvous Lo – with Loman?'

Possibly it wasn't good enough yet but I didn't want

at it, certain amount of satisfaction in having pulled out
of the spasm without having to sit down and ask for an
aspirin or anything.

I turned round, away from the wall, and looked at her.
She wasn't looking at me, looking upwards, listening. I could
hear it too.

'Not immediately.'

I didn't understand. Traces still threatening the psyche, his
upturned face and the expression on it and the way the leg
had snapped when I'd hurled the thing away, I suppose I was
a bit tired, that was all, it didn't help, not being on top form.
She was watching me. I saw what I looked like, because
her eyes showed everything, and I turned away but the
window was there with the outside dark making it a mirror,
as indeed, a sorry figure as they say, rather messed about
with, one way and another. Saw her point now. Motherly
little soul, wanted to tuck me up before the whole bloody
action had time to disintegrate.

So I walked about a bit to prove it wasn't going to.

'When's it for?'

'What?'

'The rdv.'

She was still listening to the jet, head on one side. It
sounded as though it was going into circuit above the airport.
'Later,' she said, not looking down.

'*What time?*' And she jerked her head to look at me because
I'd put a lot of force into it, fed-up with not knowing things
and not being able to talk properly or think properly, getting
better but not nearly fast enough, upsetting.

She was watching me critically, trying to make some sort of
decision. Her hands were still bunched inside the windcheater,
and the weight of the Colt Official Police .38 was dragging
it down at one side; you wouldn't have to frisk this pint-
sized Mata Hari: you could see she was armed half a mile
away.

She kept her voice low, moving closer.

'Loman has some orders for you. He insisted I didn't give
them to you unless you seemed fit enough for some more
work. Well, you're not fit but you won't give an inch so what
can I do? He's at base keeping up a signals exchange with
London in the hope that you'll be able to operate.'

'That doesn't sound like Loman. He'd grind a blind dog

into the ground.'

'I don't think it's a question of consideration.'

'More like it, come on.'

'He wants you to do something he called "sensitive" a
if you can't bring it off he said the "repercussions would
grave in the extreme". He also – '

Suddenly I was shaking her and she drew a breath a
shut her eyes and waited and when I realized what I w
doing I stopped and stood away and she didn't say anythi
for a bit, furious again I suppose because she was doing h
best and I wasn't helping. Quietly as I could:

'Just put it in your own words.'

Couldn't stand the man, that was all, a pox on his gra
repercussions, if he meant the whole thing'd blow up if
ballsed it why couldn't he bloody well say so. Besides whi
I was badly shaken because they'd wanted me to go a
report on Tango Victor and I'd done that so I'd thought t
mission was tied up and now London had got second though
on it, they never let you alone, those bastards, drive you t
you drop.

'Things have been happening,' she said. 'Soon after y
went off the air we had an alert from London. We were ask
to rebrief you for the end-phase of the mission. We did
know if you were still alive, but London said they were goi
ahead on the assumption that you could still operate.'

The whine of the jet was thinning above us as it came in
the approach path and I looked at the square electric clo
above the instrument trolley. 23.52.

'It's for tonight, is it?'

'Yes. I don't know it all. I can only tell you what I've be
instructed. You're to know that a representative of the Forei
Office was flown out this evening to meet the Tunisi
Minister of the Interior. It's been arranged that an aircr
of the RAF Tactical Command will be permitted to land he
at Kaifra tonight, at approximately midnight. Your orde
are to meet it, receive a consignment and take it to base.'

Final approach now and eight minutes early. I looked fro
the window but couldn't see anything of his lights in the sk
Then I moved away, not hurrying.

'All right,' I said. 'Anything else?'

The room wasn't big: nine short paces from this wind
to the one opposite. I counted the paces because I like know

...t things, especially about the environment I have to
operate in. I hadn't walked this far since I'd been in the desert
but the legs were holding up all right.

'Nothing else,' I heard her saying, 'till you reach base.'

The glass of the window was black and I could see her
reflection: she was standing there with her hands in the wind-
heater, watching me. The only light from below was from a
street lamp, reflecting on edges and curved surfaces.

'The immediate thing,' I said, 'is to meet that plane, right?'

'Yes,' she said.

I could hear it landing now, the jets screaming suddenly
and then fading right out. I looked down from the window.

The other side of the building there'd been a Mercedes and a
404, both with their lights off. This side there was the small
Fiat I'd seen at the Royal Sahara and a GT Citroën, no lights.
They weren't just parked: you don't leave a car like that in
the deepest shadow you can find; you put it under a street
lamp if there is one, so people won't pinch things.

I said over my shoulder:

'D'you think you could've been followed?'

It took her a couple of seconds.

'Followed?'

I came away from the window, again not hurrying, but it
didn't matter whether they knew I'd seen them or not because
it was too late to do anything about it: this place was a trap.

Chapter Fifteen

TRAP

'I don't think so,' she said.

She looked small and cold and hunched.

'Wouldn't you know?'

She didn't answer.

I hadn't meant to hurt: I wasn't even thinking about her. I
wanted facts, as many as I could get and as soon as I could
get them. She moved slowly and I said:

'No. Keep away from the windows.'

She stopped at once, looking down.

I suppose she wanted so much to show me she was a ⌐ fessional, but everything she did was amateur.

'Did you get here before Chirac brought me, or after?'

'After.'

I began walking about to get the circulation going. Ther hadn't been a psychic spasm since she'd told me about th FO sending out a man to see the President here: the end phase was being thrown at me like a fast-burn fuse and had to do a lot of thinking and if the psyche wanted to ac the bloody fool it wouldn't get any help from me.

They must be desperate in London. The RAF back in th act and unofficial negotiations at presidential level: if the went on like this they'd shake the whole thing off its bearing:

'When Loman told Chirac to pull me out he must hav known the mission was still running?'

She lifted her head and looked at me, ready to mak another mistake and ready to see what I thought of it, bracin herself.

'I don't know what you mean.'

'Oh for Christ's sake –'

Not thinking properly. Control. We were in a red secto and I wouldn't get us out of it by pushing this poor little bitc till she broke.

'Don't worry,' I said, 'they couldn't have followed you here They don't know you. They haven't seen you since you se up the base and if they saw you in Kaifra before then couldn't have meant anything: they don't know who you are

The breach of security must have been through Chirac. H wasn't a professional either and Loman had got him airborn again at short notice and he'd had to bring me here fron South 6 by road and the area was stiff with surveillance.

'All right,' she said.

She turned away with her eyes getting wet and I suppos she could stand up to me when I was being a bastard bu she didn't know what to do when I stopped.

'Listen,' I said, 'I want to know things. When Loman tol Chirac to pull me out of the desert, he must have know the mission wasn't over, right? He was still in signals wit London, wasn't he?'

'Yes.'

'Then if the mission was still running and we were mea: to keep it quiet, how could London send out a helicopter f(

...ight into the target area?'

This was something she knew about and her head came up ...ickly. 'He said that after the massive air search by the ...lgerians no one in Kaifra would go on thinking that Tango ...ictor was in the region, so a single flight wouldn't attract ...uch attention. But he told Chirac to gain full ceiling before ...e set his course, as a precaution.'

'Fair enough.'

Quickly she said: 'Is that right?'

'It makes complete sense.'

She nodded, feeling better, and I wished to God they'd ...und someone different to help us on this job, someone I ...uld have ignored or disliked, a girl with glasses and a sniff ... a yellow-toothed hell-hag with a barbed wire wig, anyone ...t this downy-armed child with her courage and innocence ...ho ought not to be here with me now, caught in a trap ...at could kill her unless I could spring it.

'Not too near,' I said.

'No.'

She turned back, keeping near the instrument trolley, the ...int farthest from both windows.

'Are we able to phone base?'

'No.' Very emphatic about this. 'Loman said it's possible ...e telephone exchange has been infiltrated. I imagine he ...eans – '

'Got at.'

I wanted to think and she sensed it and didn't talk for a ...t. Proposition: it wasn't the cell that had set up the marks-...an for me or they'd be in here by now, at least four of ...em or any number up to sixteen or more, adequately armed ...d easily capable of taking us or leaving us for dead, the ...aff of the clinic powerless to stop them. It was the cell that ...d orders to survey us, find out where we were going, so ...at when the objective was reached they'd be there too. So ...r they hadn't done very well: Loman had put me into the ...rget area and pulled me out again and they hadn't been ...od enough; all they'd done was lose a man in a ravine. ...onight they looked like doing better.

It was a proposition only: not an assumption. Assumptions ...e dangerous and sometimes lethal. They might be simply ...lding their fire till we went out there so there wouldn't be ...y fuss, nothing for the ward-maids here to clean up afterwards. They *could* be that cell: the one with the mark.., the one with orders to stop me reaching Tango Victor wher ever it was, in the whole of the Sahara. They hadn't don very well either: they hadn't stopped me reaching the targe and reporting on it and getting out again; all they'd don was mess up a Mercedes and leave it full of shells. Tonigh they were better placed.

It didn't matter which cell it was.

'You mean there's someone outside?'

I think she had to ask because she couldn't stand it an more, not knowing.

'Yes.'

She nodded.

Her little nods were expressive: just now it had meant sh felt better; this time it was acceptance. Nothing more tha that because she didn't know the whole thing, she probabl thought there was just one man, just one man watching.

'Where's Chirac?'

'He went back to the Petrocombine South 6 drilling camp Loman said he must use that as his base.'

Further operations: you don't need a base if you've finishe operating.

A spasm came and I wasn't ready and they screeched an their black wings beat at me and I shouted at them withou a sound, doing nothing with my hands, repulsing them wit my mind, half aware of their unreality, only the psych sensitized by the thought of Chirac standing by for furthe operations.

'Are you all right?'

'What?'

'Are you –'

'Yes.'

Sweat running and respiration accelerated, normal symp toms of fear. If Chirac was standing by it could be to fly m out again, drop me back into the nightmare, not ready y to stand it, even to stand the thought.

She was keeping close to me, watching me, wanting to hel

'You're all right now.'

'Yes. You know it was nerve-gas, don't you, you were the when I –'

'Yes.'

'It's the one that puts the fear of Christ in you.'

know.'

I suppose they'd heard me yelling my way out of the freighter. A bit embarrassing but it wasn't my fault: there'd been photographs, a press release at the time when the stuff was invented, picture of a mouse in a cage with a cat and the cat was terrified of it, back arched and ears flat, spitting.

'Listen,' I said and turned away from her, 'what other facilities have been granted?'

When I turned back she was just standing still trying to think what I meant, trying to answer before I lost patience again. So I said: 'The UK's had permission to land a military aircraft here but I mean what else? Did Loman ask for any kind of assistance, police, army, secret service liaison?'

'I didn't hear of anything else. He didn't tell me about anything. I was there all the time while the signals were going through, till he sent me here to brief you.'

'All right.'

Paradox: the Tunisian government was prepared to receive a plane with RAF rondels in Kaifra but I couldn't go down to the reception desk and phone the police and say there are four cars outside please have their drivers arrested on suspicion. But it wasn't quite like that: the Tango mission had been ultra-sensitive from the start and a visit from the Foreign Office type with a request for immediate military overflying and landing rights could have tightened things to the limit. We were strictly on our own.

The thing that worried me most was the timing. The plane was down and the crew was expecting me and I was here in a trap and I didn't know how long they'd wait or what they'd do with the consignment I was meant to receive.

'What is this thing, d'you know?'

'Which thing, please?'

'Whatever the RAF are bringing in.'

'I don't know. Loman called it "the device".'

'The what?'

'"Device". It's the word he used for it in signals.'

'You didn't get any clues? Chemical antidote? Some sort of destruct system? Gas-mask?'

She thought back and then said no. This was logical because if Loman had been allowed to tell me what the thing was he would have briefed the girl, instead of which he'd obviously made sure she didn't pick anything up during the signals exchange.

I kept on walking, the mind exercising the organism,
wouldn't be possible in this condition to do very much if they
came in for us, effort required, keep on walking and do it
properly.

'Is there any kind of a deadline on this?'

'He didn't say so.'

Logical too: the military aircraft had landed and I ought
to be there to meet it because there'd be no point in letting it
hang about the airfield. The deadline was already past.

I stopped by the window, the one at the front of the
building, and looked down as I'd done before. It presented
them with a model target, a silhouette with back-lighting, but
that was all right because if they wanted to pick me off they'd
have done it the first time and in any case they wouldn't have
sent four vehicles with crews numbering up to sixteen if all
they wanted to do was make a small hole in a skull.

It wasn't easy to see things through the reflections on the
glass but the white oblong down there had a cross on the
side and a pennant mounted on the windscreen pillar, French
style. It was parked about halfway between the gates and the
front entrance of the clinic and from this angle I couldn't
see if it was in sight of the Merc and the 404. They were in
the shadow of the palms on the road outside and there was
a hedge of desert tamarisk in their general line of vision: if
they could see the ambulance at all it would be through the
gateway.

'How many are there?'

I shortened focus and looked at her reflection in the glass.
At this distance I couldn't see her eyes but her voice had
sounded steady enough, just a degree strident as if she'd made
herself say it. She was young and inexperienced and would
make the worst possible agent material and if they ever pushed
her into a mission where she had to operate solo for five
minutes that'd be as long as she'd live, but she looked as
though she had guts and I thought the safest thing would be
to tell her what the actual situation was so that she'd have
a chance of saving herself if I forgot to duck.

'There are at least four cars.'

Her reflection gave a little nod. She didn't say anything.

I looked through the glass again. Conditions outside were
the same as last night when I'd walked out of the Roya

..a to the Mercedes: bright starlight, still leaves, moonless
d windless. Low natural visibility without haze, acoustic
adiation conditions somewhere near a hundred per cent
th the hygrometer down towards zero and the air totally
tic. I would have preferred low cloud and a moist wind,
e dark to hide in, the wind to take sound away.
I turned and began walking again.

'What's the code-intro?'

She was watching me with very bright, very alert young
es: she didn't understand what I meant and was trying
rd to think and get it right and not look stupid.

'What's the code-introduction when I meet these RAF
pes? Password. What do I –'

'Oh yes – Firefly. They'll be carrying photographs of you
d you'll be asked to show them the scar on your left arm.
ou must destroy the photographs immediately.'

'My Christ, is that all?'

She just shut her eyes and stood there hunched up but I
sn't even thinking about her because London had covered
e code-intro with actual pictures and a physical feature so
wasn't just a gas-mask they were handing over: it was
mething so classified that the Air Ministry wouldn't deliver
before they'd forced the Bureau into providing treble-check
entification. They couldn't be standard aircrew on that
ane: they were seconded from DI6 or Liaison Branch, or
e Bureau wouldn't have let those photographs out of the
es.

I suppose she thought she'd got it wrong again because of
e way I'd said was that all. She only knew half of what was
ing on and whenever I asked her anything she'd only got
fifty-fifty hope of coming up with the right answer and it
as wearing her down.

'What car did you come in?'

She opened her eyes.

'The Chrysler.'

'Loman's?'

'Yes.'

'You came from base direct?'

'Yes.'

'You know the way back?'

'Past the mosque.'

'That's right.'

167

It was a three-minute trip.

If I could get her out of here she could be back in co
within three minutes but three minutes wouldn't give her a
thing like enough time to flush a tag and she hadn't b
trained to overshoot base and take him on to neutral grou
and do what I'd done to Mohamed. With four vehicles wait
out there I thought they'd probably just take her somewh
for interrogation and she wasn't trained to cope with tl
kind of thing either.

I'd have to leave her here and tell the staff to look af
her while I drew off the opposition.

'What are your orders?'

'Orders?'

'What were you told to do, once you'd briefed me?'

'Get back to base.'

She'd already briefed me: FO involvement, Tactical Co
mand sortie, rdv, code-intro, there wouldn't be anything el
it was a simple pick-up job. So now Loman wanted her ba
at the Yasmina to man our communications and leave h
free to make neutral-ground contact with Chirac and perh
others so I *couldn't* leave her here and ask the staff to lo
after her while I tried to break out.

I'd have to take her with me.

'Are you frightened?'

'Yes,' she said, 'very.'

'That's good.'

She wasn't exactly shivering: there was a tension in l
body that was making her contract, hunching herself into t
windcheater as if she were cold. It was the classic anin
posture in the face of a predator, the body drawn in
itself to protect the vital organs and present a smaller for
the limbs at the same time contracted in readiness to str
or spring if defence were changed to attack.

'Why is it good?'

'You're producing everything you need: adrenalin, musc
tone, sensory alertness. No one else can do it for you a
you can't get it out of a bottle.'

She nodded.

I took another walk and passed the window and glanc
out and went on. There wasn't any sign of life down ther
the Mercedes and the Peugeot 404 made blocks of shad
among the trees and the ambulance showed up as a blur

...e against the tamarisk hedge. In the building here I could ...ake out voices but they were distant; twice since I'd regained ...onsciousness I'd heard the lift working just outside this ...oom.

'Has the thing got a full clip?'

'What thing?'

'That gun. Has it got a full magazine?'

'Yes.'

'Is the safety-catch on?'

She had to look, tugging the thing out of her pocket as if ...omeone had said give me that bag of toffees, I've told you ...efore. Then she nodded.

'Yes. It's on.'

She was pleased because she'd got her lessons right and ...thought oh you bastards if you rope in a child again to help ...s in the kind of work we do I'll have your thumbs off first ...nd then mind your eyes.

'Do you want it?'

She was holding it out to me.

'No. Put it away.'

'All right.' She got it back into her pocket and looked up ...t me again and the fear was still in her eyes, I suppose ...ecause I'd made her think we were getting ready for some ...ind of trouble. I'd only wanted to check on the safety-catch ...ecause she might have to run and if she tripped and the ...hing fired it'd blow her leg off. I would have taken it away ...rom her altogether and dropped it into a waste-bin before ...e left but it was just possible she could save herself with it if ...hings got rough.

'Diane.'

'Yes?'

'We're going.'

'All right.'

'There won't be much trouble.'

'I see.'

Light eyes and a firm mouth and her bright hair in a ...andeau and out there in the night a bunch of thugs who'd ...o what their orders were to do, shoot her down or take her ...omewhere and put her through forced interrogation, any-...hing they were told to do, anything they wanted to do. I'd ...y her chances were fifty-fifty, the same as my own.

But the alternatives I'd come up with were riskier still and

I wanted to try the break-out before the opposition co..
decided to send them in for us. We'd be better off in th
open, with room to move.

So I told her to find a couple of white coats, the line
things the doctors used, and she drew blank in the cupboard
here and had to go out and across the landing and try he
luck over there. I could still hear voices from somewher
below in the building but they weren't loud. It was almos
midnight and activity in the clinic was at a low level.

She came back.

'Will these do?'

'Yes. Leave them here for a minute. We're going to wal
across the room, past that window. Just slowly, talking.'

'All right.'

'No, this side of me.' I took her arm. 'I want them to se
you closely. But don't look out of the window.'

We got moving and before we reached the window she'
begun trembling.

'Do I do all of the talking?'

'No. We're just in conversation. The main thing is not t
look out of the window. This way a bit, a few inches thi
way.'

If she passed too near the window she'd only present a
almost black silhouette and if she were too far from it th
reflected light from the walls would strike her face. I didn
want them to see her face but only the pale blue windcheate

'Don't look out.'

'How do you know I want to?'

'You want to see for yourself who they are. A bit slowe
But you wouldn't see them anyway, it's only a couple of ca
parked under the trees.'

'You said there were four.'

'The other two are at the back of the building.'

'I see. It's giving me gooseflesh, knowing they're watchin
me now.'

'Don't worry.'

The trembling was still in her arm, under my hand.

'Why are we doing this?'

'They know you're with me here, because you must hav
passed this window a few times before I told you to sta
clear of it. They could even have been outside when you drov
up. I want to remind them, as late as possible before we leav

, that you're wearing blue.'

We reached the wall and turned round and started going
ack, the window on my side now. She said:

'Why did you tell me to keep clear, before?'

'I thought there was a chance they'd shoot you.'

'Why don't you think so now?'

'Because I'm still alive.'

The other window wasn't important because from the Fiat
nd the Citroën they couldn't see the ambulance. She was
till trembling and I said: 'You'll feel all right once we get
oing; it's only the delayed action affecting your nerves. Can
ou drive a DS 90?'

'Yes. We've got one at the Embassy.'

'Fair enough. There's a DS ambulance outside. I want you
o go and start it up and bring it over to the front steps.' We
ere clear of the window now and put on the white linen
oats. 'Keep that thing tucked well in: I don't want them to
ee any blue. All right, we'll take the lift.'

There was nobody in the main hall. Posters about inocula-
on against cholera, preventive hygiene to fight sandfly
achoma; a pair of sandals lying in a corner near the door;
rtificial flowers on the reception desk with a faded ribbon
n them. Sand gritted under our feet; there is sand every-
here in Kaifra, even inside the buildings.

'Take off your bandeau and put it in your pocket.'

'All right.'

'See the ambulance?'

'Yes.'

'I'll wait for you here on the steps.'

She went down them and I stood watching her.

There wasn't anything else we could do but this; nothing
at had as much hope of working out smoothly, provided
ey didn't get too close a look at us. I wanted to keep the
ction down because she had all her life in front of her and
e had a mission to run and I wasn't in fit condition to risk
major mistake.

She walked nervously, her step springing a little, but she
asn't looking around her though I knew she must be wanting
. They couldn't see her yet: it would only be when she
rossed the gap made by the gates that they might see her.
could think of no reason why they should shoot. It was
st that she looked small and vulnerable out there where there

171

wasn't any cover and I wished I'd gone with her but it
too late and anyway impractical because this was part of th
whole set-up: a change of image as convincing as we coul
make it.

She got into the ambulance and the sidelights came on an
the engine started up and the pennant gave a couple of laz
flaps as she locked over and came towards the steps.

'I'll drive.'

She slid across and I got behind the wheel as quick as
could because one of the voices I'd heard on the groun
floor would belong to the ambulance driver and he'd kno
the sound of this vehicle and wonder what was going o
I would have preferred to let her drive: she'd already estab
lished the image behind the wheel and now we'd altered
but if they weren't satisfied with what we were giving the
they'd tuck in behind and we'd have to lose them and sh
wasn't trained for that.

'Seat-belt,' I said.

She pulled it across and buckled it.

The fuel was at three-quarters. I turned the facia-lam
rheostat to medium power, getting enough of a glow to sho
up my white coat but not to light my face. Then I put th
heads full on and drove through the gates and turned le
so that if they decided to follow us up they'd have to mak
a half-turn first. I could see the blue flash of the roof eme
gency lamp in the mirror-frames and thought about usir
the hee-haw but there was no traffic and it might be ove
doing things.

There was a slight clang from behind us, probably th
chrome-armoured tube of the oxygen unit against the cylind
because we were leaning in a close turn; and there wa
another sound, fainter and underlying the first and not ea
to identify: possibly a piece of equipment shifting.

'You all right?'

'Yes thank you.'

'Don't worry.'

'No.'

I really thought they'd accepted the image and then som
lights swung from behind us and I knew the sound I hadn
been able to identify had been the first of them starting u

'Keep low in the seat.'

'All right.'

172

kicked the throttle to bring the ratio down and the rear
tyres lost traction on the sand but we weren't even picking
up useful revs before the lights showed me the Citroën GT
moving broadside across the road in front of us. There wasn't
anything I could do because this was an avenue of close-
standing palms and there was no point in trying a slide U-turn
because there were lights in the mirrors now.

Their orders hadn't been to tag us. They'd been told to set
up a pincer trap for anything that moved, and we were in it.

Chapter Sixteen

HASSAN

No, this is Angela, with Robert.

They'll be coming over to see us while you're here and I'm
longing for you to meet them.

Yes, aren't they? And always hand in hand – they weren't
posing like that for the photographer. Deeply in love, and
we're so very happy for them.

On Tuesday, coming down from Cambridge. They're just
dying to meet you – of course we've told them all about you.

No, that's our youngest. She – she was a lovely child.

Yes, I'm very sad to say. It happened in North Africa, one
of those mysterious and dreadful things that sometimes
happens to people when they're abroad.

We never really found out. It was sort of – hushed up,
and even our own Embassy advised us to let the enquiries
drop. Yes, all very strange.

Murdered. But no one was ever accused. They say there
were just some Arabs, and it was night-time, and – well we
don't let ourselves think too much.

Oh not a bit, no. That's why we keep her picture here,
with the rest of our little family. She was such a lovely girl
and it sort of helps, to talk about her to people. It makes
her seem – well – still a little bit alive.

The Citroën GT was backing and turning.

The term in the personnel files is 'an assault on the person
designed to extract intelligence'. If you've held out against

it you get the 9 suffix to your code name but it's not exa
an award for meritorious duty or anything: it just mear
they can give you some of the high-risk jobs in the hope tha
you'll do the same again, refuse to expose the mission or th
cell or the Bureau even though the light blinds and the fles
burns and the scream is private inside your skull, for pride
sake.

An assault on the person. Your own person. No one else'

Backing and turning and coming in this direction, no longe
blocking the road entirely, leaving me enough room to g
through if I wanted to. But there wasn't any point: the Fia
was farther along the avenue with a muzzle poking out of
side window. The lights of the Citroën came on, full heads, an
most of the scene was blacked out because of the glare.

'Shall I shoot at them?'

'No.'

'Why not? They –'

'When you're outnumbered, the thing is to think, not shoot

I turned my head sideways to avoid the glare. She wa
looking at me, her skin silvered by the brightness of the ligh
her eyes exaggeratedly blue because of the contracted pupil:
She would have made a good photograph.

'What will they do?' she asked me.

'Nothing much. They want some information, that's all.'

Because if they'd intended to kill, as the other cell ha
intended, they would simply have sent a marksman to wai
for me to leave the clinic or they would have ordered a
armed group into the building to do it summarily. And i
they'd intended to put mobile surveillance on me they wouldn'
have used four vehicles to set it up: they couldn't hope t
do it without my knowing and in a small town like Kaifr
it wasn't even necessary.

They wanted me for interrogation.

This idea would have worried me in the ordinary way, bu
not too much. I had twice explored this psychological terrai
in earlier missions and I knew roughly what to do: the onl
possible way is to remove the mind from the body and t
look at the situation objectively – the pain is expressed i
the nerves and is perfectly natural but it doesn't have an
significance; it's totally physical and there's no message; yo
merely want it to stop and you could say the word but yo

...n't live with yourself afterwards so you might as well
...e now and if you're prepared to die then they've had it
...cause once you're dead you're no more use and they know
...at.

The worry would have been about the unpleasantness, that
...as all, not about whether I'd break. And at the moment they
...ouldn't have a lot of success because there were bruises
...erywhere and the effects of the gas were still hanging
...ound and they'd only have to push me a bit too far and
...I flake out and they wouldn't learn anything.

But there was a new factor involved tonight. I didn't know
...ow long I'd be able to hold out if they went to work on
...iane instead of me.

The Citroën pulled up and someone got out and walked
...p to us holding a sub-machine-gun. For a moment his
...adow grew immense, flitting across the bonnet of the
...nbulance; then the light blazed again and he came to the
...le and stood there waiting for something, the muzzle aimed
...my head.

I turned to look at him. Except for the man who'd died in
...e ravine this was the first time I'd seen anyone from an
...position cell because they'd worked covertly for the most
...rt: the bomb in Tunis, the marksman here in Kaifra. This
...an wasn't of any interest because he was just a factotum
...t I looked at him so that I'd know him if I saw him later.
There were footsteps on the loose sand and another man
...me up from one of the cars behind us and stood looking in
...Diane.

'Get out of the car.'

I noted that he was an Egyptian, with a Cairo dockside
...cent. I told her:

'You only speak English.'

'What?' she called to him through the window.

He jerked his sub-machine-gun.

'Get out this side,' I told her, 'with me.'

'All right.'

I opened the door and the one who'd come up from the
...troën got worried and jerked his gun at me.

'Get your hands up!'

'Oh bollocks.'

He was Egyptian too. I suppose Loman must have known

the UAR was involved but hadn't been allowed to te‖
on the grounds that the less the ferret knows the longer ‖
lives.

Diane followed me out and we stood waiting. Two oth‹
men came up, one from the Fiat and one from behind u‖
and both had guns trained on us. Only one of them wore
fez: the others looked inferior material, capable of subdui‖
or killing but nothing more. By their speech they were a‖
from dockside Cairo and they called the man in the fez ‖
the name of Hassan.

'Bring the Fiat here,' he told one of them. Then he turne‹
to me. 'Give me your gun.'

'I haven't one.'

I spoke in Arabic because at least one of the oppositio‖
cells had a dossier on me: Loman had warned me about tha‖

'Search him! Get his gun!'

Hassan was very nervous and I placed him fairly high u‖
in his cell or even in the network: he had the intelligen‹
to know his responsibilities and to know that if I got out ‹
this trap he'd probably get a chopping.

One of the thugs frisked me and I didn't make it diffic‖
for him.

'He has no gun, Hassan.'

'He must have!'

I was frisked again and they dragged open the doors of t‖
ambulance and ransacked the compartments and then one ‹
them said it was the woman – she had my gun. Hassan look‹
at me to see my reaction when they tugged the Colt .38 o‖
of her pocket and I looked suitably upset.

'He gave the woman his gun,' said a man, 'but we fou‖
it!'

Hassan told him to shut up and turned away and spo‖
to the man who'd brought the Fiat alongside.

'Is Ahmed coming?'

'Yes.'

The transmitting aerial went on waving, slower and slowe‹

I thought that Ahmed wouldn't be likely to come alon‹
he was obviously higher in the cell and would have at lea‖
one trigger-man. So far there were only the four of the‖
here, unless there were others who'd stayed in the Merced‖
or the 404 and I doubted this because Hassan was nervo‖
and would have brought every one of his men in to gua‖

176

There was no hope of estimating how long it would take Ahmed to reach here from their radio base but it would need only ten minutes to cross the whole of Kaifra. He could be here within sixty seconds.

Hassan was watching me.

'Where is the rest of your cell?'

I said I was operating freelance and there wasn't an actual cell, and he just shook his head and didn't take me up on it. I think it was just a random question to try me out. He looked like a hardworking field executive, the eyes alert but unimaginative, a man who had reached the position of lieutenant in a small cell operating overseas. I thought he would put the requirements of the operation before everything else, and would work well with Ahmed when the grilling began. I would have given a great deal to know whether either of them would have the intelligence to use Diane as the means of persuasion; I believed they would, because it had two immense advantages over a single interrogation session: a man might easily hold out if the pain was his own but might as easily break if he had to listen to someone else going through it, especially a young girl; secondly the girl could be brought again and again to the point of mental unbalance while the man was left with a clear head and the ability to answer questions.

It would depend partly on how well Ahmed and Hassan understood the European attitude to things like this: an Arab would entirely ignore the suffering of a mere woman and it wouldn't be worth touching her.

'Where is the aeroplane?'

'I still can't find it.'

The answers had to be acceptable: it was no good saying what cell, what aeroplane, so forth. He knew I was an agent operating in the local field and he knew I was assigned to the UK Tango Victor mission and if I could give him some answers that would fit in with what he already knew it might get him to think of a few more questions. The more I could persuade him to talk, the more he'd tell me.

'Do you think the aeroplane is somewhere near Kaifra?'

'Well,' I said, 'I don't know about near. We certainly thought it was, but it looks as if we were wrong.'

He seemed about to ask me another one and I waited but he shut up and began stamping his feet impatiently, looking

177

THE TANGO BRIEFING

along the perspective of the palm-trees to see if Ahmed
coming. I thought it was interesting to note that this was a
Egyptian cell and not the one controlling the marksman; als
that one of the other cells was Algerian and working a
government level with immediate-category liaison, becaus
Chirac had brought in five squadrons of desert-reconnaissanc
aircraft just by mooning around up there at dawn th
morning.

'Feeling all right?'

'Yes,' she said.

She was looking pale, the gold skin losing colour.

'Do not talk!'

Hassan had swung round nervously.

'You mean don't talk in English?'

'Yes. Talk in Arabic.'

'But this woman doesn't understand Arabic.'

'Then do not talk.'

His olive-black unimaginative eyes stared at me to mak
sure I was getting the message; then he turned away an
looked for Ahmed again.

He wasn't trying anything subtle: he was energetic an
efficient but not educated and it was almost certain that hi
henchmen didn't speak anything but their own crane-hoo
argot but it'd be too risky to rely on that so I asked her i
English:

'Did you leave the other gun in the ambulance?'

I didn't expect her to have time to answer: she hadn'
heard about any other gun and anyway she'd be throw
because I'd just been told not to speak in English and her
I was doing it.

He came round very fast, Hassan, and his teeth flashed i
the light as the animal mouth delivered its speech, the ex
pression more explicit than the words.

If you talk to the woman in English again we will kill you
I will not have my commands disobeyed, if you do it agai
you will die, so forth.

But I'd got the information I'd wanted because the othe
three had closed in on me almost by reflex action when they'
seen him swing round, and their sub-machine-guns had com
up to the aim. So they didn't understand English and Hassa
didn't understand it either or he'd have told them to searc
the ambulance for the 'other gun' instead of telling me off.

178

ust hoped Diane would work things out and make a
ueful note: I'd told her they wanted to interrogate me and
e knew you can't interrogate a dead man so if we had to
lk to each other urgently we could do it in English.

Hassan was still glowering at me and I could see he'd like
shoot me here and now just for disobeying his orders: he
as terribly nervous about the whole situation and didn't
ally trust in his ability to keep me subdued.

'Oh come on, Hassan, I bet you talk a bit of English, if it's
ly Coca-Cola.'

He spat, not too far from my shoe. We could hear a car
mewhere, its exhaust-note muffled by the phalanx of palms,
d he jerked his head to listen, watching the end of the
venue. I was worried because there was so little time and
cause this situation couldn't be expected to improve. One
an and one sub-machine-gun would be enough to keep us
mobilized, and this force – already overwhelming – would
e augmented as soon as Ahmed arrived.

And I didn't like the thing about Diane.

I could only save her by getting her away and I didn't
ink I could do that. Once they'd got us in the confines of
a interrogation chamber she wouldn't have a chance. Nothing
ry important of course would happen: a fledgling agent
conded from an embassy to an active cell would go into
e reports as fatally injured during the course of a mission
d the incident would be passed on to those responsible for
reading the blackout. Two young gentlemen with diffident
ices and polished nails would call at the flat in Lowndes
quare to break the news, bearing the personal sympathy of
e Foreign Secretary and hoping it might be a consolation
know that this very courageous civil servant sacrificed her
fe for the sake of others, adding that since her duties had
en of an exceptional kind it would be unfair to her memory
any demand were made for enquiries that could only prove
ortive and at the same time undo much of the work she
d so assiduously accomplished in the cause of active
plomacy.

We never really found out. It was sort of – hushed up, all
ry strange. They say there were just some Arabs, and it was
ght-time, and – well we don't let ourselves think too much.

The avenue was still empty: the car was moving at right-
gles to it, a good mile away, its note rising and falling as

179

the sound was trapped and released among the bu
Hassan turned back to us and fumbled quickly for a cigaret
breaking the first match before he could light it.

Nothing very important and it happens two or three tim
a year to experienced executives like O'Brien and Fyson a
we never know how many smaller fry are neutralized. It w
infinitely more important that when she began sobbing
should remind them that I hadn't yet been able to loca
Tango Victor, that when she first screamed I should repe
that I was only a freelance without a local base, and th
when she failed to respond to resuscitation I should tell the
they'd been wasting their time simply because they had
believed me, and that they would only waste more time
they put me through the same treatment because if I did
know where the freighter had crashed then I couldn't t
them.

Hassan went and leaned into the Citroën GT and put t
headlights down to dipped so that he could watch the ro
without having to move away from us beyond the glare. T
smoke from his Egyptian cigarette drifted on the air, tar
and perfumed. He was smoking it nervously, flicking aw
the ash before it had time to form more than a millimet
I watched his cigarette.

Diane was yawning quietly, being afraid. It happens in t
trenches and behind the *barrera* of the bull-ring: the intake
oxygen for the muscles, the release of thyroid secretion f
the nerves. I looked at her and nodded and said:

'Okay?'

'Yes, thank you.'

Hassan jerked his dark head to look at me but okay w
international and that was why I'd used it and he didn't sla
into me this time. I said in Arabic:

'The woman doesn't know anything. Why don't you let h
go?'

He shook his head again, taking me seriously.

'We will find out what she knows.'

I let it go at that and moved my feet around a bit, as
was doing, my hands behind me. The snouts of their gu
moved, keeping me lined up. I wished I could help her g
through the waiting, saying a word or two; but she was
meant to understand Arabic and if I spoke English again
might tell one of them to go for the face or the diaphrag

ake sure I understood and that wouldn't do any good:
didn't think I could save her but it wouldn't make her less
rightened if she saw how helpless I was.

I stopped moving about and leaned with my back against
he little Fiat, listening to the faint sounds of traffic on the
ar side of the town where the highway linked the airport
ith the drilling camps. I couldn't hear the sound of any
articular vehicle nearing. Hassan was listening too and I
hought it probably wouldn't be long before he used the radio
o ask his base where Ahmed was.

That was the principle of the thing, anyway: whatever
hey did to her, I wouldn't give them information. Whatever
hey did to me, I wouldn't talk. They could afford to work
n her as far as the point where life ceased and the odd
hing was that I was absolutely certain she'd hold out for as
ong as I did: it hadn't occurred to me that they'd get any-
hing out of her. I could of course have been wrong but I
idn't think I was.

She was watching me and glanced away but realized I'd
een her and looked at me again, one eye clear and amethyst,
he other in deep shadow, the down on her face silvered in
he light from the Citroën, her soft hair shining. One day
he'd be a beautiful woman, would have been, yes, as you
ay, a beautiful woman, but there we are and I suppose there
ren't many families without something to grieve for, it's
ngela, really, who felt it the most, they were very close you
now, terribly fond of each other, almost like twin sisters,
ut I mustn't go on like this the minute you arrive.

A query in the quiet regard: what's going to happen?
I don't know.

Cursed them again till the sweat came and I looked away
rom her because I ought to have reassured her but couldn't
anage it, cursed them for bringing in a child just because
he machine they'd set up was running too fast, sweating in
he cool night air, not wanting to make the effort I would
ave to make and very soon. Not only her life involved,
utterflies are pretty too, you find them flattened in window-
ambs and the world goes whistling on, but my own life as
ell, not that I've ever thought of dying in bed, thank you.
wo lives and a mission. Made you sweat.

Physical condition not up to standard: the bruising had
eft me wanting to keep still, every movement making it feel

181

as though something was going to snap, a bone, a te..
Mentally fed-up of course, the horror still there at the fr..g
of consciousness, their talons hooking and the farmyard stin
of them, quite apart from the worry about what was goin
to happen. Put it this way, the organism wasn't in awfull
good shape for survival.

'Hassan.'

I was still leaning against the side of the Fiat and I didn
straighten up when he came over to me. I was dead beat, h
could see that. I said:

'The woman doesn't know anything.'

'You have said this, but we will see.'

'Let her go and I'll tell you everything I know.'

He laughed, just a quick flash of his teeth in the brow
skin, and turned his head to look at Diane, the cigarett
flattened between his fingers as he raised it and drew th
smoke out, the glow of its tip reflected like a spark in his ey
and then dying.

They would use a cigarette like this one. Probably one c
those in the pack he'd pulled out just now. What is th
longitude, what is the latitude, or she will not see anythin
again, the glowing tip against the amethyst, tell us. The
would use other things; they would be selective, efficient.

'You will tell us everything you know,' he said, 'in any case

He'd laughed because I'd said something at last that h
couldn't take seriously: if they let her go I'd tell them les
in the end, not more; and he knew that. Anyway the whol
thing was academic because he was a professional and h
knew that any man can be reduced to a gibbering loon
they take it far enough and it doesn't need more than a
hour. The only drawback is that he might not be, at tha
stage, too articulate.

'You can't say I didn't try, Hassan.'

He turned to me, his teeth flashing again.

'You tried,' he said, nodding his dark head, 'yes.'

He dropped his cigarette end, putting his black pointe
shoe on it, the loose sand gritting. Then he stood watchin
the roadway, listening.

The three men hadn't moved for minutes. Most of th
time they watched me but turned their heads now and the
to see what Hassan was doing, one of them staring at Dian
until he saw me watching him, one of them looking sometime

g the road's perspective. Their sub-machine-guns had
llen away from the aim since Hassan had told me off for
eaking in English but this was normal for the situation:
ey were standing at ease, in the military sense, to avoid the
nset of syncope that sends our guardsmen toppling with such
mbarrassment at the Trooping of the Colours. Their guns
uld swing up and fire within a tenth of a second and at
is range the shells would go through me and through both
des of the Fiat and there wasn't anything I could do about
: Hassan was running an efficient little cell and this trap
as man-tight.

Near the end of the avenue a dome turned white and then
arkened again as headlights swept across the building, and
assan's thin dark body stiffened, straightening. We could
ar the car but it wasn't coming in this direction and he
laxed after a while, shifting his feet and getting the packet
cigarettes, pulling one out.

'Don't worry, Hassan, he'll get here.'

He put the cigarette between his lips.

'Oh yes,' he nodded, 'he'll get here.'

'Can I have one of those?'

He came over to me and I got some matches out, striking
e for him. When he'd lit up he held the packet out to me
d I took a cigarette, putting the tip between my lips and
riking another match. It occurred to me, in one of those
ray thoughts that pass through our minds at unlikely
oments, that it wasn't a very easy death I was giving him.

Chapter Seventeen

MARAUDER

hey were Unicorn Brand but that was all I knew about them.
he important thing was that they were British made and
erefore likely to have fewer duds among them than a
ontinental make, so that the odds against this kind of
peration succeeding were considerably lower even though it
as a strictly one-shot set-up without a hope of another go.

The oxygen carrier might have been anything, potassium

chlorate, manganese dioxide or possibly lead oxide, wi
usual sulphur for the flame-burst medium mixed with dextr
powdered glass and so on for the binding and striking agen
The actual splint would have been treated with sodium silic
or ammonium phosphate as an impregnation against aft
glow and although in this climate it was tinder dry I decid
to throw directly into the fuel tank orifice while igniti
was still in progress rather than wait for the flame to beco
established because the air rush could blow it out.

There was an area of danger during the actual setting-
of the operation. I had gone to lean against the Fiat inste
of the Citroën GT because there wasn't a hinged panel ov
the petrol cap: a panel would have made a noise springi
open and I would have had to stand slightly away from t
bodywork to give it room, which would have exposed
hands and the panel itself. With nothing more than the ha
turn cap to take off it had been a pushover even with r
hands behind me and no one had seen what I was doi
because finger movement alone was necessary, the forea
and wrist remaining perfectly still.

The area of danger had involved the petrol cap itself on
I'd removed it: I couldn't put it into my pocket witho
their seeing it, so I'd had to leave it wedged between r
spine and the body panel in order to leave my hands free
get the matches and strike them; and the whole operatic
would have been abortive if for any reason I'd had to le
away from the car because the petrol cap would have dropp
with quite a lot of noise.

There'd been a certain amount of strain on the nerv
because the fact was that two lives and the end-phase of
priority mission were now depending on a blob of chemica
literally as small as a match head and this resulted in qui
normal but dangerous purpose tremor when the time can
to bring out the matches: my fingers weren't steady as
struck the first one and I had to get over this by consideri
a simple enough fact: that if nothing at all had depende
on doing this thing properly I could have done it at the ve
least a dozen times with perfect success. In other words I w
on an odds-on favourite at twelve to one so there wasn't a
real need to worry.

I think my fingers had been quite steady again in the insta
before I struck the second match but there wasn't time

it any attention. The operation was now in final sequence and almost automatic: the match had to be moved through a hundred and eighty degrees laterally and downwards approximately forty degrees from the horizontal and the eye would pick up the target at once because it was well defined as a dark hole in a light-coloured panel. The actual timing was critical but presented no physical problem: all I had to do was swing half round with my right hand moving downwards during the ignition phase, allowing almost two full seconds for the manœuvre – more than twice as long as I needed for the muscular commands and responses.

The ignition was normal and I waited for the oxygen release from the carrier and the formation of sulphur dioxide with heat increase before I turned and threw the match into the fuel orifice. At this stage the chemical process was becoming rapid and the final oxygen release almost explosive and I got clear and let the petrol cap drop to the roadway.

Hassan didn't have any time to react. The mental process involving the sequence of surprise, suspicion, comprehension and physical avoidance commands was much too long and I doubt if he'd done more than assume the startle posture, head forward and shoulders hunched, before the fumes caught. He was standing, in effect, directly in front of a flame-thrower.

The timing of the main explosion wasn't important. Both Hassan and one of his men were in the immediate flame area and were thus technically out of action as soon as I threw the match. My target was the man standing seven or eight feet away towards the Citroën GT and I went for him in the same movement that got me clear of the explosion.

He didn't have a chance and I knew that. His surprise phase would last much longer than it would take me to reach him: two seconds ago the night had been quiet and he had been party to a situation affording him absolute power and he was now faced visually with a conflagration that covered seventy-five per cent of his static field of view and mentally with a reversal of concepts difficult to accept without a sense of unreality. He was moving instinctively into a half crouch when I spun the sub-machine-gun to break his hold on it and flung it clear and dropped him and went for the other man.

There was bright flamelight now and a lot of noise. Hassan was screaming and trying to roll over but he was a torch and the petrol was still flooding across the roadway and making

185

a sea of fire and I had to keep clear as I went for the f[...]
man. The one who'd been standing near Hassan wasn't makin[...]
any noise and I think the initial burst of flame had asphyxi[...]
ated him and sent him down without any chance of gettin[...]
away. I saw Diane still standing near the front of the Fia[...]
and starting to move for the ambulance and then I wa[...]
coming up on the fourth man and having to dodge becaus[...]
he'd begun pumping his gun as a reflex action and the stuf[...]
was going into the roadway and sending up clods of ta[...]
before he saw me and swung round and I felt the blast o[...]
three successive shots as I went low and got his legs.

Sudden rattling almost as loud as the gun itself as the aim
went wild and the shells began hitting the Fiat behind me[...]
sharpness of cordite in the lungs and somewhere in the middl[...]
of everything the unmistakable sounds of Hassan dying an[...]
then my hands closed and I dragged the fourth man of[...]
balance with his feet kicking upwards, split-second image o[...]
his face terrified in the flamelight then I chopped once an[...]
took the gun and slung it skittering across the sandy roa[...]
and finished him and started back towards the ambulance.

Fell against something.

Oh Christ someone saying, fumes very strong, myself sayin[...]
it, get up but my hands slid, part of the Fiat, front end[...]
couldn't get up.

The effort demanded hadn't been great but total resource[...]
had been called upon suddenly and factors like oxygen need[...]
and blood supply to the muscles and brain had become in[...]
volved, bad enough if I'd kept up the effort till the organism[...]
rediscovered its rhythm but worse because the relative fall[...]
off in terms of effort was precipitous: all I was having to d[...]
now was move from the flame area to the ambulance and i[...]
didn't take much doing and reaction was getting time to set in[...]

Roaring and the red light blinding, hello we'll have to watch[...]
that won't we, hitting something again, bumpers, up but [...]
couldn't then bloody well try again or you'll burn alive, [...]
sleeve of the white coat catching you're in for it now if yo[...]
don't take an interest but the fumes choking and the hea[...]
fierce look out that's the wrong way, this way or you'll fry[...]
and *get* that coat off, *get it off*.

Lights through the dark, the billowing dark of the smok[...]
and the lights flooding through it, greenish and very clea[...]
and not the orange-red colour of the fire, somebody movin[...]

...r coming nearer, the ambulance why don't you *bloody* *ell get up.* Yes better now, the air more breathable. The tars spinning headlong across the roof of the night and *look where you're going for Christ sake,* that's better, steady now here's no need to panic, everything's under control.

Door swung and I pitched in and slammed it.

She drove hard and just before we left the area I saw them ying there, three of them blackening, one of them still trying o crawl through the dying flames. This was satisfactory and t had been easier for them, even this, than what they would have done to her, and later to me.

She drove well but the sobbing wouldn't stop and she had o keep straightening up from the wheel, her tears bright in he back-glow from the headlamps. She hadn't seen anything ike that before and the spasms kept shaking her and when could manage it I said all right, I'll drive now.

Sorry I'm late.'

'We've only just got here ourselves.'

I thought it was civil of them. They were both in their flying-suits, one short, one tall, no indication of rank or ervice branch, strictly incognito, but the Mk XI Marauder utside on the tarmac had the standard roundels on it: I'd een it in the docking bay when I'd driven into the airport.

I suppose they felt they shouldn't go on looking at me like his without asking something about it because the short one aid:

'Have you had an accident?'

'Not really.'

It annoyed me because I hadn't had time to clean up since he petrol tank thing and I didn't have any time now so they ould keep their bloody remarks to themselves.

'Are you Mr Gage?'

'Yes.'

'Would you like some coffee?'

'Yes.'

We were in the bar alongside the Metropolitan Departure ate: they'd been waiting here because they couldn't miss me when I came through the main doors of the building, and heir own coffee hadn't long arrived.

We sat down at the little table and I said don't wait for me o they started stirring and the short one said:

'Lovely weather, isn't it?'

There weren't many people around: the boy making the coffee behind the bar, a holy man wrapped in his *gandoural* and his dreams in the corner by the Kodak stand, a young French couple perched half-asleep on a pile of baggage, a clerk in a fez coming through the doors and crossing the hall There was no sound of any flying.

Thoughts not a hundred per cent coherent because the pressure had come off, total energy output in progress fifteen minutes ago and now I was waiting for a cup of coffee and the nerves were having to adjust. But present situation comfortable and that was a help and besides she'd have reached base by now: I'd dropped her as near as it had been possible without exposing the image of the ambulance all over the place, no this one's Diane, our youngest, we've just had a call from her today, as a matter of fact, from Tunisia, she sounded quite homesick but otherwise fit. Yes, isn't she pretty?

Satisfactory.

'What?' I asked him.

'I said the weather's nice.'

'Yes. The trouble is it brings the insects out and you get them all over the windscreen, one firefly after another.'

So the tall one got the envelope out and gave it to me and I opened it and looked at the three photographs, mug-shot coverage with two profiles and a full face, and began tearing them up while they drank their coffee.

Everyone still looked all right, but the clerk in the fez had gone into the phone-box near the check-out counter and occurred to me that they could have been his headlights I'd seen in the mirror when I'd turned into the car park.

I drank my coffee. It was hot and bitter and I could taste the caffeine and I needed its heat and its alkaloid and I took it into my mouth slowly, as if it were ambrosia. They talked to each other about nothing in particular, a wonderful place to bring their wives, all those stars and palm-trees, talked to each other as if I weren't there or wouldn't be interested, letting me drink in peace, perhaps, and gather my strength.

Presumably without significance: a lot of people would come here to the airport to use the phones, the post office wasn't open at this time of night.

'How big's this thing?'

'I'm sorry?'

this thing you've got for me. How big is it?'

I was getting fed-up because one or two bits of glass were trying to work out and I smelt of singed hair and they were obviously wondering where the hell I'd been and I wasn't going to tell them, none of their bloody business.

Then they were talking in short embarrassed sentences and the penny dropped and I pulled my sleeve up higher, looking at my watch, after all they'd got their orders and they'd brought something pretty deadly for me in the Marauder.

'We could go and look at it,' the short one said. 'I expect you've been told it's flashpoint-zero freight.'

'Well, I didn't think it was a piss-pot.'

They shut up for a bit and I finished my coffee, wondering how far he'd been, Ahmed, from the scene of the fire when I'd left there: he'd been on his way and the ambulance was a distinctive vehicle and I hadn't been feeling bright enough to worry too much about headlights in the mirror so long as they didn't come any closer.

I didn't know what he looked like, Ahmed.

Incipient torpor and I was aware of it objectively, didn't feel at all like making an effort but there was a lot to do and I jerked my head up and thought watch it you're not safe.

'Let's go and look at it then.'

They said all right and we got up and they paid and the added nylon legs of their flying-suits made a faint *zoop, zoop, zoop* as we walked through the hall.

The clerk in the fez had left the telephone-box and was crossing towards the main doors. I didn't know whether he looked like a clerk in a fez, Ahmed.

It was better in the fresh air and I lost the dangerous urge to fall asleep as the caffeine began working on the nerves. There was a police guard on the Marauder, a young Tunisian with a peaked cap and white gauntlets and a holstered pistol, very smart and rather self-conscious because he wasn't used to being on special duty. We walked into the smell of kerosene and hot alloys and PVC and the short one climbed aboard so I assumed he was the pilot and the tall one ushered me on to the metal step and followed me up.

The flight cabin was roomier than I'd expected, with a chart-table and an astrodome and two freight lockers: the Marauder Mk XI was a modified version of the original Mk X short-range bomber and Tactical Air Command used it

for the kind of work that the standard models would n
jibbed at.

'Shut that door, will you?'

'Right.'

The pilot opened the lockers and brought out two black
rectangular containers with top and end grips and brass com-
bination locks, one of them looking lighter than the other
by the way he handled them. Both had Bostik airtight sealing
with rip-wire opening provision but there weren't any labels
and I assumed it was because anyone in charge of this cargo
would know what it was without having to read about it.

I picked them up one at a time. The smaller one was very
heavy, about four times the weight of a medium portable
typewriter but not much bigger.

'What are they?'

'M'mm? Not sure, actually.'

'Oh for Christ's sake can't you –'

'No, we can't. Awfully sorry.'

Typical armed services security attitude, so bloody coy
about everything, of course they knew what this cargo was.
In any case I didn't want more than three guesses because in
London-to-base signals exchanges it was called a 'device' so
these were obviously two components of one unit and you'd
have to fit them together before they'd work. The only thing
I didn't really know was why Control was sending me a
nuclear bomb with no prior instructions.

'I'll bring the car over.'

'Fair enough.'

They slid the door back for me and I climbed down and
began walking across the tarmac and saw a pair of headlights
just dimming out among the trees on the far side of the car
park where the ambulance was. Three more cars had got
here since I'd arrived and I could see movement along the
road from the town: a string of vehicles using only their
sidelights. So he did in fact look like a clerk in a fez, Ahmed,
and he'd called in the whole of his reserves and there wasn't
a hope of getting that device as far as base, not a hope in hell.

Chapter Eighteen

CHRONOMETER

Receiving you.

Shook him a bit: he was having to think.

Q-Quaker high Rharbi imp trans mat awheel.

Dation?

Croydon indigo.

I'd had to get him on the Embassy wavelength and use speech-code because this thing hadn't got an auto scrambler. Chirac had either left my KW 2000CA in the desert or brought it back for Loman to pick up and whichever it was he'd know I couldn't use it so he would have shut down that wavelength while he was in signals with London through the Embassy.

UMF?

I asked one of them and he said twelve minutes.

Synchronize please.

Double-oh two nine.

Plus twelve.

UMF double-oh four one.

He didn't say anything for a minute and I left him to it and looked down at the lights of a village as we began turning. The pilot had agreed we ought to set our course for Malta because that was where he'd told Kaifra he was going. Then we'd turn back and make a loop across the desert and go in from the south.

'Are we off their screens?'

'I don't know their range at Kaifra but fifty miles ought to be good enough because there's no other traffic.'

He was in the navigator's seat, the tall one. They were both cheerful enough but we all knew it was going to be a real swine and some of the jokes had got a bit thin since we'd taken off.

I watched the glow of the village and the white dome of a mosque reflecting the starlight as we came round in the turn.

I suppose we needn't have taken the trouble to head for Malta before we got off their screens but the Ahmed cell was badly up against it and they might decide to go into the control tower and ask questions at the gun-point.

Loman was still sulking. He'd been thinking everything wa all right because when I dropped her I told her I was goin to the airport to keep the rendezvous and pick up the devic and now he knew everything was all wrong because I ough not to be somewhere over Rharbi at ten thousand feet an he was having to face an entirely new pattern of hazards a zero notice. Well, that was what he was for.

'Feeling the cold?'

'We're not going to be stuck up here forever.'

'Frankly I wish we were.'

He laughed but we didn't join in. They'd jibbed at first bu I said they'd got to try so they'd worked things out and th pilot had said all right we'll have a go but this dolly weigh sixty-three thousand pounds with the amount of fuel she' have on board at our ETA and if we can't pull up she'll dra half the strip into the desert, so long as those oil-drilling chap don't mind.

It occurred to me that base might have gone off the air.

Hear me?

Hear you.

Is Fred all right?

Perfectly.

Reprimand in his tone and he could bloody well keep it Fred was the standard speech-code name for any third mem ber of an active cell and I wanted to know how she wa because the last time I'd seen her there'd been tears runnin down her sooty little face and if anyone of us survived thi trip I'd see those scaly bastards wrote her off the books befor they did anything else.

My eyes kept shutting and the navigator said somethin and I missed it and got my head up again.

'What?'

'Is there any chance of a flarepath on that strip?'

'No. They don't night-fly.'

'I see.' He said it rather stiffly.

'You've got landing-lights, haven't you?'

'Fortunately, yes.'

He didn't like me any more than Loman did but I couldn' help that. I think he was trying to find an excuse to call u the Air Ministry through Malta and get official permissio for the captain to hazard his ship but he couldn't do it i

of me because it'd be embarrassing: they'd been
ᴜered to make this rdv with an over-ranking contact and
at meant that whether they were pilot officers or air-vice-
arshals they still had to do what I told them, otherwise
ey'd have turned me down flat about the South 6 thing
d I knew that.

Quaker.

Hear you.

Friday Croydon indigo.

Roger.

I gave them back the headset.

Friday was rdv so he'd meet me at South 6 and presumably
wouldn't have to lug these rotten things as far as base and
at was something.

Then I suppose I just went to sleep because there wasn't
ᴀything else I had to do. She was rolling about in the flames
d I was trying to pull her clear and he was saying we'll
 down in three minutes so you'd better get into this thing.

'What thing?'

He was rigging some fabric stays across the freight-locker
ction and I gave him a hand because even if we didn't hit
ᴀything we were going to turn on an awful lot of decelera-
ᴏn on a strip that short and I didn't want to go through
e front window.

'Have you got room to turn round?'

'Just about.'

'Okay, then turn round and squat down with your back to

The pilot moved the flaps and we began running through
ᴅerdowns and they were both rather young considering their
sponsibilities so I said:

'I'm sorry about this.'

'Oh that's okay. It's just that these dollies are so terribly
 ᴩensive and we're always being told about the tax-payers'
ᴏney.'

ᴀe noise was pretty hellish because of the surface and the
versed thrust and I thought the nose-leg must have folded
.ck on impact but the angle was still roughly horizontal.
ᴀen the brakes came on and I was pressed backwards into
e fabric sling like a pea in a catapult and one of them was
ᴏuting to the other one, something about *distance* but I

couldn't hear the rest of it. A lot of low-pitch vib
coming in as the air-frame took the strain, smell of
rubber, be awkward if we hit a bad patch and the locke
burst open, not that anything could go off but we'd been
a lot of trouble getting it here, vibration starting to hamm
and someone yelling *won't make it* and I thought oh Chri
can't we ever get anything right, the front leg taking th
brunt of the shocks and everything trying to shake loose
the flight compartment, of course they'd known it would l
like this and that's why they'd looked at me as if I wa
barmy when I told them we'd got to do it.

Hit my shoulder when they dropped me through and a han
caught at me and then there was a dreadful quietness an
there was Loman sitting sideways on the front seat with h
arm hooked across the squab and his pale eyes watching m
and I said we got down all right did we?

'Yes.'

He didn't look very pleased.

I absorbed the environment: Chrysler. I was on the bac
seat with a rug over me. Zenith: 00.56. The ETA had bee
00.41. I don't like gaps in the timing.

'What happened?'

'In what precise way?'

Talked like a schoolmistress. He was very rattled.

'To the aircraft.'

'They wrote off the undercarriage.'

'Is that all?'

'It's quite sufficient.'

There was an engine starting up somewhere but I couldr
see anything. We were parked alongside the hangar and th
echo was coming back, sounded like a chopper. I listened
it and Loman didn't talk: he'd stopped looking at me no
and sat watching the road that ran from the main gates
the camp to the south end of the airstrip where the windso
drooped against the starfields.

'Is it for me?'

'What?'

'That chopper.'

'Yes.' He sounded edgy, even for Loman.

I suppose the waiting was getting on his nerves. The Ahm
cell had seen the Marauder go up and it wouldn't be lo

...e they heard it had come down all over the South 6
...ip instead of Malta and they'd get here as fast as they could.
...man knew they were on to it because if there'd been no
...e getting in my way at Kaifra Airport I would have left
...ere by road.

The helicopter was being warmed up, a comfortable *throp-*
...rop-throp from its rotor, aurally hypnotic, my head going
...wn, then she said London wanted to know the position,
...r voice about normal, not still upset or anything.

Loman said he'd send it direct.

...Situ Croydon indigo point skygo redmins point Q-Quaker
...le light-time standby ending point object present go con-
...ters point Tango out.

I thought he was being a bit optimistic but I suppose he was
...rried about getting a blast if he sounded too doubtful: they
...re already having to absorb the Marauder switch into
...ir thinking and it didn't take much to send them hysterical.
...e whole of this area was on the plotting table at the Bureau
...d they'd just received a situation signal and in spite of
...man's optimism they knew we were in a distinct red sector
...cause the Marauder had made a lot of noise coming down
...d every opposition cell would have been alerted: they'd
...t me out of the plane before anyone had come along to
...e what had made the crump but quite a gang of day-shift
...llers had gone down the airstrip from the living-quarters
...d the crew were still there explaining about engine trouble
...d forced landing conditions and all that cock and it
...uldn't be long before every camel-driver in Kaifra knew
...at a foreign military aircraft had gone into South 6 by
...ght.

...London would be sweating because what ought to have
...ppened was that I should have taken the device by road
...m the airport to base for Loman to brief me on it and
...at had happened was that I'd arranged for us both to be
...ting here with the thing on our lap and hoping to Christ
...body found us before we got airborne. At the first sign
... an adverse party in this area Loman would quietly melt
...o the middle distance because the director in the field is
...ver actually meant to operate *in* the field but only from
...al base, on the double principle that he's not trained in
...armed combat and if a mission blows up there has to be

195

someone to take home the pieces and have them an...
in the hope that one fine day someone's going to profit fr...
the lesson.

Loman would take the device with him because it w...
expensive and injurious and that would leave me on my ow...
to do what I could but I wasn't in a condition to do ve...
much and although he'd told them that Q-Quaker was al...
they wouldn't think much of my chances. So London w...
having the sweats.

Tango.
Tango receiving.
Embassy wants a repeat on 'redmins'.
They can have it.

She went off the air.

'Is that my end of the blower you've got there?'

'No,' he said.

I believed the little bastard. He'd told Chirac to leave ...
transceiver in the desert when he'd picked me up becau...
I'd need it again and there wasn't any point in dropping it...
second time in an area where there were rocks that co...
bust it up.

'Are you sending me back there, Loman?'

'We don't know yet.'

'Oh yes you bloody well do.'

Throp-throp-throp.

01.17.

Chirac shut off and the rotor began slowing above o...
heads. I hadn't taken a lot of notice when I'd come abo...
but I had a look around now and saw that the little necessit...
of life were here all right: two parachutes and the two bla...
containers.

'What's in that thing?'

'Cous-cous, mon ami.'

'I'm not hungry.'

'You will be,' Loman said. He sat peering through ...
curved Perspex like a goldfish in a bowl. From what I co...
see of it we were in a *gassi* between low dunes.

'Where are we?'

'In a *gassi*.'

'I know that.'

Chirac set the fuel taps at off. 'We are ten kilometres fr...

...combine South 5 and eleven kilometres from Kaifra.'

tried to think where that was, but any kind of mental ...rt induced a kind of grey-out and I gave it up because ...idn't seem to be anywhere in particular.

...Why here, Loman?'

...t's neutral ground.' He'd stopped peering through the ...spex bubble and was watching me critically. 'You have ...ee hours in which to get some sleep, so I suggest you do ...t.'

...Ie looked so depressed that I felt sorry for him, as far as ...I can feel sorry for a man like Loman.

...All right.' I wanted to ask him a few things because it was ...y 01.18.55 on the Zenith and he was going to let me sleep ...04.18.55 and that meant he'd got me lined up for a dawn ...p unless Control threw us a new one during the night; ...if he was in the mood to give me any answers I didn't ...at to have to work them out, singing in the ears, a sensation ...floating, the tick-tick-tick of the chronometer near my ...d. 'Loman.'

...fes?'

...Have we still got a mission running?'

...Ill I heard as his voice went faint was something about ...don and I suppose he was saying depends on.

...st stage, second stage and detonator.

...Ie showed me three times: annular clamp, by-pass conduit, ...n body-locking with three-start threads. It was easy enough ...I didn't object to the repetitions because you had to do ...roperly or the thing wouldn't go off.

...t's essential that no sand enters these threads.'

...Noted. How powerful is this model?'

...t has the equivalent of one hundred tons of trinitrotoluene. ...e Americans have used similar devices in the Sahara for ...ting wells, but this one has been modified for a ground-...st operation, reducing fall-out and giving a low Mach ...ve with a relatively small residual radiation range.'

...n figures?'

...One thousand yards. In still air with low humidity you will ...safe at one mile, and should set the timer accordingly.'

...o it was a mini but the soot-black finish and the castellated ...ining nuts and the knowledge that it would bring down the ...t Office Tower at one blow gave it a potent aspect. It was

so very quiet, standing on its flat end with the three ⌐
crouched around it.

'Pouf!' said Chirac, 'hein?'

He turned away and opened the polyester picnic box
took out the Thermos of *cous-cous*. There was no meat ⌐
it and we used two of the plastic bowls. Loman said ⌐
eaten not long before we'd made the rdv at South 6 and
had Chirac probably but you'll get a Frenchman joining
at any time and in any place and with whatever kind of m
but especially an hour before dawn in the Sahara if it's c
cous.

I'd slept for most of the allotted period but Loman
been talking to London quite a bit and I'd partly heard s
of the panic: a lot of the trouble was that the signals had
to go from here to Kaifra to Tunis to Crowborough
London and back and had involved three automatic scr
blers and two codes and the normal telephone delay betw
Crowborough and Control, but most of the panic was ⌐
the need to liaise the Bureau's international monito
facilities with the controller running the mission and to
it within the few hours left before dawn. The local situa
here was known and the risks calculated, but addition
London was using what amounted to a scanner that wo
pick up any event internationally that might have a bea
on the end-phase of the Tango mission: if for example
president of the United Arab Republic happened to be as
sinated at any given moment then London would get the n
almost immediately through the monitoring facilities
Control might realize straight away that an Egyptian
operating in Kaifra could conceivably get orders to cease
action.

I didn't think it would happen. Nor did London and
was why London was having the sweats. I wasn't long ou
sleep but it didn't take a lot of brain-think to see that Lo
was now driven to mounting a last desperate throw, bec
the Marauder thing had made it clear to every local opposi
cell that I was still very much in business and therefore
UK was still certain that Tango Victor was somewhere
this area. Chirac had made the short hop from South ⌐
the *gassi* here without picking up a tag from any one of
airfields around Kaifra but when we took-off for the ⌐

…t we'd be running a gauntlet of ground observers and
…ustic units.

…oman had said I'd need something like forty minutes after
… drop to set up the device in safety and trigger it and if
…irac could fly me into the target zone and leave me with
…t amount of time to work in without drawing in a whole
…ck of opposition agents I thought he'd be bloody lucky.

'What's that glow?' asked Loman.

'The moon rising.' Chirac spooned his *cous-cous*.

'Why is it diffused like that?'

'It is a sandstorm over there.'

'Will it affect your mission?'

'*Pas du tout*. It is two hundred miles away and moving to
… west. I have been watching it and there will not be any
…uble.'

…oman drew the spigots and freed the clamp and boxed the
…vice into its separate containers. I decided not to look at
… watch so frequently: it was becoming a habit and it was
…sign of nerves. If we took off at the appointed time we
…uld do it in eleven minutes from now.

'So what does London say?'

…oman didn't look at me. He doesn't like briefing you until
…re's precisely time enough left to give you the whole story
…hout leaving an interval before the go, and he's perfectly
…ht because it allows a psychological sag and you'll start
…lling over the things and asking silly questions but I
…ldn't help that. There were things I wanted to know and
… was going to tell me.

'London?' he said blandly.

'That place with the clock.'

'The end-phase has been approved.'

'Oh come on, Loman, give me the bloody information.'

…Voice rather sharp and Chirac flicked a look at me and I
…s very annoyed because my nerves were more touchy than
… thought and that's always dangerous and I'd have to do
…nething about it. It was the snivelling little organism, that
…s all, saying we don't want to go back there with all those
…rid birds and that nasty gas, always worrying about its
…n instead of the job in hand.

…oman went on sulking for half a minute and then said:]
'The objective has to be obliterated.'

He meant I'd got to go and blow up the freighter.

'Why?'

There was no technical problem: he wasn't obliged to s
anything that couldn't be said in front of Chirac and I co
do what I liked about that.

'It's the only way of dispersing the gas.' He checked
watch and looked back at the diffused glow on the horiz
'The heat of a nuclear reaction is required.'

I finished the *cous-cous* in the bowl and Chirac went to d
me out some more but I shook my head.

'Is there any protein?'

Loman fished in the box and gave me a square packet a
I peeled the skin off and ate it slowly: by the taste, it v
mainly processed soya. I said:

'You know some Arabs found that aeroplane, don't yo

'Of course they didn't.' Still upset because I'd spoken
him like that in front of Chirac.

'What did they die of then, those Arabs in the clinic?'

'Nerve-gas.'

He wanted me to ask him how they could have be
exposed to the gas without finding the freighter and I was
going to: Loman had the knack of making you as pet
minded as he was. I said:

'Some of the drillers think it was ergot. There's a medi
unit testing the bread supplies. The nurses at the clinic s
it was a magnetic storm.'

He waited long enough to let Chirac see that I didn't kn
what the hell I was talking about.

'The properties of Zylon-4-Gamma are peculiar. By
nature it is humid and – as you discovered – heavier than a
and in addition it is given pronounced surface-adhes
characteristics by the manufacturing laboratory, enhanci
its effectiveness as a weapon of war. When Tango Vic
came down and a gas cylinder was damaged on impact, so
of the gas remained in the aircraft, but some was eviden
released by overspill and formed the characteristic bubl
This was invisible, freely afloat at ground level and of cou
subject to the influence of winds. It seemingly was blo
across the caravan track between Ghadamis and Kaifra, si
within twenty kilometres of Kaifra there were fourteen Ar
found dead, also their camels, also sundry birds of prey t
had flown down to feed. The Arabs who died in the cli

inhaled considerably less than their companions, and
ere able to reach Kaifra.'

So that was why I was still here.

Their situation had been different from mine: they'd been
aught in the open desert and couldn't escape but I'd been
aught in a confined space, and could. They hadn't known
here the gas was and they could have run deeper into it
hen they'd tried to run clear; inside the freighter I'd known
here the stuff was and I'd known where to run to get away
om it. There'd been other factors in play: moving slowly
nder the open sky, as they'd been doing all their lives, they'd
en taken utterly by surprise and must have thought in terms
f a visitation by fiends at the behest of a disapproving Allah,
eir fear transfixing them. My mind had already been con-
tioned to think in terms of a toxic gas, and inhalation had
en blocked immediately by reflex as I'd started to get clear.

'Isn't there any kind of gas-mask available?'

'You would have been given one, in that event. So would
e crew of the aeroplane.'

Their situation had been different from mine and from the
rabs': they'd been conditioned to the risk of a toxic gas
ak but the crash landing had slowed their escape, either
cause they'd been partly stunned or the door had become
mmed, possibly both.

'Who's been making this bloody stuff?'

Loman said nothing so I left it. There wasn't anything new
e could tell me about that gas: when I went back inside
ango Victor I'd know what to expect.

'Where was it being delivered?'

'This is not the time to discuss – '

'I will go away, *mes amis.*' Chirac opened the starboard
or and swung his feet through the gap.

'There is no need, Chirac. There's nothing to discuss in any
se.'

'*Comme même,* I shall stretch the legs.'

He dropped through and I watched his dark compact figure
oving away against the starlit flank of the dune.

'Algeria,' I said, 'or Egypt.'

Quickly: 'You've identified a cell of the UAR network?'

'Yes.'

It'd be a signal for London.

'There are probably more than one.'

'More than one Egyptian cell?'

'Yes.'

I finished the protein and screwed up the paper and flicked it through the doorway. 'This gas was made in England, was it?'

'Clandestinely, of course.'

'By private initiative?'

'Certain members of an otherwise reputable laboratory have been interviewed by the Special Branch. Unfortunately the laboratory had been placed under government contract and although the production of this gas was made in secret by criminal elements, you can imagine what would happen to the reputation of the UK itself if Tango Victor were found by – shall we say – an ill-wisher.'

'And what's going to happen to the reputation of the United Arab Republic when we tell everyone they've been buying BCW material within six months of the Geneva banning?'

He turned slowly to look at me.

'What reputation? The difference is there. In any case it won't occur. The UK will tell nobody, since the gas was unfortunately made in England and any accusation would of course boomerang.'

'There'll be a public trial for the people who made the stuff.'

'Unavoidably. The image of the UK will receive a certain degree of damage. Regrettably, a criminal element has been manufacturing and selling a deadly chemical warfare material. Nothing more. We shall hope to avoid the disastrous outcome of much more serious revelations.'

'You mean those poor bastards in the clinic have officially died of ergot in the bread supplies.'

'You would oblige me by remembering that.'

'And the outbreak in Mali? What was the death roll?'

'Three hundred.'

'Jesus. An outsize bubble on the move. Was it lobbed there?'

'There's an Algerian missile site in the south Sahara and the gas was being tested for the United Arab Republic.'

'*In vivo.*'

'How otherwise would its precise effect be known? But in fact the Mali batch was too powerful: the intention was to induce an incapacitating state of anxiety for a period of a few days. The batch in Tango Victor is less lethal but still

oo strong. What Egypt would be seeking is of course the
onvenient dilution providing this effect, enabling her to take
ver control in Tel Aviv without casualties and therefore
vithout too great an international motion of censure.'

He looked at his watch.

In the background silence the tick of the instrument-panel
hronometer was insistent, its illuminated dial sharply defined.
There were four minutes to go.

'You'd better brief me.'

'Yes.'

He shifted his position on the observer's seat as he opened
he map, and the Alouette moved slightly on its suspension.
rummaged in the rations box and found some dehydrated
oney tablets and peeled one off the strip.

'Chirac will be using a flight pattern designed to confuse the
coustic observation posts as much as possible. You will go
rom here to the Petrocombine South 5 drilling camp and
verfly the airstrip, setting course for this point here in the
Roches Vertes complex and then flying for three kilometres
long the scheduled air route from Ghadamis to El Oued
cross the Algerian desert. You will then proceed at 203°
direct to the target area.'

I checked it twice and asked him where the listening-posts
vere meant to be.

'From local intelligence we know there are four posts in
his line from South 5 to No. 2 Philips radio tower. There
nay be others farther west.'

I looked up from the map.

'What d'you think our chances are, Loman?'

He must have been expecting it but tried to look surprised.

'Of doing what?'

'Reaching the target area without bringing a whole pack
of tags or interceptors into the air.'

I'd made my point and he had the grace to give me a
straight answer without pretending to consider the actual
odds.

'Unpromising.'

I suppose he was spiritually exhausted or physically over
the edge of fatigue because he suddenly sagged, his hands
resting loosely on the spread map and his pale eyes closing
for a moment.

'That is the only possible flight pattern we can use.'

'Taking us within seven kilometres of this end listening post.' I'd begun sweating. 'What d'you imagine their effective range is? About fifty?'

'Perhaps.'

He was sitting perfectly still and I knew he was waiting for me to blow up in his face but I wasn't going to do it because it wouldn't help us and Christ we needed help and a new question was coming into my mind and I tried to get rid of it before it could do any harm, before it could bring down the last few bricks of the mission that still appeared to be standing. But it wouldn't go.

Question. When does a director in the field start losing his sense of proportion? When does the strain of watching the slow demolition of his plans begin to tell on him and take him beyond the point where reason can only be ignored with fatal results? *When does he break?*

Perhaps it is when he finishes up sitting in a helicopter on the edge of the Sahara in the early hours of a sleepless night and awaiting the dawn of a hopeless day, his hands lying unnerved on a map where the only uncharted feature is the ruin he knows is there but refuses to recognize: those last few tumbled bricks of the thing he was trying too hard to build.

I wouldn't expect a man like Loman to abandon a mission if success or even survival looked unattainable. I would expect him to keep on working at it, no longer for what he could make of it but for its own sake, once it had gone beyond the stage where any useful purpose remained. I would expect him to become obsessive, to make a shrine of it: and I would expect him to regard his executive in the field as a natural sacrifice.

'Loman,' I said, 'when did you get London's directive on this end-phase?'

He was now genuinely surprised, couldn't follow me.

'Just before 03.00 hours.'

I didn't think he'd actually lie about a thing like that. I didn't think he'd lost his reason: I just thought reason was now being subjugated to the point where he might have me killed off for nothing.

'Have they been given total intelligence on the disposition of those listening-posts?'

Then he saw what I meant.

'I'm sorry, Quiller. The objective has to be destroyed.'

ondon insists.'

'For what reason?'

Because you can ask questions if you think your life is being
oved into a specific hazard: they don't bind your hands
ehind you and drive you blindfold against the cannon.

'There are two reasons,' Loman said. He sounded perfectly
alm and I thought this is how they sound when their fantasies
ave had to take control of them to save them from the
ality they can't any longer face. 'It requires several days of
xposure to the ultra-violet rays in sunlight to alter the
omic structure of Zylon-K-Gamma and render it harmless.
' anyone attempted to move the cargo in that aeroplane,
ot knowing what it was, enough gas could be spilled to
ipe out the population of Kaifra, particularly since the *Ghibli*
a south wind. The United Kingdom would be responsible.
econdly a nuclear explosion would not only change the
omic structure of the gas instantaneously, but would obli-
rate the aeroplane: and this is essential. It will be known
at a new BCW weapon was being manufactured in the UK
ng after the banning of such weapons by the Geneva
onvention, and even though it was done clandestinely it can
ly be embarrassing and the Government will have to explain
ow it was allowed to occur. This is bad enough. It would
e disastrous at this moment when Israel and the Arab world
onfront each other if it were also known that a consignment
f chemical warfare gas had been flown from the UK to
orth Africa. Allow me to borrow the old cliché of a spark
a powder barrel.'

I watched his reflection in the glass of the black-dialled
ronometer. He was looking at me, waiting. His face was
s calm as his speech had been: reaction-concealment was
cond nature to him and that was why I was worried when
e'd suddenly sagged a few minutes ago.

He would remain perfectly calm, I assumed, after his mind
ad slipped its focus. He would give careful and cogent
asons for driving his executive headlong against the cannon.

Decision necessary: stay with the mission or get out. Trust
is efficient and merciless little bastard all the way or take a
ep back and see him for what he might be: an intelligence
irector turned psychopath.

Chirac, a dark figure against the pale flank of the dune,
aiting. The chronometer ticking in the quietness, the face

205

of Loman reflected on the dial, waiting.

Do what he says and do it even if you know it's likely to kill you, even if you know he'll never grieve. Or save yourself, tell him no.

The scream of a ferret in the dark.

Or refusal.

Chapter Nineteen

EPITAPH

The slam of the wind and the known world gone, the sky on the ground and the sand overhead, spinning.

Sink rate rising.

Tumbling now and a lot of noise and the collar of his flying-suit flapping because the zip had pulled open when I'd jumped. Chirac had lent it to me, helping me on with it in the pre-dawn cold. A good man, Chirac, a man I'd like to see again and probably never would. *Adieu, mon ami.*

It was a low level drop at low speed and the conditions were different from the first time: he'd only given me two hundred feet to do it and that wasn't much, even over sand, but he said there was rising ground towards the north-east, the remains of an eroded escarpment, and it could conceivably bounce our acoustic irradiation and fox the scanners, you never know your luck. You've got to try everything when you haven't got a hope in hell, everything.

Blood pooling in the head, the eyes swollen, the air noise very loud and the terminal velocity coming up close to a hundred knots so pull the thing, lying awkwardly face up but there's not much room left so *pull it.*

Canopy deployed.

Pendulous oscillation setting in and I tried to control it with the shroud lines but couldn't, hadn't the strength, because the opening shock had jerked me upright like a puppet and the harness webbing had bitten into old bruises and all I could do was hang in the air getting my breath, nausea threatening because of the oscillation, fight it.

Swing, swing, swing.

Cheer up, the worst is over, so forth.

Very queasy and I got hold of a line, two lines, pulled on them, an improvement, going almost straight down like a shuttle-cock. Don't think about the ground: it's not going to be comfortable so we'll just settle for that and shut up about it.

I caught sight of the supply 'chute three times during the drop, lower than I was because I'd shoved it overboard before I'd jumped, and not bad timing: it was nearer the rock outcrop, almost on top of it.

It would have been nice, yes, if Chirac could have landed me in his Alouette and waited for the estimated forty minutes while I fiddled with the thing and then taken me away before the bang went off, a civilized approach to the end-phase of a mission, a taxi for the executive in the field. But the listening-posts were going to pick us up on their scanners unless the rising ground to the north-east diffused our sound-wake enough to fox them, and there was a chance they'd take us for a prospecting crew or one of the Algerian desert-reconnaissance machines.

But if Chirac put her down they'd get an immediate fix on our position and I wouldn't have time to set up the bang before we got smothered in ticks. No go.

Sand coming up fast don't think about it.

The first light of the day was spilling across the horizon, touching the tips of the rocks with rose and colouring the crests of the dunes and leaving the last of the night pooled in the hollows. Chirac had done his homework and the timing had been precise. With the opposition cells alerted by the Marauder's switch to South 6 we couldn't hope to repeat a night approach by sailplane: this time we had to go right into the target area with a zero margin of error so that I could set up the device as soon as I landed, trigger it and leave an escape-delay on the detonator sufficient to get me clear.

Nor could we night-fly the mission all the way because dead-reckoning was out of the question: it would demand a margin of error and we couldn't afford one. Chirac had to see the rock outcrop, home in on it and overfly, and do it without altering speed so that the doppler factor would remain constant on the scanners. Nor could we fly by daylight all the way without being seen, even if we flew at dune level from the south.

So Chirac had flown through the last of the dark with an ETA of dawn plus one over the target area and he'd got it spot on.

I could still hear him, heading south-west for Ghadami on a decoy run before he turned back to Kaifra.

Estimate five seconds to go, relax or you'll break a joint.

I tried to turn bodily but it set up the first swing of an oscillation and I didn't want to land at an angle so I stopped. In any case there was no problem: the supply 'chute had been close to the rocks when I'd last sighted it.

The decision had been made rather formally. He is like that, Loman. Even when the chances of a successful end-phase are almost nil and he's staring straight into the brick dust as the mission collapses he remains rather formal.

The situation, Quiller, is simply this. Even if we have only a one per cent chance of completing our mission, London would appreciate our making the attempt.

Then he'd got out of the observer's seat and dropped on to the sand and walked away in the direction opposite from Chirac's, to stand there with his back to me. His gesture was symbolic, accurate and characteristic: he couldn't go far from the helicopter because if I accepted the end-phase we'd have to take off in three minutes, so he went as far as he could and indicated by turning his back that he was to all intents and purposes out of sight. The final decision was to be my own and no pressure was to be put on me by my director in the field, even by his presence.

Ground close watch it.

The situation, Quiller, is simply this. Even if you have only a one per cent chance of surviving the end-phase, London would appreciate your making the attempt.

One always has to paraphrase just a little, with Loman.

Then I'd called to Chirac to start up and I was here because I was an old ferret sharp of tooth and I knew my warrens and I'd run them before and I'd run them again because the chance I believe in is the one-per-center and that is the way of things, as I see them. Pure logic, of course: the high risks of my trade drew me to it and that is why I ply it and the greater the risk the more I am drawn and when the risk is expressed as a one per cent chance of survival then I'm hooked and damned and hell-bound and don't get in my way.

Their small heads, I suppose, were raised there among the

hadowed crevices of rock as I drifted down, a great circular
betal reflected in their gold-rimmed eyes.

Side of a dune and I was badly placed and pitched flat and
he sand burst and I blacked out.

The supply 'chute was draped across a spur of rock like a
heet hung out to dry. The shroud lines were badly twisted
nd I had to cut some of them before I could free the two
ontainers, and with each jerk of the knife everything went
ed again and I had to rest, leaning on the hot surface of the
ocks. When I could manage it I dragged the canopy down
nd folded it and stuffed it into a fissure: all they needed
vas a landmark but we were all right at the moment because
here were some vultures coasting not far away and they'd
ave sheered off if there were any aircraft about.

When I'd looked at the containers I went across to the
iche in the rocks where I'd left my camp. Chirac had found
he transceiver when he'd come for me last evening, and
towed it here out of the sun's direct heat.

Tango.

Loman wasn't going to like it.

He would have been trying to call me up, I knew that, but
hadn't set to receive before I'd dragged the canopy out of
ight. Chirac would have picked him up in the *gassi* an hour
go and dropped him somewhere near base and since then
te'd been trying to call me and by this time he'd be certain
ve'd failed and he was right and he wasn't going to like it
vhen I told him.

Tango receiving.

I could hear them scuttling, perhaps in fright at his voice,
harp and metallic and amplified.

I said I was in the target area.

What was the delay?

Bad landing.

Are you injured?

No.

Then I saw the vultures drifting away and knew that there
vasn't any doubt left: we'd hit a dead end. We'd thought this
nission had an all-or-nothing end-phase, either I'd blow
Tango Victor off the face of the earth or the opposition
vould get her and kill me before I could do it. The idea of a
compromise hadn't occurred to us: that I'd get here for

nothing, and too late.

I would appreciate your situation report.

Talked like a bloody schoolteacher. I'd soon stop that.

We've had it, Loman. The timer's been smashed.

Five seconds.

Please repeat.

I suppose he had a point. When you're sending the last signal of a mission you might as well make it clear what you're saying, if only for the record.

The supply 'chute came down on the rock outcrop and the impact has smashed the timing mechanism.

A longer pause. I waited, listening to the sky.

My lips tasted salty, had blood on them. It had been dripping on to the shale and I'd only just noticed it and I wiped my hand across, well, what would you expect, I'd hit the side of the dune with my face and opened the stitches.

Loman asked:

What is that noise?

Helicopters.

Silence from the black speaker-grille.

In his mind he was trying to reorganize the end-phase, signalling London for directives, recreating the ruins I'd just told him about. And he couldn't do it.

How long have they been there?

About a minute and a half.

How far away?

Five kilometres, maybe six.

I watched them. There were three of them.

What is your situation appraisal?

I wiped my hand across my mouth again.

They got us on the scanners but not too accurately. They're starting a square search due east of me, three of them.

Are they moving towards your position?

No. Directly away, at right-angles.

I didn't see it could matter. I didn't see it could matter to him or the mission or London because if they found me I was a dead duck and if they didn't find me there wasn't anything I could do here. I wished he'd stop asking questions, too tired for it, not on form.

Are they military aircraft or civilian?

Oh for Christ's sake Loman we've had it, I've told you the timer's been smashed, didn't you hear me?

Are they military, or civilian?

I shut my eyes, let them water, sand had got into them when
d hit the dune.

Ten seconds.

I can't see from this distance. They're close to the sun.

I am going off the air for thirty minutes but please keep
en to receive.

Silence.

Thirty minutes: he'd signal London now for a directive, ask
em what to do, but there was nothing to do. He'd tell Diane
use the phone and contact Chirac and request him to stand
y with the helicopter but it'd only be a gesture because
hirac wouldn't be able to pick me up without exposing the
rget area and if he came in after they'd found me there
uldn't be anything to pick up anyway, nothing alive.

I opened my eyes and squinted towards the horizon. The
ree choppers were moving back along their initial course,
rther south by one prescribed strip of their sweep. They
uld see these rocks but they couldn't see me because I was
shadow and sighting through a gap in the shale. I'd buried
y 'chute under the sand before I'd come here, and last
ening Chirac had taken down the fabric shelter I'd set up
ar the plane, so there was nothing for them to see.

The birds had come down five hundred yards away and I
atched them. They'd obviously been there when I'd landed
d the 'chute had startled them and now they were back,
eding on the pilot and navigator. The helicopter crews
uldn't have noticed them or they'd come to investigate
cause they'd know that the presence of vultures marked
e presence of recent life.

Urge to sleep now overwhelming. I took a final look at the
ner to make sure it hadn't been the subject of hallucination
t it hadn't changed: two of the brass lugs were snapped off
ar the flange and half the main body of the mechanism
d been so badly impacted that I could see one of the inter-
ediary gear-trains lying askew and thrown out of mesh.
rictly no go.

I crawled deeper between the rocks because of the dark
ghtmare shapes over there: they reminded me of terror
d I didn't want them to see me, to come for me in my
ep.

My eyes closed and the great weight of my head came to

211

rest against the rock-face, a last thought, we got close, te
London we got close.

Said I could hear him.

Caught me in a low sleep-curve, groggy.

Zenith 06.31.

I have been in signals with London.

They were still there, I could just catch their distant purrin;
throp-throp-throp.

Can you hear me?

Hear you.

What is the position of the helicopters now?

Damn his eyes, won't ever leave you alone.

I reached for the water bottle and got the cap off and dran
tasting the blood on my mouth. The sun's heat was beginnin
to strike into the niche and I couldn't get my legs in the shad
Took my time, thirsty, and he said could I hear him and
didn't answer till I'd finished my drink because that was mo
important. Then I told him:

They're shifting to a second square.

How clearly can you see them?

About distance shot.

Could they see you, if you went into the open?

No.

Of course I should have known.

*Will you please verify that the timing mechanism is out o
action, irreparably?*

Verified.

Is there any damage to the main components?

No.

Please verify.

I should have known by his insistence on these things.

There's no external damage. The timer took the shock.

What is your physical condition?

I need sleep.

He considered this.

*Are you capable of carrying the device as far as th
freighter?*

Should have known, shouldn't I, what he was going to d
to me.

Perfectly capable.

Silence for half a minute. I thought he was calculatin

omething. Maybe he was.

Quiller.

Hear you.

London would like you to proceed with the end-phase.

How the hell can I do that if the timer won't —

I didn't finish.

Got it now.

The sun was burning on my legs and I drew them up, orcing myself higher against the rock-face, the effort in-reasing the circulation and bringing me fully awake. I would ave to think about this. He was saying:

Control has asked me to point out that your action would e seen as generous, and therefore much appreciated.

Death sentence.

Civil of them.

He didn't say anything; I suppose he was giving me time to aink. They were all being very considerate.

Give me ten minutes, Loman, will you?

Of course. There's no immediate hurry.

I clipped the mike back and stared through the cleft in the ocks. They were still at it, their ragged plumage fluttering s they jerked about, hooking at the meat. That, at least, I ould be spared.

Of course the potential expendability of an executive is part f the contract and we know what we're signing. The Bureau the sacred bull and its first credo is that the mission is aore important than the man, otherwise you wouldn't be sued with a capsule if you wanted one, on your way arough clearance. And after all, providing you accept the act at any given time during an operation that you've become xpendable the actual means of despatch don't matter: all e ask is that it shall be quick and the only thing quicker aan a cyanide pill is putting your thumb on a nuclear etonator.

I couldn't assess my chances when they shifted their search ver this area and found me: the thing was that I'd want initiate some kind of hostile action and they'd finish me nyway. That situation was entirely academic in any case ecause if London wanted me to complete the mission I'd ave time to do it before I was seen.

And I didn't have any choice. I had contracted to hazard ay life if the needs of a mission demanded and that was that.

213

I was only taking time out to think about it because if the
was an alternative I wanted to use it, but I knew there was
one: Loman would throw me to the dogs if it suited h
purposes and his present purposes were to go back to Lond
with his instructions carried out and Tango Victor obliterate
Technically there wasn't an alternative because we didn't ha
time to send for a new delay-mechanism and without one t
only way to detonate was to press the button myself.

Sense of unreality creeping on me because the whole thi
was so calculated: I'd come close to dying in Tunis amo
the flying glass and in Kaifra when the marksman had me
his sights but there'd been no time to think about it, and no
there was.

Bloody little organism up on its back legs and whinin
don't want to die, *shuddup*.

My ten minutes wasn't up but I'd had all the time I need
and it was no good sitting here with this strange hollo
feeling, the almost physical sensation of the life blood begi
ning to drain away. Possibly normal: a question of mi
over matter and when the mind knows that death is immine
the body starts dying automatically, it happens in Africa, p
a curse on a man and he'll die without a mark on him.

Irrelevant.

Mission running, end-phase initiated, instructions perfect
clear, so go on, pick up that mike.

Loman.

Receiving you.

Just tell me again, will you, what exactly I'm going
achieve?

No change of tone when he spoke. He'd known I'd have
do it. He'd known, earlier this morning when he'd walk
across the sand and stood with his back to me, that I would
refuse. And so had I.

They're bastards in London, mean with the money a
slow on promotion and that sort of thing, but certain gestur
are made in the name of decency: despite the contracts v
sign they like us to feel that we're not irrevocably committe
that when the crunch comes we'll still have a part in t
decision-making. But it's only a gesture, the same as bei
asked if you'd like a blindfold before the bolts click back.

It is less a question of what you'll achieve than of what y
will vouchsafe your country to avoid. If the objective is r

*estroyed, the influence of the United Kingdom at the inter-
ational conference tables will be greatly enfeebled, and her
ork for peace tragically undermined.*

I waited but that was all he said. The second half of the
quation was tacit: compared with these disastrous even-
alities, what value had the life of one man?

All right, Loman.

Pause.

You are prepared to complete your mission?

Did you think I'd back out?

No.

Never make a mistake, do you?

Wished I hadn't said it but an hour from now he'd be alive
nd I wouldn't and I hated him for that, for that alone and
or nothing else.

*The most important mistake I could have made, Quiller,
ould have been to choose an executive in the field with a
ense of responsibility less admirable than your own. Please
ccept my compliments.*

A certain style: the man had a certain style, give him that.

Good of you.

She'd be there, I supposed, listening and not liking it, her
wn fault, she shouldn't have looked for work in this trade,
er downy arms and her sooty face and her quick little way
f nodding, all I knew, really.

Loman, is that girl there?

Yes. Do you want to —

*No. Just do something for me. Get her out of it when this
ission's over, get her out of this bloody trade, it's not for
er. Do that for me.*

Then it occurred to me that this was the final signal, so I
nded it the way the little bastard would want me to, right
ut of the copy-book.

Tango out.

215

Chapter Twenty

DETONATION

They flew up screaming as I neared them, one of them wit
meat hanging from its beak. I remembered them from th
nightmare, and had to stand still for a while, the swe
running on me, until something inside the spirit of a dyin
man was roused to his last needs, and I managed to go o
towards the freighter, the weight of the two containers slowin
my feet through the sand.

The birds didn't go far away: I'd interrupted their feedin
and by the time I reached the doorway they'd settled agai
I thought it odd how the chemical processes of life were sti
going on: a minute ago I'd drunk the last of the water, an
these birds were busy absorbing nourishment, but very soo
we would no longer exist. The scene was surrealistic: a ma
and some birds perpetuating the motions of life in a dese
landscape, without purpose.

*The influence of the United Kingdom at the internatione
conference tables,* so forth. Purpose, yes.

I took great care going into the freighter because some o
the cylinders had been lying at an angle and could fall if
caused vibration. This is characteristic of the end-phase of
mission: you take pains to see that at the eleventh hour yo
don't wreck everything you've been working for.

I didn't think I could go into the actual freight section an
set up the device without the risk of inhaling gas: the move
ment of my feet could stir up the bubble pooling there. Th
flight-deck wasn't contaminated because it was at a highe
level, so I carried the containers inside and slid the doo
closed after me, switching on the torch.

Stifling heat, tendency to claustrophobia, not because th
cabin was small but because I knew I would never leave it i
the form of a living creature. Rapid increase of sweatin
pulse accelerated, mouth dry: the organism mortally afrai
and the forebrain alone driving it on, forcing its hand
arranging the movement of its fingers, performing the nece
sary motions that would assemble the black-painted com
ponents as required.

Annular clamp, the brass threads smelling of silicone lubricant and an additive, the toggle action precise and almost silent as I brought the levers home and set the pins.

By-pass conduit, the channels lined up by a sprung ball-and-socket: I listened for the click and the lingering musical tone of the spring.

Main body-locking, the three-start thread fairly coarse, but even so there was provision for alignment by sighting, to avoid the risk of crossing them. Push-fit pin location, precise to less than a thousandth: the entire mechanism was built to maximum-security specifications, giving me confidence in it.

It had to perform with absolute satisfaction and somewhere in the last confused interplay of thoughts I felt adamant about this: since I was prepared to detonate it I didn't want it to fail me because of slip-shod work at some stage during its manufacture.

Oven heat.

Aware of my breathing, rather loud in the confines and faster than normal. Sweat in the eyes, stinging. Some area of the brain noting the immediate environment, instinct plus training: appraisal of physical factors in hazardous situation. Instruments and controls, parachutes, pair of tennis shoes in the open locker, carved teakwood statuette, copy of *Playboy*, so forth. Nothing significant.

As I worked I could hear them cackling outside. The sand was still piled against the Perspex windows and I couldn't see them but they were much in my mind, adding to the incipient terror that was trying to overwhelm conscious thought.

Cackle cackle.

The awful thing was that I couldn't hear them without seeing them in my imagination, tugging and pulling as they fed. If they'd been doing anything else, if they'd simply been flying around like ordinary birds, they would have kept me company in these last minutes. As it was, the world I was leaving had the aspect of nightmare.

But I was ready now.

The activator was a cylindrical spigot, not very different from a press-button but two inches across, its surface grooved to mate with the grooves I'd seen on the timing-mechanism. The extent of travel was less than half an inch, the extent by which the activator stood proud of the casing. Thumb pressure would suffice: the mechanism of the timer had been sensitive rather than heavy. I put my thumb on the grooved surface.

The organism was at this point in a state of excitation: the blind instinct to preserve itself was in fierce conflict with the will. I think it would have been easier for me if I'd been in fit condition: there wouldn't have been this need to drive a bruised and terrified subconscious into contributing to the final act of extinction. In the confused cerebral state there was only one area with any kind of ability to reason, and here the technician in me was observing the situation in his own terms and noting things like the complementary factors of requirements and facilities available, the requirements being to press the activator and detonate the device, the facilities being my thumb and its motor nerves.

At some time this idea became linked with philosophical considerations containing a marked awareness of self: the activator has to be pressed, therefore all we need is pressure; I can exert pressure with my thumb, but I'd rather it were something else because if I press this thing with my thumb it's going to kill me.

Cerebration is very fast and I doubt whether more than half a minute had passed before the whole idea took shape. I could still hear them cackling, and another sound, a kind of secret laughter, gloating and vengeful, rising from the vortex of my own subliminal.

Vaguely aware that I was laughing at the birds out there, the horrible sounds inside me echoing theirs, but not a lot of time to think about it, the need was to move back from the edge of clinical hysteria and perform acts.

The first was to remove my thumb from the detonator.

Of the various objects on the flight-deck I thought the carved teakwood statuette was most suitable. For a little while I held it, feeling its shape with my fingertips. It was a couple of feet long, the carving quite good except where the tool had slipped and one of the feet had been narrowed; or it could have been damaged at some time and the break smoothed off. It was Nahudian, obviously a god, wide nosed and with tribal markings on the forehead, a burning brand held at the side: perhaps it was N'Gami, god of lightning.

Other material was available and I wedged the nuclear

device on its flat end between the seats and moved the throttle levers parallel with each other, driving the feet of the statuette between them to inhibit lateral movement. At the other end I used the parachute packs as lateral guides, so that N'Gami's body lay horizontal, his head resting on the grooved activator. And while I made these simple arrangements the unnerving muted laughter went on inside my skull, echoing the noise of the birds outside, perhaps defying them.

Because it would be difficult to do what I would have to do now. I had done it before, to save my life; and I would do it again, to save my life; but this time it would be more difficult because I would have to make myself do it, in cold blood. Nevertheless, I would do it.

The daylight struck in as I slid the door open, and for a minute I stood listening, my eyes closed against the glare. But the noise of the birds overlaid the more distant sound and I had to go outside before I could note the difference in volume: the helicopters had moved westwards and were flying the same north-south pattern. I could see them more easily now because they were nearer, but their configuration was much larger than mine and I discounted the immediate risk of my being seen on the ground.

On this side of the freighter, the lee side, the sand had barely drifted across the top of the cabin, and I climbed there, feeling the solidity of the mainplane root somewhere under me. As I dug with my right hand, bringing the sand away, I saw that Tango Victor had been overtaken by a storm and had turned to head into it, some time before landing blind: the flight-deck windows were abrased to the point of opaqueness. But they were translucent, and that was all I needed.

Then I came down and looked at the birds against the glare coming up from the sand, nausea starting in me and bringing doubts whether I could do it. The heat pressed on my back and I stood swaying, watching them.

All right, they were merely feeding and we all do that, all living creatures have to feed; but it was their ruby-red eyes and the fact that their meat had once been man.

Sleep was trying to blot everything out: fatigue plus the soporific after-effects of the gas, and this was dangerous because there was a chance of staying alive if I made an effort, pity to let it all, slope of sand and my hand to break the *get up* spin of the blinding sky *get up you bloody fool*, near one.

That was a near one all right.

Stupid bastard, get moving, do what you've got to do, think where you are: no more water left and the tissues already drying out, helicopters moving closer, a matter of half an hour before they're over here, you going to stand here till you drop, stay here till you fry, Christ sake put some effort into this thing or you've had it and you know that.

Still hadn't moved but now I did, going down the slope towards them, jerk jerk, cackle cackle, towards them.

When I was within a dozen yards of them the nearest one flew up, shrieking its alarm cry. The others chorused it instinctively, some moving away but all turning to face me, one lifting its ragged wings and waddling towards me, threatening.

I dropped on to my knees and rolled over and lay face down with the sand's heat burning under me and the sun's heat on my back. Already their cry had changed from the alarm to a desultory cackling and the one that had flown up came drifting across to rejoin the others. I lay watching them, catching their foetid stench on the air. There'd be no danger if I fell asleep. If I slept, they'd wake me.

Cackle.

Very close and in front of me.

Sense of *déjà vu*: I'd lain here on the sand before, in this or another lifetime, and the bird had come for me, cackling. It voiced again and I opened my eyes and from between my fingers I saw the thing standing close to me on its wide-straddling legs, the head forward and the hooked beak open, the wings raised, menacing, the guttural racketing in my ears.

Difficult not to move, not to yell at it, not in some way to show defiance. But I mustn't even show life.

Others were coming, encouraged. They came waddling, their heavy bodies moving from side to side under their bald white necks and heads, their red eyes brilliant. It was the biggest of them that had come over to me first, and now it came closer, taking a single hop with the black wings spreading and folding again as it landed and stood over me. I felt the draught it had made, and began taking slow shallow breaths because of its smell. It voiced again, uncertain of me, knowing that minutes ago I'd been alive and moving. As the sound rattled from its throat I saw the sharp red tongue stiffened in the gaping beak and the small eyes glaring.

Lie still.

The others came waddling and I heard the hiss of the sand as their feet displaced it; but the big one, standing over me, gave a low cackle and lifted its head; and they stopped. This was the leader, and according to the protocol of the flock it would be the first to take meat.

Lie still.

Peck.

Shocking in its force, part pincer and part hammer blow, numbing my wrist. I didn't move. I could do it now because the thing was close enough but it was still uncertain, hopping back after taking the first trial peck in case I reacted. Now it came closer again, more boldly, the hooked beak half open for the strike, this time to feed.

Then I took it.

The beak struck but I went for the legs and got a grip on their scaly hardness and held on and tried to stand up but its weight stopped me and I rolled over and buried my face against an arm as the shrieking broke out and the wings beat in a frenzy to churn the sand and send it clouding and scattering, the strong legs tugging as I held them and one pulling free and its talons hooking at my face and hooking again, the gross body swinging from its single tether while I found a purchase on the sand and stood up, lurching and snatching for the free leg because the talons were murderous and if the other leg snapped and the thing got free and flew away I was done for.

Then I got it and held on and let it struggle, the wings thrashing and the beak striking and striking again and again at my wrists and arms as I walked with the thing to the aeroplane while the rest of the flock wheeled screaming overhead.

I had left the sliding door to the flight-deck fully open and now I hurled the bird inside and shut it in and came away and dropped to the sand and began walking, began lurching into some kind of a run towards the rock outcrop, hearing the mad shrieking behind me as the thing battered at the windows for escape.

Cerebration minimal now but I knew that I'd done what I'd meant to do: the rest would depend on chance. If the flight-deck had been totally dark the bird would have fluttered aimlessly, disorientated, and that would have been dangerous. I'd cleared the windows so that it could see the daylight, and for a while it would beat uselessly there until its frenzy tired it, leading it to look instinctively for a perch.

N'Gami, are you a god for me or for them?

The screaming was fainter now because of the distance.

I took the transceiver from the niche among the rocks and cradled it against me and tried to run with it but couldn't manage, had to make do with a shambling lurch through the sand, stopping sometimes to listen. I could hear the distant cries of the flock as they circled the freighter, disturbed by what had happened to their leader. The one distinctive cry, with its note of panic, was no longer audible. Perhaps the bird was tiring now.

A throbbing was in my head as I made what pace I could, in my head or in the sky, and I stopped again, turning to look back.

The helicopters had broken off their search and were moving into the target area at dune height: they'd seen the vultures and knew from desert experience that there must be carrion below, or some kind of living prey. When they landed I would go back there and talk to them, a voluntary captive parched for water, and show them the freighter, telling them what I'd found inside it, and arranging at the most convenient moment that the little god should summon his lightnings.

I thought I was already beyond the residual radiation range but I turned and went on again because if they landed I would hear them. I would give myself until then.

The weight of the transceiver was dragging me forward and I fell twice, the second time pitching down off balance and lying prone, a flashing in my head as I got on to all fours and dropped again, sudden rage rising, can't stand being feeble, *Christ sake get up,* trying again and hanging on the sand like a dog, *get up and get on,* trying again, no go, trying again as the dunes in front of me turned dazzling white and I squeezed my eyes shut, dropping again and groping for the transceiver, hitting the switch.

Slowly the white light was dying.

Beneath me the desert shuddered.